Those around him

Brett Shapiro

Simon Press

ISBN 978-1-7952551-1-0

Cover photo by Tom Ewell

Book design by Jen Gordon

About the Author

Brett Shapiro is an American novelist and author of the best-selling *L'Intruso* – a memoir published in Italy (Feltrinelli) that was later produced into an award-winning film and theatrical production. He is also the author of two children's books, one of which was the recipient of Austria's prestigious National Book Award. Several of his short stories have been performed in theatres throughout Italy, where he lived for 25 years, and his essays and articles have appeared in numerous magazines and newspapers in Italy and the United States. Brett is a veteran writer for the United Nations and currently lives by the beach in Florida.

"The writer's joy is the thought that can become emotion, the emotion that can wholly become a thought"

– Thomas Mann, *"Death in Venice"*

PART I - THEN

"…Nothing is stranger, more delicate, than the relationship between

people who know each other only by sight… Between them is

uneasiness and over-stimulated curiosity, the nervous excitement of an

unsatisfied, unnaturally suppressed need to know and to

communicate…" Thomas Mann

CHAPTER 1

The house was flooded with light, especially in the living room, whose seven original windows had all been enlarged in an effort to blur distinctions between outdoors and indoors. Without the sloped ceilings, which were nevertheless very high, and the central air-conditioning (a necessity), and the smooth cool white ceramic tile flooring throughout the house, perhaps little if any distinction would have been discernible. Even so, when Andrew stepped outside of the brightness and cool, dry air of his father's house into the greater brightness, heat and humidity of the outdoors, he felt a weight of oppressiveness lift. He tried not to feel it (focusing on the invasion of oyster grass leading from the walkway to the driveway and spreading its gloom around the perimeter of the house, and whose spiked leaves gave shades of green and purple that resembled shadows of colors, or colors that had recently been extinguished after a long and dreary life, rather than the colors themselves, in their prime), because any feelings about this relative sense of lightness couldn't help but point a finger in the direction of his father inside, who was ailing, failing, would soon die.

In the western sky, the predictable low-lying black clouds were gathering like a football huddle, almost a daily occurrence in these parts and at this time of year. Sometimes they continued floating eastward, unhampered by the wind from the ocean pushing them back, and spilled their contents beachside. Sometimes not. One never knew how the interplay between cloud and wind would pan out. Andrew welcomed these frequent and intense afternoon showers. He thought of rehydration, cleansing, nourishment, the "ahh" of relief as the sun-broiled vegetation soaked up this dampness. But they were also a bit of an annoyance: never knowing whether they would actually arrive directly overhead, he couldn't make his afternoon beach walk a de facto part of his routine. All had to be decided with a certain degree of risk, at the last minute. Andrew was not an especially risk-averse person. His job alone took him to hot spots around the world – Rwanda, Congo, Kosovo, Iraq. However, his willingness to accept risk depended on there being an alternative plan in place in the event the risk manifested itself. To his family, friends and acquaintances, he was the enviable adventurer, the "yes" man, always on the go to the most far-flung places. Andrew knew better. He was no adventurer. He was as much, if not more, a creature of routine as anyone else. His routine simply took place in many unorthodox places. No, he was not adventurous. He lacked one essential trait: impulsiveness. He calculated everything exhaustively before deciding, before acting. But the rapidity with which he was able to calculate (practice makes perfect) rendered the process invisible to his family, friends and acquaintances, who thought him wildly adventurous, and also "lucky" in the outcomes of his antics, not realizing that the so-called luck was actually the result of his exhaustive calculations. Andrew let their observations ride. He secretly relished the grand and somewhat pathetic irony to be found in people truly believing that someone is one way, when in fact the person is subtly and secretly, but radically, something else. If his family, friends and acquaintances only knew how constricted he was in his single path of rationality, his rapid-fire deliberation, if they could be privy to this invisible process by means of some as yet uninvented instrument on which they could place their eyes and peer into the map of his brain, they would step back, look at him, and say, somewhat embarrassed, "Excuse me. I mistook you for someone else."

Andrew expected the indoor brightness to strike from the moment he stepped inside. The front door encased a large pane of translucent glass, with a tall and slender ibis etched into the entire length of the right side. The foyer had two domed skylights in the ceiling, capturing the sun's direct rays in mid-afternoon and throwing spotlight parallelograms onto the floor. But inside, Andrew had to remind himself for months, his father was ailing, failing; the steady downward trajectory had begun, taking the power of the indoor light with it. Charles was eighty-five. His eyes resembled ripe blueberries just on the verge of beginning their shrivel. They were without age. To see only his eyes would be to witness a possessor of perpetual wonder, one with a thirst for knowledge, a desire to love, to guide, to be always engaged, vital, vibrant.

After giving his father a tight hug and telling him he loved him, Andrew left. For decades they had embraced each other and told each other they loved each other every time they were saying good-bye; it was an important ritual, and one that didn't slip into a banality over time, since both men took great care to say "I love you" as three distinct and emphatic words, and directly into each other's eyes. Charles turned his walker away from the front door and toward the dining room table, where he sat for a while and read another section of the *New York Times* before preparing himself an afternoon snack – cottage cheese with sliced avocado, a dish of trail mix, and a slice of rye bread, browned in the toaster whose three left-hand slots were no longer used.

As soon as he positioned himself comfortably in his "recreational" car (a black used Mazda Miata convertible he referred to as his mid-life-crisis mobile) and before backing out of his father's driveway, Andrew gave his sister Sheila a quick call to let her know that he'd paid Dad a visit. It was his way of intimating that she was off the hook for the day, in case she had other things to do (or not), even though he visited almost every day when he wasn't traveling. He told her that everything seemed fine, except that Charles's feet seemed bluer and that he might have a hernia. One or two hours with Charles each day made him feel both young and old. His black convertible did the same, with a touch of foolishness. Andrew was fifty-six, middle-aged, a term he despised. Everything made him feel young and old. Middle age. Middle class. This "middle," or "middling," status – implying neither here nor there, a coming from and an arriving at, but a vast limbo in the vast meanwhile. It was purgatorial.

He drove out of his father's neighborhood – modest cookie-cutter style homes, each with the slightest of a variation (a double or single garage, a double or single front door, a screened-in or bare entranceway, terracotta or mint green window trim) to render it "unique" – eager to arrive at the causeway, that splendid arc that took him from the mainland, where his father lived, to the beachside, where he lived. Andrew felt a surge of the dramatic every time he approached the causeway. He knew it would convey him from the manicured green-hued suburbs to the slapdash blue-hued bungalow beachside, where everything was a bit ramshackle and in varying degrees of erosion and corrosion from the trio of sand, sea and surf. There was a scrappiness and scruffiness to the beachside that struck him as a mean, almost tribal, way of paying homage to some higher, natural, raw purpose. Or perhaps it was something simpler: the old Florida versus the new Florida.

The clouds were intensifying in the west. No matter. His plan: He would stop at the grocery store to pick up a piece of fish to grill for dinner, drive home to park his car in the driveway, drop the fish off in the kitchen sink, and then head to the beach, a five-minute walk from his home.

Andrew moved to Florida two years ago, ostensibly to keep an eye on his father (his mother had died a number of years ago, riddled with a host of complex conditions, although the cause of her death was quite simple: she was old and very overweight). He knew that that construct, although not a spurious one, appeased his friends and family, thus alleviating him of the burden (to them as well as to him) of articulating why he had made the move. After all, migrating from Paris, where he'd lived for twenty years, to a small town in a refurbished swampland in Florida, where he'd only made obligatory annual family visits, hardly fell in the natural order of things. Other rationales could be offered as scaffolding – the desire to return to the U.S. after twenty years as an ex-pat; the prohibitive cost of moving to one of his destinations of choice (New York City, Los Angeles); the impulse to relinquish urban life for beach life. These were also not spurious. But neither were they on the mark, individually or collectively. They seemed to orbit around some larger, more essential sphere, something having to do with lightness and leanness, a gradual but deliberate desire to pare away everything that hinted of excess or distraction or insidious accrual. Zen would be too new-agey a term for Andrew; at the same time, whatever the nameless yearning was, it was strong. Strong enough for him to cross the ocean after twenty years, leaving behind his partner (a relationship that had subtle but telling indications of heading towards an inevitable end but wasn't yet there), friends close enough to decipher his words and gestures (to themselves as well as to him), and to start anew with less, and wanting to want less.

As he drove home, with each right or left turn he made, the corresponding variations in light in his rear-view mirror seemed to both age and rejuvenate him. At times, his crow's feet and cheek rifts vanished, and his teeth gleamed as white as they had before he began smoking some thirty years ago; at other turns, with the sun in front of him, the lines seemed to have been etched in black, and his teeth to have been dipped into paint the color of tapioca. As he picked up speed going down the far end of the causeway, he wondered whether, between these fluctuations that he saw in various reflections – from a mirror, a window, a puddle on white asphalt – there was one appearance that was fixed for all those outside of himself. And if so, which was it? Andrew was certain of one development as he headed home: he could no longer work his looks the way he used to; they were no longer there to be worked. He felt the brevity and indifference (so unintentionally cruel) of the glances of those who glanced at him, who were few. They were not looking at his looks. They were simply glancing at him as they did any and every object – a parking meter, a recycle bin, a sidewalk bistro table (peopled or un-) – that they passed, because it was in their range of vision and they couldn't not glance at it. He tried to remember the last time when someone's glance lingered an extra second or two, captivated by something about his looks. He thought about his father, attached to his walker, and alone.

After returning home, he decided to drive back up to the Mobil station, which was across the highway from the beach entrance, and to park his car between the station and the Dunkin' Donuts parking lots (four diagonal parking spaces, never occupied, that seemed to define a space that belonged to neither) to take his ritual afternoon walk on the beach. He dashed across the busy four-lane highway and arrived at the entrance, barely visible between a condominium complex to the left and a luxury home to the right. The path, two feet wide, was arced by sea grapes, creating a long dark tunnel before opening onto the dunes, the sand, the ocean. In October and November, the rising sun was framed by the tunnel opening. If he were lucky during those two months, as soon as he broke through the tunnel he might see newly-hatched leatherback turtles scurrying toward the water to increase their chances of survival to twenty percent.

Once arrived at the sand, he said to himself with a certain conviction: let me go just a bit farther this time, to that house over there in the distance, the one with the tiki bar jutting out onto the beach, where I keep saying I'll get to but never do. And he got to that house and in front of it (but probably having nothing to do with it) was this tall guy standing erect at the water's edge like some ostentatiously solitary lighthouse. Andrew didn't register him in any particular way, except for the phenomenon of his height, so it was with a natural and neutral politeness that he responded, "Pretty good, and you?" to the guy's "Hey howya doin?" It wasn't unnatural either that the guy then looked at him just a bit harder but with disarming gentleness and continued the threadbare conversation: "Doing great. Look at all this in front of us." And it was only then that Andrew saw astonishing light in his eyes and shine in his teeth as he spoke, and that he imagined for some reason, or better yet for no reason at all, how he might sit with this guy's head in his lap, on his favorite sofa in the living room, stroking that rainforest of hair (defiantly unwashed) as if to coax him to be still, here, just for a moment.

He stopped walking, paralyzed by the sight of such a creature, and the attention, however cursory, that the creature was directing at him. But he quickly turned his head back to the beachline he had just traveled and whose colors were beginning to gray and pinken as the sun set in the west. In the distance he could make out two elderly couples, a young girl with her dog, and possibly one of his neighbors with his son, and was struck by what we find to love in order to love and be loved. He started to head back toward the sea grape tunnel, his car, his house, the piece of fish sitting in a bowl of cold water in the kitchen sink that he would grill for dinner, and to yet another quiet evening that the routine of his particular solitude, along with the advancing of his years, had crisped into an age-hardened rind.

He heard the voice behind him. "This is the best time of the day to be at the beach. I grew up here and still think it's amazing." He stopped again and turned. The voice was still being directed at him. "Are you new here? I've never seen you before."

Andrew explained that he walked the beach every afternoon at this time, but had never ventured this far.

And that on the way back home he liked to stop at the Dunkin' Donuts to pick up a cup of coffee.

"I've got some coffee here in my thermos if you want some."

Andrew peered over at a ratty piece of beige fabric that was neither blanket nor sheet nor towel and looked like it had never been smoothed out or de-sanded, not even when first spread out. On top of the fabric were a tablet, a cell phone, ear buds and an overstuffed backpack. "I'll take you up on the coffee, but would you mind if we stand here instead? I sit too much. And besides, you can see more of the sunset standing from here. The dunes don't get in the way."

The youth scurried back to his blanket, poured a cup of coffee, and returned to Andrew. "Here you are. Cheers."

And so they stood, touching lightly on many things – music (he writes lyrics and composes songs, soft stuff), cooking (he wants to learn to cook; good nourishment is so important for body and soul), school (he does intend to go back and finish his undergrad), homes (when he has his own, he wants to have a Zen garden as a living room), politics (he's a sucker for conspiracy theories), friendship (he has outgrown his high school friends), life (he wants to make a difference). Andrew sipped on the cold, weak coffee, letting the creature do most of the talking, which required little effort. This youth's youth was a floodgate and in a half hour was able to reawaken in Andrew, no reanimate in Andrew, intensity – of thought, of feeling, of love, of life. Of being in Love with Life. His presence cast a shimmer on everything around him.

"You know, you're a really nice guy. I mean, decent. Nice."

Andrew smiled. "What makes you think I'm decent? And what do you mean by decent?"

The young man smiled back, with eyes averted. "Man, you know how to ask the questions. It's hard to explain, and I don't want you to think I'm some weirdo."

"Is there something intrinsically wrong with being a weirdo?"

The young man brought back his smile, and raised his eyes to meet Andrew's. "Okay, okay. It's like this. First off, there was something about your posture when you were walking. Your back was so straight and upright and your shoulders were so pushed back. And your head was always looking out or up, not down or kind of inward, if you know what I mean. It made me think of," and here he allowed a blip of silence as he sought out the words, "of expansiveness, of being at peace. Solar. You know, super-positive energy kind of stuff."

Andrew was at a loss for words. "How old are you?"

"Why do you want to know?"

"No reason. I'm not an actuary. I don't like statistics. I'm not a numbers person. I don't really believe in numbers, even if they can give an extremely false sense of extreme comfort. So it's okay. Promise. I just want to hear the number."

"Well, if you insist."

"I do."

"Okay. Here goes. But if…"

Andrew interrupted him. "If what? How do you think I'll react if you say you're thirty? As opposed to eighteen? Or a googolplex?"

"Okay. You win. Twenty-three."

Andrew watched him watching him for a sign of how the number resonated. "Thank you."

"And so?"

"So what?"

"You know."

"No I don't. I don't ask a question if I already know the answer."

"So how does it sit with you?"

"Tell me how you think it should sit with me. Or let's let it find its own way."

They stood there, the two of them, face to face, frozen under the heat and humidity of the sun, which had now begun its dip under the horizon line. The creature's impossibly thick hair was wet-waved. Andrew wondered whether it had been done purposefully (the young man dipping his hand into the ocean and raking it strategically through the mass and letting it set) or naturally (after hours at the beach and salt spray gathering in his hair until one unconscious rake of his hand did the trick). The key – what of him is about innocence and what is about knowingness? – was buried precisely there, in that sun-bleached mane. The thought was disrupted by a sudden breeze from behind the young man, which sent his hair in endless directions, with equally endless tiny shafts of light flickering and fading among the strands, like an orgy of fireflies.

"By the way, my name is Andrew. And I really should be getting back to my car."

"I'm Alexander. Most people call me Lex."

"And the others?"

"A couple of people call me Ex."

"I'll call you Ex too, if you don't mind."

"Sure. Can I ask you another weirdo question?"

Andrew nodded his head.

"Can I come back with you? Don't get the wrong idea. I just think it would be cool to spend some more time together. I can walk home afterward, if you're not too far away. I live close to here."

Andrew looked beyond this tall magnificent specimen

toward the sliver of remaining sun. The sky was pale blue, oh so peaceful, the soft regular crashing of waves behind him oh so steadying, this familiar cloak of beachside-sunset safety that enfolded him and protected him against change. For one dangerous instant, when the possible revelation of that instant was seeming to abate, along with the excruciating agitation of Andrew's body and mind, he thought of declining. No explanations, no summings-up, no attempts whatsoever at closure. Just a tip o' the hat and walking away. What would it be like, he wondered, to slip away before the mess sets in? He glanced at his feet. A small sand crab burrowed into a hole nearby. He knew Ex was waiting. But Ex was twenty-three and had all the time in the world. Andrew gazed at him and, in the face of such towering and luminous beauty, could no longer see the sky nor hear the waves. He was powerless to do anything except nod his head, then say "Okay."

CHAPTER 2

Andrew loved his father. Most people did. Charles enjoyed talking, but he enjoyed listening even more, and most people relish being listened to when they are saying whatever it is they are saying. He never interrupted, didn't make pronouncements, didn't offer opinions as truths, rarely responded with a sentence that started with "I," and knew how to relate some incident or make some point without getting washed away by a flood of delirious detail. He was a sweet, smart, thoughtful man, a consummate lover of life in its simpler forms. He went to classical concerts, built furniture, enjoyed an occasional un-idiotic television show, read the New York Times, researched high-end electronic gadgets and accessories that he never bought, and occasionally but with intelligence waxed philosophical. He didn't read books, though, which was odd.

Sheila loved him too, but her love was weakly stoked by the time-worn "Honor Thy Father" decree. Whatever prickly arrogance Charles possessed (and he, like everyone, did possess some, which he reserved for his children) seemed to crest immediately above her, suck her into its tumble, and give her a good thrashing. He made her feel small and inadequate. To her every B on a report card, he reminded her that an A had been eminently possible. For every skirt she purchased at the nearby mall, he brought out the retractable thirty-foot tape measure from his workshop, and a small transparent plastic box of pins from drawer of the Necchi sewing machine table, and started measuring and marking to make sure that the hem arrived no higher than the middle of her cheerleading-bruised kneecaps. Her boyfriends were sub-optimal choices, all of them, whose future trajectories he envisioned only as flat or downward. No doctors or lawyers among them, to be sure, as he saw it. No, their collars would at best be blue. Sheila lived with this imprint of imperious scrutiny and disapproval carved deep into her core. She relished hating him for exacting such a prodigious level of excellence from her but, even more, hated herself for continuing to need and seek out an approval from him, or some other man (she had married and divorced three), that she knew could never be granted.

Andrew's love for his father was less fraught. A certain temperamental and intellectual compatibility saw them easily through potential rough spots, even when Andrew had told his father, decades ago, that he was gay. Charles didn't spare Andrew his predications over his son's imperfect achievements, but unlike Sheila, Andrew didn't particularly care. He had enough of a reserve of confidence, or perhaps arrogance himself, that his father's brow-beatings were no more abrasive than a feather duster making its way across a polished mahogany surface.

Charles started to be dying recently. Even when his

wife (Sheila and Andrew's mother), Edith, passed away at seventy-nine – by which time Charles had already suffered prostate cancer, mild neuropathy, a mini-stroke and was undergoing drip chemo once a week for Myelodysplastic Syndrome (an alleged killer pre-leukemia) – he was not dying. The cancer had been removed, the neuropathy cured, the mini-stroke inadvertently revealed during an MRI performed a year after the stroke had occurred, and the chemo had in no way prevented him from going to the gym or the tennis court on his way back from the treatment, where he sat each session for three hours in a burgundy faux-leather lounge chair, listened to classical music on his MP3 ("Everyone else sits there with their eyes shut, they look like they've already died right there in their chair") and nibbled on Ritz crackers with some kind of mauve granular spread, crunching gleefully to the rhythm of the symphony cascading out of his earbuds. So until recently, these were simply breakdowns of old parts that needed adjusting in one way or another. They were hideous signs of aging, to be sure, but not of dying. At least not to his daughter and son.

Sheila was two years older than Andrew, a difference which at certain early stages of their life seemed generations apart, but from the age of about sixteen (when Andrew was about fourteen) melted away completely and forever. If anything, starting at that age, Andrew felt like the older brother, forever giving her silly advice about her boyfriends and helping her cover her tracks when she ventured into delinquency. During a certain short-lived fashion trend, he woke up an extra fifteen minutes early to iron her already straight auburn hair until it looked like a well-sanded and varnished door. Sheila treated him as the older brother and confidante, and did so with a mix of gratitude (thank God I have you to talk to), embarrassment (I can't believe I'm telling you this) and resentment (Why are you the only one I can tell these things to?). At fifty-six and fifty-eight, they were united in their struggle to cling to the beginning edge of middle age themselves, before that final thrust into the sixties and, heaven forbid, beyond.

Sheila immersed herself in dance lessons of all kinds – samba, ballroom, tango, Viennese waltz. Andrew wasn't sure whether immersion in anything would be a toxic-free elixir for him. Charles thought the dance lessons were just plain silliness.

Sheila's son Jason had his bar mitzvah a year after Edith, his Bubba, died. Sheila had little choice but to hold it in an event room of a hotel, since the outdoor temperature was reaching eighty degrees by ten a.m. (it was May, in Florida) and a beach bar mitzvah was simply not done here or anywhere. As much as she may have tried otherwise, it was a perfectly conventional affair, and one that her father couldn't possibly find fault with, since, when it came to his rare forays into organized Jewish life, he cherished the glue of convention and ritual reaffirming themselves in minute detail, from the circling of the Torah to the buffet of lox, kippered salmon and whitefish laid out on white-linen-covered tables whose under-surfaces gave the roving hand a barrage of plywood shrapnel.

Sheila was confident that her father was rejoicing in the affair, and somewhat relieved that her mother wasn't around to glower at all those who didn't pay homage to her above all. She also considered it likely that, although her brother's meanderings from table to table to dip into conversations were impeccably gracious, Andrew was at that level of remove that she envied and that would cause her to reflect for just enough time to believe that, once again, unlike her brother, she hadn't quite come through.

"Mom, when will Zee be here?" Jason asked. He was an only grandchild and, if such a thing is possible, over-loved. When he was born, the generations-old tradition of calling one's grandfather "Zayda" didn't quite take root. By the time Jason was able to form almost-complete thoughts, if not sentences, it had morphed into "Zee."

"Don't worry, sweetheart. Zee wouldn't miss this for the world. You know how much he loves whitefish! Forgive me, but…" and she pinched his cheek.

Charles sat front-row center, flanked by his two children (neither of whom had had their bar- or bat mitzvah) and took it in, moving only when it was time to *daven*, and once to center his Windsor knot and once to make sure that his yarmulke was still set squarely on his head (he'd lost the clip at his wife's funeral, thinking that it might have fallen into the hole when he knelt to kiss the coffin). He didn't know Hebrew or the cantillations, and simply let exotic made-up sounds and oscillating pitches escape his mouth in a hush so that he could permeate the form without disturbing anyone else.

When the guests were liberated from their metal folding chairs to head to the reception room, Jason found his way to his grandfather, who gave him a hearty squeeze. He reached into the inner breast pocket of his navy blue jacket, pulled out a small, square light-blue envelope and handed it to his beloved grandson. "This is for you. You hear me? For you. Don't give it to your mom for her to put away in some college fund or something. You are now a man. It's yours."

As Charles spoke, Andrew watched Jason fingering the

envelope in one hand behind his back, as if he was trying to feel its thickness and glean the monetary equivalent. "Thanks, Zee," he heard his nephew say before the lad ran off to join his friends, who were hovering by the improvised dance floor, replete with miniature disco ball suspended from the drop ceiling, eager for the music to begin so that they could abandon all things Jewish and sweat out their budding male and female hormone energy.

Sheila made her way to Andrew, who had positioned himself against a support beam that had been painted a textured white, as if to resemble a Doric column. He had a plate full of delicatessen. "I'd say it's a great success. Just look at Jason. And Dad, too." Andrew smiled and nodded his head. She added, "It probably seems a little cheesy to you, but hey, this is what you can get here. The Hilton, the Crowne Plaza or the Marriott."

"Actually, I haven't tried the cheese yet. I've been hoarding the kippered salmon. And it is a success."

Sheila looked at her brother and held her gaze. "You really piss me off, you know that?"

"What did I do now?

"It's just that supercilious attitude of yours. It makes me want to bash your head in."

Andrew rested his fork on the plate. "You know, Sheila, you set yourself up for it this time. If I'd agreed that it was cheesy, you'd have gotten all bent out of shape. And if I'd said it was a success, as I did, you'd have called me arrogant, or a snob, and gotten bent out of shape, as you have. I guess you just want to be bent out of shape. My only question is, why here, at Jason's bar mitzvah?"

Sheila moved closer to her brother, cupped her hand lovingly around his ear and whispered, "Fuck you."

The disc jockey started playing the selections that Jason had chosen, under the loose guidance and not-so-loose approval of his mother. All of the selections were upbeat, and sequenced in waves of energy designed to turn up the heat, offer a respite and turn up the heat again. The thirteen-year-olds were on the floor within the first bar of music, and a few of the older guests soon joined in, while the majority remained at their tables or hovering at the buffet.

Andrew remained standing at the column, observing what seemed to him to be three basic categories: the dancers, the standers and the sitters. The dancers were primarily of bar and bat mitzvah age; the sitters were grandparents, great aunts and uncles; the standers were those between twenty and fifty and represented a distinct minority. Andrew didn't approach the dancers (why would they be interested in him?), had already made the rounds of the sitters (so nice to see you; you're looking well…), and didn't know any of the standers. One of them, a man in his late thirties or early forties, was positioned at an adjacent column. He wore a fitted suit, charcoal colored, a black shirt and a burgundy necktie. His shoes were dark gray buckskin and his legs were crossed at the ankles, revealing a thin stripe of gray and burgundy argyle sock; one hand was in his pocket, and the other held a glass of red wine. He looked like an Israeli bodyguard, or an advertisement for some musky robust cologne, although, strangely, he looked too calm to be posed and there was nothing seductively forbidding in his face. It was a handsome face, not quite chiseled but the features were strong, and his dark hair, with hints of gray at the temple, lacked the sense of composition that the rest of him strove to suggest. Andrew was thinking about how to end up standing near him and what to say to get a conversation going when the man was joined by a woman, who kissed him on the cheek. Andrew focused on their hands. They had twin wedding bands.

Charles was standing by a column near the dance floor talking with Andrew's younger cousin Jill. His foot was tapping to the music, and when Jill kissed him on the cheek and headed off, his shoulders started to sway to the music as well. He wasn't watching anyone or anything in particular as bit by bit his entire body started to move in a tentative, self-conscious way, as if to say "Will some woman come please join me and take the pressure off?" But when the band started playing a fully charged version of Robin Thicke's "When I get you alone," he was no longer in control. The combination of disco and Beethoven entered his bloodstream like an injection, and Charles was soon writhing and convulsing around the column like a pole dancer. Those nearest to him stopped their conversations to watch, and his audience quickly fanned out in a concentric circle, clapping to the rhythm and goading him on. When Charles grabbed the column with both hands and started doing the bump, thrusting his pelvis against it as if he were raping it, Andrew had to turn away. He had never seen his father so unleashed. It was breathtaking, enviable and pathetic.

When Andrew called Sheila from his car to let her know about the blue feet and hernia, Sheila suggested that maybe the time had come for their father to move in with her. "If I put his house on the market, I could sell it within a week." Andrew shifted the gear back into Park.

"I'm sure you could. So that's not really a problem. Dad knows he can move in with you – or even with me, for that matter – whenever he wants to or feels he needs to or is ready to."

"But you know Dad, the stoic."

"I know. But it's his life and he has to decide. The only thing we can do is remind him from time to time that he has these options."

"Christ, you're so reasonable, Android."

"We'll talk about it later." Andrew knew that eventually his father would need to be coaxed to make the move. Who wouldn't need to be coaxed into removing themselves from the shelter that had housed them for most of their life and all the objects and smells and sounds that had accumulated in that shelter because of their life, into a smaller, reduced and almost unknown place? Who could possibly do that without hearing death pounding at the door? And Andrew also knew that it would fall on him to eventually do the coaxing since, as his sister herself had just said, he was so reasonable; just as it would be to his house that their father would ultimately move since it had no stairs (Sheila had a duplex, with both bedrooms on the second floor), and one of the bathrooms didn't have a perilous bathtub to climb in and out of, just a large shower stall. Andrew sometimes wondered whether Sheila's effusive generosity about having their father move in with her was possible because she knew that, in the end, it wouldn't be possible. He may have been reasonable, but it was also a stall tactic. This "coming full circle" or "closing the loop" thing – the aging, diminished parent returns, like a child, to his child, to be soothed and coddled – horrified and repulsed Andrew, with its under- and over-tones of slow agonizing deterioration and absence of dignity. It also struck him as a supreme inconvenience. No, he wasn't ready to cohabitate with a dying man, let alone his own father. As he shifted the gear back to reverse, he looked in the rear view mirror at his blue eyes, brilliant in the sunlight, and thought, Christ, am I ready for this? And am I ready to be simultaneously an orphan, a patriarch, and the next in line?

CHAPTER 3

"Come in."

Andrew opened the door to the narrow front porch that lined the front of the house, a modest beach bungalow built in the 1950s. His was the only house that had the front porch screened in. It was a last-minute decision during the renovation, when he realized that without the screening the porch would probably not be used because of the mosquitoes and no-see-ems. It also allowed him to keep the front door to the house itself open most of the time, allowing for brisk cross-ventilation.

He flipped off his sandals beside the neck-high paradise palm to the right of the front door, whose white frame encased a large pane of glass. A piece of white brocaded fabric was drawn over it from the inside. Ex started to kick off his flip-flops. "You don't have to take your shoes off if you don't want. I just like walking around barefoot." Andrew was relieved when Ex continued. His flip-flops were coated in damp sand, and Andrew could tell from the deep impressions that his toes had left on the upper soles that the flip-flops were very old. The tops of Ex's feet had a light dusting of dark grains. His toenails were clipped, although not freshly, since they lacked the sharp edge or two that one day's growth would smooth out. The heels of his feet were smooth too, and pink.

Andrew relished opening the front door to first-time guests after they'd opened the screen door on their own, passed through the front porch and rung the doorbell. Guests had been few so far – a neighbor, a rare visit from an out-of-state or out-of-country friend (but they had already seen photographs), infrequent hook-ups materialized from so-called dating sites, who were acceptable enough for one encounter, perhaps a few, after which, like ice floes, they found their way back out to sea. It was a rhythm that Andrew was accustomed to, one that he even encouraged, although with some ambivalence. There were hook-ups, there were partners, and there was the vast in-between. He no longer wanted a partner (two long-term relationships had been sufficient for him) and he didn't understand what the vast in-between really consisted of. Dating? To what end – partnership or parting of the ways? Friends with benefits – and how long do the benefits last? Friends? Surely there must be another route to friendship besides swiftly spent sexual craving. He relished the reaction that his visitors would have when they saw the open-air space, so incongruous with the box-like 1950s bungalow exterior, which he had intentionally maintained to suggest, from the street, small, low- and popcorn-ceilinged rooms that had accrued unchosen hand-me-down furniture taken from a death, a move, a find on a street corner. The reaction was always one of positive surprise, confirming to him the achievement of his vision, not perfectly articulated, but that was something along the lines of the redolent banality "Beneath the surface…"

He unlocked the door, gave it a slight push, and let it swing open as Ex stood at the threshold.

"Wow." He entered, then looked back at Andrew as if awaiting instructions from a tour guide. "This is awesome." Andrew was thinking the same thing as he watched Ex's face directly, and his torso indirectly.

"It was a fun project. Thank goodness I wasn't living in it when the renovation was going on, and that I wasn't in a hurry. Otherwise it would have been a nightmare. It took almost a year to complete." He explained how the four small rooms of the original day zone – kitchen, living room, dining room, den – had been laid out before he had decided to knock out all the walls and enlarge all the windows.

Ex rotated slowly. "Awesome."

Andrew noticed two small holes in the bottom right leg of Ex's blue bathing trunks as he turned. He moved in front of Ex and headed toward the large translucent glass dining room table. "This is my favorite spot." Ex followed him to the table and looked out the giant picture window. The pool was centered in its frame and went length-wise toward the back of the yard. "Can I get you something to drink?"

"Would you have any kind of juice?"

"I should." They headed to the kitchen area, which had a high, sloped ceiling. Ex hit his head against one of the suspended lights. Andrew smiled. "Now that's a first. You really are tall." He opened the small black refrigerator. "I have apple and cranberry."

"Cranberry? Let me try that."

Andrew suggested they sit out on the deck while there was still some light.

Ex lifted his glass. "Would you mind if I went swimming out there?"

Andrew raised an imaginary glass. "Of course not. That's what the pool is for."

The back door was identical to the front door and positioned in the same place on the rear wall. Before stepping outside, Andrew hit the switch to illuminate the pool, whose water reflected the turquoise of the pool's surfacing, a granular white-turquoise-deep-blue mix. A trace of pink was still visible to the west, above the tangerine and jacaranda trees (the only two trees that had been in the yard when Andrew purchased the property). Ex gazed at the jacaranda. "We had one of those in my back yard too. I almost lived up there when I was a kid. I'll have to climb it later."

"Do you still live at home?"

Ex's lips curled in. He shook his head, set his glass down on one of the small rattan tables, and peeled off his t-shirt and bathing suit. His "Do you mind?" was shouted out in mid-dive, and before Andrew could finish replying "Of course not," Ex was already submerged under the water, naked, spinning and propelling forward like a lithe and sumptuous torpedo.

Andrew sat at the edge of the pool, his legs in the water up to his kneecaps. He watched Ex, mesmerized by the indisputability of his youth, and the improbability of the two of them together, and knew that any future memory of having been with him would take place in solitude, unshared and unshareable with anyone. He watched as Ex shifted to butterfly, thinking so forcefully that it felt like he was screaming: when he is no longer in my life, which could be within the hour, the "halo effect" of memory will cast a long dark shadow on all others. Whereas for him, who has so so many more minutes and hours and days and years to accumulate minutes and hours and days and years of life on its still steep incline, "us" will tumble and land toward the bottom of the cistern, to be quickly obliterated by all that tumbles and settles above it. How and why is it possible to cling to someone so tenaciously when you know that the almost unbearable fullness he awakens will be vanquished by an even more unbearable — and one-sided — bereftness when he inevitably slips away, drawn toward the rest of his life and leaving you with a palpable nothing? I am so much older than he is, but I still don't have answers, if they are to be had.

"Aren't you coming in?"

Andrew wanted to be the type of person who would just strip down and plunge. Instead, he told Ex that he should probably think about throwing together some dinner, adding, "You're welcome to stay, if you'd like."

"Sure."

"Then let me get started. You do eat fish, don't you?"

"What kind?"

"Let's see. How about guppy sushi?" The quip went right over Ex's head, and with more strength than he'd needed to muster in a long time, Andrew turned away and walked into the house. From the kitchen window, he could make out a small wedge of the pool. The water was rippling lightly from Ex's movements, which was enough for him as he washed the grouper and thought how he could prepare it to be enough for two. Perhaps marinated in a pan with lots of diced plum tomatoes, calamata olives, capers, olive oil and garlic, and with an abundant side dish of basmati rice steamed with pine nuts. Quick and easy, and all prep could be done on the counter in front of the window, where he could keep an eye on the small wedge of the pool, where the water continued to ripple lightly from the fantastical presence of a twenty-three-year-old creature who, fewer than two hours ago, hadn't existed and was now there, in his pool, naked, and moving about with a such a sense of delight that it seemed as if he had always been there, were it not for a new agitation that Andrew was feeling as he opened the jar of capers and held it up to his nose to see if they were still fresh. He coaxed a caper out with his index finger, put it into his mouth and bit down, thinking: if this is doomed, let me die tonight, and it will be fine.

The sun had sunk below the horizon. The sky was pitch – it was a new moon – and the stars were out in full force. Small solar lights dotted the deck and vegetation in the yard. Andrew heard the sound of the outdoor shower running and walked to a window where Ex would be able to hear him but where he wouldn't be able to see Ex.

"Dinner's almost ready."

CHAPTER 4

"I'm certain I can convince him. It's an excellent price. And a cash offer. Deep down he knows that he'll be moving in with me sooner rather than later. You've nothing to worry about. I would suggest you take care of any paper work that you need, while I take care of things on my end. You have my word that we'll be able to go to contract within two or three days." Sheila wished her client an awesome day, hung up the phone, and immediately redialed her father to let him know that she'd had a solid cash offer on his house.

"So what do you think, Dad?"

"I think it's something to think about."

"It's a great deal, and quick and easy too. We could probably close within a couple of weeks. And they're a lovely couple. You'll like them a lot."

"I'll think on it." Charles hung up the phone, walked over to his stereo unit and turned up the volume. He had put on Rachmaninoff's Piano Concerto No. 3, and the *Intermezzo: Adagio* was about to begin. He sat back down in his dark green leather lounge chair and closed his eyes, trying to imagine every detail of every room in the house. Not this house, but the house before this house, the one in the suburbs of Philadelphia that he and Edith had bought shortly after they married, the four-bedroom split-level where they'd raised their two children, watched them begin their own adult journey when they went off to university, confronted their separate and joint solitudes in rooms no longer resonating with youth, and which, in the end, they sold when they moved to Florida some twenty years ago.

"We'll start over," Edith said. "We could sell all of this dark heavy furniture and buy teak and glass and bamboo. It would be lovely."

Charles knew that there was no use in trying to persuade her otherwise. Edith thought that changing one's mind was a sign of weakness, something she couldn't suffer in others, let alone herself. Moreover, Sheila had been pushing them to move to Florida ever since she'd relocated there from Ohio three years before, she herself having started over after her divorce from husband number three. Better to relent, he thought. It's inevitable anyway. But he insisted on taking the entire contents of his workshop and garage – every tool, piece of wood (including over one hundred twelve-foot two-by-four planks of redwood he'd bought to build an atrium/sunroom on the house), scrap of sandpaper, paint stirrer, jar of screws, nut, bolt, rubber band…it was all to come with them.

"Sweetheart, I yield to your folly. You yield to mine. Let's not argue for a change."

They did not argue about it. But their bickering about anything and everything else went on as before, until they separated.

*   *   *

Their very late separation might have gone on beyond seven months had Edith not decided to doll herself up and go to the Friday dance at the senior assistance-optional community where she'd moved. Her lipstick ("Tawny Glow") was stubborn at first, but with a slightly more forceful twist, out it came, like a wounded but eager tongue. Lisa's bat mitzvah was the last time she'd remembered using lipstick, even though she didn't remember whether Lisa was a second cousin, a cousin twice removed, or something even more unrelated. All those Maybelline cosmetics – the mascara, the eyeshadow, the blush, the rouge, the toner – painstakingly applied only to end up being displayed at yet another of those banquet halls with a basement smell, drop ceilings and plywood tables covered by coral-colored sateen cloth. Each time Edith went to a bat or bar mitzvah or wedding, she would locate her place setting and slip her hand under the table to feel if it had that same rough texture as Charles's spare plywood sheets stacked against the wall in the garage. And each time it did. There wasn't a real table to be had at those affairs. And not a real ceiling to be exposed. Edith felt the table and viewed the ceiling with disdain, although her own drop ceiling (the one she and Charles installed in the converted crawlspace of the home they bought when Edith was pregnant with Sheila and they wanted out of inner-city row homes) filled her with pride. They had installed it together one summer; boxes and boxes of chalky panels stacked in the utility room, next to the vat of garden pickles soaking in brine waiting for the cooler weather to arrive. Charles suspended the white metal tracks one foot below the original ceiling and Edith slid the panels in, one by one, until the entire ceiling, previously higher and white, became a drop ceiling, now lower and white. She tried to remember what it was that the drop ceiling was supposed to be hiding. Nothing that she could think of.

As she applied the lipstick to her upper lip, she calculated that Lisa had to be about forty-five years old. She was married again and had one, or maybe three, children. Lisa had married young, like her, although in Edith's day it was expected. In Lisa's, it was suspect. Was she pregnant? Without career prospects? Or just plain daft? Oh the things she could have done, her infinite potentials stopped dead in their tracks as soon as she yielded to motherhood. Edith was twenty-four when she married Charles. One year before her marriage, she was worrying about being a spinster. At fifty, she was wishing she had never married Charles. And at seventy-eight, she left him.

Edith placed a sheet of tissue paper between her lips to blot. The red imprint was thinner and more intricately veined than she had recalled it ever being before. She was tempted to face the mirror and take a good hard look at herself, but decided against it. She had avoided mirrors for decades, glancing at them from the forehead up as she quickly brushed her white, wavy and slightly out of control earlobe-length hair. She always tried to confine her glance to her hair only, pretending that she was brushing the hair of some other woman whose extraordinarily rounded face and extra chins were not hers. It was one of many denials – my body is a prison, my marriage is a prison, I am unhappy – that she had perfected over the decades of avoiding mirrors. Until one month ago, when she and Charles separated.

She studied her teeth in the mirror, to check for micro-panes of lipstick. Her teeth. They had been removed –

gum problems – and capped twenty years ago by the less expensive dentist in their suburb. Dr. Gilmore's waiting room had unframed reproductions of soothing classics thumb-tacked to the paneled walls: "Sunflowers," "Water Lilies," "Moulin Rouge." Charles had offered to go with the more expensive and reputable dentist, but Edith had insisted, "If we want to move to Florida when you retire in two years, now is not the time to think about high-end dentists. I only need teeth to chew." Besides, she looked forward to losing herself in the reproduction of Degas' "Dancers in Pink" as she sat in Dr. Gilmore's chair, the sound of the drill muffling into silence under the layers of ballerina taffeta. Somehow, the excruciating pain of a dancer standing on point, extending a straightened leg to meet the head and form a perfect line, diminished the pain of the root canal and tooth extraction. Theirs was the pain of arriving at sublime beauty, hers merely of salvaging old parts. The less expensive caps were not the same shape as her original teeth. Over time, they modified the bottom half of her face, the lower jaw jutting out further, the space between the upper lip and nose narrowing: a mildly bulldoggish face, no longer Edith's face, yet faithfully exuding the ever-growing contempt she had for the world around her and the world within her as she mastered the art of hurting, wounding, hating, an art from which she derived such a pleasure that it overpowered all others. Its force, revealed in the downcast eyes or the rearing up of her victim, presented itself as a kind of victory that she couldn't resist. She trusted it entirely, reliable as it was, like a family dog grown old and weary but faithfully and lovingly under foot. It was her only means to not be condemned to the mediocrity that assailed her.

Under pressure from Sheila, she and Charles moved to Florida one year earlier than planned, and all the spare lumber moved with them. Charles had already dreamed up six projects as soon as he signed the contract on the new house. He set up the garage as his workshop, relegating their two cars to scorch in the driveway (although Edith would give up driving, and her car would be sold, one year after the move).

"I guess I'm as ready as I'll ever be," she said to herself as she turned from the mirror, grabbed the black beaded purse lying on her bed, and hung the straps of the purse on the hook of her walker. She headed for the front door of her apartment. Before opening the door, she stopped, raised her hands, plumped up her breasts, and thought about the dance floor in the Activity Center that she would be on in five minutes, imagining her dress swirling as she moved with her partner. Aloud, she asked: "How is this possible?"

The density of clientele at Lonnie's on a Friday night was enough to keep the cocktail lounge afloat the rest of the week, when the bar area alone was never more than half occupied. There were alternatives to Lonnie's: Allen's Bowling Lanes, The Ice Cream Inn, the weekly non-denominational church supper and dance, an occasional firehouse bazaar. However, something about the harsh lighting of those places and the predictability of their attendees (there were always neighbors) prevented Edith, who was twenty at the time, from allowing her thoughts to meander into imagined romances. There was no sense of stepping into some "other" world, as there was at Lonnie's. It was a very small and simple establishment – a long bar, small thick pine tables stained to resemble a darker, richer wood, rounded banquettes in the corner, and a sunken dance floor in the center – but the smoky haze and the dim lighting coming from the faux-Tiffany chandeliers severed the focus on the week past or the one to come. Strangers appeared. People from other places. A new flux of elements – including a few Coloreds and Spanish, as Edith called them then and now – mixing and combining in new ways each Friday night. Lonnie always greeted Edith personally. "Here comes our local Ginger Rogers with black hair, looking as beautiful as ever." Edith relished his welcome, taking it as a kind of pronouncement that she was waiting for the rest of the world to appreciate. At first, she would blush, but in time she responded, "That's me," for all the world to hear, and hoping that all the world was already aware of it.

Bernie, Manny, Lou, all of her boyfriends took her to Lonnie's. After one night with her on the dance floor, they all proposed to her, she said. She could have had any of them. But she didn't. Something inside told her to wait, to hang on just a while longer, that these men would make fine husbands and fathers, but that she deserved something special, beyond the role of provider that their jobs, prospects and softening bellies vouchsafed. She deserved affinity of souls. She was convinced that she would know it instantly.

"He's a really sweet guy," said her friend Grace. "Shy, but sweet. And skinny as a rail, but an adorable pixie face." Edith was interested but was trying to seem indifferent. "I've already told him about you. I hope you don't mind that I compared you to Elizabeth Taylor instead of Ginger Rogers. I mean with your hourglass figure and all that fabulous dark hair. And those Ipana teeth. Can he call you to make a date?"

"Sure, it's fine. Nothing to lose but a Friday night."

"I really think you'll like him, Edith. There is something very quiet and unshowy about him. By the way, he doesn't dance. And I know you pretend to not care about these things, but he goes to Penn. He's an Ivy Leaguer."

When Charles showed up at Edith's house, the rain had been teeming for over two hours. Her parents were still at the produce store. They worked late on Fridays, to prepare for Saturday, the main shopping day, and her younger and much despised sister Pearl was at the movies with friends. She opened the door to find a waif of a man wrapped in a drenched and oversized raincoat. He had no umbrella. His hair was matted to his head and rain was dripping down his face and shoulders.

"It looks like we're not going anywhere until you dry off and warm up a little," Edith said to him after he had introduced himself. As she spoke, she was trying to understand his shape and his face through the surfeit of wet cloth and hair. They never did go out that evening. Charles sat on one side of the sofa, she on the other. The mugs of hot cocoa Edith had prepared lasted long enough for them to negotiate the necessary snapshot histories, laundry list of likes and dislikes, all edged with a subtle keening on Edith's part for the subtext. What should have been the moment for Edith to have filled the inevitable pause with, "Shall we go?" was instead claimed by Charles, who glided into an unfettered autobiography. Ten hours later, he was lying on the sofa with his head in her lap, fast asleep. Edith was gazing out the window at the rising sun, certain beyond the shadow of a doubt that, after dating hundreds of men (she said), she had found the one. Any man who could open himself up as Charles had done, she thought, had to be the one. Four months later they were married. Many had assumed it was a shotgun wedding, but Edith's belly never grew. She claimed that their rush to marry was precisely because they were not sleeping together, and Charles was such a nervous wreck over their abstinence that it was interfering with his studies.

Diane was the director of the Fountains, one of several retirement communities that Andrew had taken her to visit, once he was able to convince her to allow for the possibility that perhaps love was not enough, especially when it came to his mother and father. He made it a point not to meddle in his parents' psychological script. For thirty years he had diagnosed their unhappiness as severe but benign. For the following eight years, it was a precarious on-the-threshold act. And in the past two years, it had crossed over. Six months ago, he started to gently intervene, with Sheila's permission, administering regular doses of interrogation along the lines of:

"What is it that you want that you don't get?"

"At my age, I demand respect. And he doesn't give it to me."

"Well, Mom, respect needs to be earned, even at your age. And you know how you can be sometimes."

"But I'm only asking him not to give me that look every time I say something."

"I suspect you might be asking for much more than that. And why do you think that he looks at you that way? What do you think could be provoking it, Mom?"

"I know that I can be too harsh sometimes. I just speak my mind. But he should know that by now. And he should know what I mean when I say something."

"In other words, you want Dad to become a mind-reader. That should be quite a feat. And what will you become in exchange? If he's going to change, then you need to, too. It's only fair, right?"

Mini-sessions of this type were regular, deliberate and systematic. Andrew pulled from an endless supply of

Edith's harshnesses in an effort to make her understand that perhaps she too needed to make a change or two if she wanted things to be different. He would start with the Kentucky Blue Grass incident, as it was light and not particularly threatening. When in company, and with Charles present, Edith couldn't resist telling about how Charles had gotten it into his head to plant Kentucky Blue Grass in their yard, right before winter was setting in and while she was pregnant. The story itself could have been charming, but Edith's rendition did not have charm as the point. Rather, the sheer stupidity of her husband was the point, and she beamed every time she arrived at the line, "Can you believe what a moron he can be? And this is what I have to live with." When this example failed to rouse whatever introspective proclivity Andrew hoped Edith might have, he would select something more unequivocally harsh. Like the time her first and favorite grandchild, Ilana, went into rehab, and Edith pronounced in front of the whole family gathered around the Thanksgiving dinner table, "Christ, she'd be better off dead."

"Tell me, Mom, how are we supposed to interpret that differently than the way it came out of your mouth? And how is respect supposed to find nourishment in opinions like that? Do you see what I mean?

"No I don't, Andrew. In some ways, you're just like your father."

These mother-son crescendos took place after Andrew's lunchtime visits. When the three of them had finished eating, Charles would head for his workshop to tinker, leaving Andrew and his mother at the dining table. Edith's son was gently persistent in these forays into pushing deeper, until after a few months Edith couldn't help but realize that the kind of changes she was hoping for and counting on were simply too radical, too fantastical, to happen. What she called pipe dreams. Once she had settled in with this bit of reality – that what she had with Charles was immutable – Andrew introduced the idea of a separation. And Edith was not unreceptive.

Diane was in her thirties, quite beautiful, and had fine-tuned her role as Director of The Fountains. Her mastery of eye contact, active listening, body language, empathy, open questions was so seamless that Andrew scrutinized her every word and movement, not so much to learn from her as to hope to exchange a momentary glance of complicity, which didn't come.

"Can I get you anything at all to drink? Some coffee, tea, juice, water? Or some delicious cookies that Janelle our receptionist made?" she asked as Edith sat in the plush armchair in front of Diane's simple desk.

"No thank you, my dear. I never snack between meals. And I never eat lunch. Just breakfast and a simple dinner." (Confabulation.) "And I am always very careful about what I eat." (Confabulation.) "I'm diabetic, you know."

"How do you like to spend your days? What are your interests, Edith?"

Edith, whose days had long been reduced to bickering with Charles and reading large-print romance novels, didn't know how to respond without seeming pathetic. She lowered her eyes, hoping to give the impression that she was formulating the best sequence in which to describe her rich medley of pursuits.

"That's okay, Edith. I'm sure you have many interests, and I certainly hope The Fountains will be able to cater to them. We'll take a walk around the premises soon, but I thought it would be helpful to first get a sense of who you are and what you are looking for. It can be such a difficult transition, but we truly understand this at the Fountains, and we are quite remarkable at making the transition an extraordinarily pleasant one. I really speak from my heart when I say this Edith. This place is truly special. You'll see in just a moment."

She was simply uncrackable, and Edith was spellbound. She was delightful, and her ability to delight was terrifying. Andrew was grateful that Diane was not a Scientologist.

The amiable conversation continued for fifteen minutes. Then, Diane tilted her upper body forward, as if to bridge a gap with Edith, who lowered her eyes again, hoping to avert the question she feared was inevitable.

"Tell me Edith, how long were you married?"

The inevitable question wasn't framed in the way Edith had imagined. Nevertheless, it hit upon the subject that Edith had been dreading since the moment Andrew told her that he had scheduled the appointment. It was one matter to keep this separation business confined to the immediate family; quite another to set it free in the cruel and chaotic world. If she had been seventy-five years younger, she would have run to the credenza next to Diane's desk and squeezed underneath it, refusing to come out and screaming "Make this all go away!"

"I am still married," she said huffily. "Almost sixty years. And my husband and I still love each other deeply. We just can't live together any more. We don't see eye to eye on the important things. You see, Charles..." but she stopped herself.

Diane activated a trace of a smile. "I understand what you are telling me Edith, and you will be surprised at how many of our residents are in the very same situation. I hope you will have the opportunity to discover that for yourself if and when you decide to become part of our community. I think you will find yourself completely at home here. It is all about quality of life, regardless of our age."

Andrew's patience was being tried to the limit. He felt as if he were reading an interminable Hallmark card. "How about we take a look at the facilities?" he asked as kindly as possible.

Before Diane or Edith could reply, he went to help his mother out of her chair. He met Diane's eyes. She winked at him. He wasn't sure which of two messages she intended: "Thank you for helping your mother out of her distress" or "I'm pretty damn good at this, aren't I."

They passed through a maze of corridors and their various intersections into what seemed like indoor plazas – all carpeted and with mildly baroque seating arrangements. Clearly the theme was plush – to muffle noise, to cushion falls. Edith greeted each resident she passed with a smile and a "Hello." She was a bundle of nerves. She could feel all eyes on her, the newcomer, making snap judgments about her and her acceptability into this enclave. So concentrated she was on each person she passed that she barely registered the three restaurants, the library, the gymnasium, the Olympic-sized indoor pool, the Wii Room, the Lecture Hall and the rest.

It wasn't until her eyes caught sight of some parquet flooring through the window of one door that she regained her composure, her sense of where she was.

"Is that a dance floor?"

"Yes it is, Edith. We have dances two or three times a week. Some of our residents are pretty spectacular on their toes. And others play instruments and sing. This is where we try to bring it all together. It's definitely our most popular activity."

Edith remembered body heat, muscles stretching

beyond normal limits, sweat, breathlessness, a slow-building sexual intoxication that felt almost chemically induced. Lonnie's.

"Shall we continue, Mom?"

Edith's gaze remained fixed on the empty dance floor. "Charles never really did learn how to dance. He was always so stiff. I've had some of the best dance partners in the world. I know what it's like when a man can dance. Believe me, I know what it means. But Charles..." Andrew took her by the elbow and started to lead her away from the window. "Let's go take a look at the different apartments, Mom."

When Charles laid his head in her lap, Edith jumped. Not by this sudden cheekiness. In fact, for the past hour she had been trying to will proximity -- there was something about the way Charles was recounting his upbringing that made her want to enfold him entirely and never let him go. She jumped because his hair was still damp and cold. He didn't look into her eyes as he spoke, so inwardly concentrated he was on letting unspeakable things latch onto words, things he had never spoken about: his illegitimate birth, being placed in foster care, a younger sister who was not only not placed in foster care but was spoiled rotten. Edith didn't mind his glazed eyes. She was certain beyond a doubt, by the modulations in his voice, the soft but irregular breathing, a perpetual licking of dry lips, that this was the first time Charles spoke of these things, and that she had been chosen for such intimacy. She had expected an affinity of souls to arrive with a slow gentleness of angels' wings, a floating-upward sensation, not this sledge-hammer variety. Nevertheless, she was stirred beyond her wildest dreams by this man.

The more vulnerable he allowed himself to become to his past, the more heroic she found him to be. She gathered all of her courage and started to stroke his wet hair, running her spread fingers through it comb-like, from the forehead back to the crown, and occasionally letting her bottom palms reach as far down as his eyebrows.

Most intimacies bring together, but eventually they can also pull apart. As Charles unburdened his onto Edith, coaxed on by fingers raking his hair in a soothing, regular rhythm, his unimaginably (to Edith) irresponsible mother, his absent mother, his non-mother, opened up a gorgeous void that Edith would fill: she would open the dual floodgates of wifely and motherly love. At last, she could be everything for a man, whose happiness would be entirely hers to craft, mediate, modulate – control. It was an exquisite feeling. What Edith didn't realize until right before Sheila was born was that Charles had maintained a relationship with his mother. "Why? How?" she would hurl at him every time he set off to visit Hannah, taking Sheila along, and then Sheila and Andrew. She refused to have anything to do with her. She was so close to total possession of him. That this undeserving woman should be the thing preventing the total possession made Edith wild. She hated Hannah, and the hate soon spread to Charles's sister Laura, even though it wasn't her fault that she had been spoiled rotten. There was something intoxicating and powerful about this hate, and Edith soon found herself experimenting with it – and with disdain, contempt, hubris – on other people, places and circumstances. In varying degrees, a sense of satisfaction was always the result. These irresistible wedges gradually but persistently pulled Edith and Charles apart, until the only things they shared were meals. And even then, they prepared them separately. Edith liked large, heavy fare –

eggs, bacon, potatoes, toast and butter for breakfast; large steaks, veal chops, roasts for dinner – while Charles was a clean eater – fruit and yogurt for breakfast; grilled seafood and steamed veggies for dinner. They had figured out a way to maneuver through the kitchen without killing each other so that they could prepare separately but eat together.

Breakfast was unfraught. The newspaper was delivered on the driveway each morning, stuffed inside a transparent plastic bag to protect it from Florida flash storms. Charles would spread its sections out over the four empty table settings. He would read the news sections, and Edith would scour the sales and coupon inserts. Whatever conversation leaked out was about some item in the paper and sounded more like they were talking out loud than to each other. She: "They're having a sale on Triscuit." He: "Getta load of that. Ashkenazy may have to cancel because of the flu." Harmless wisps of facts, far from the perilous terrain of opinion or judgment. Dinner was another story. Anything could, and did, happen. It didn't take much (sometimes nothing) for Edith to spin off into a rabid trajectory of loathing or contempt (for others, for the world) or of pity (for herself, for being unappreciated or, more frequently, un-understood). Dinnertime was a mine field and Charles had learned early on that you could escape alive but never without serious injury. To respond in any way to her was to experience being slowly cornered by some kind of wild beast – a cheetah, a jaguar, but without the stunning finesse. To not respond was to lead to accusations of being uncommunicative and closed. But it was futile to call Edith on this. As uninhibited and explosive and vulgar and uncensored as her outbreaks were, three tiny but potentially redeeming phrases were altogether missing from her lexicon: I don't know, I was wrong, I'm sorry. And without part or all of this triumvirate, it boiled down to putting up or bailing out. Charles put up, aided by an iPod he bought when he was seventy-three.

When Andrew was born, less than two years after Sheila, the bliss and divine call to motherhood began to lose its patina – a kind of fall from grace into white metal pails of diapers soaking in royal blue Purex, and pale green canisters of powdered Similac baby formula continuously needing to be measured into bottles. Charles was at work, in the shop, reading the paper, paying the bills. Supportive but elsewhere; for her, but not with her. Edith couldn't understand why two adult lives that set out to create and manage a household had to establish such non-intersecting roles. She knew it was the way things were done, but it didn't feel normal. Not by any stretch. Such hustle and bustle in the house. But such isolation and loneliness. They only merged in bed. But with two babies only one thin wall away, their bedroom was hardly a place of abandon or communion. It was a place for each of them to have a moment of peace before quickly drifting off to sleep. Even in the double bed they shared, peace was a his-and-hers peace, carried out individually. Charles was the first to fall asleep, after which Edith would get out of bed, turn off the television before the end of the nine o'clock movie, check on the babies, get back into bed, switch off the lamp by her night table, and lie awake trying desperately to believe that the self-sacrifice and self-enclosure of mother- and wife-hood were precisely what made them so sacrosanct. Once or twice a week she would dream that she was jitterbugging with an ease, agility and frenzy that was almost like flying were it not for the presence of a man who was spinning her, tossing her in the air, catching her in his arms, hoisting her over his shoulders, standing rigid as she descended, coiling around him like a python. She would wake from these dreams exhausted, rejuvenated and with an assortment of feather-light dream residue: the minty smell of Bernie's neck, the sweat that gathered on Manny's wrists, the pained twinkle in Lou's left eye when her legs were wrapped around his waist and both of them felt the playful but ardent pushing to fit that was taking place between their thighs.

"This is it!"

As soon as they entered the third apartment, those three words burst of Edith's mouth. The unit's configuration and appurtenances were no different from those of the other two units they had seen and which Edith had scrutinized without much commentary: foyer, living room, kitchen, bedroom, bathroom, three closets, utility room, screened-in patio, lots of windows, off-white carpeting, white appliances, white walls, white trim, white tiles. White. Clean. Straight-edged. A typical Florida preface to a cookie-cutter habitat, waiting for something, anything (a boldly colored toss pillow, an iris in a stem vase) to breathe life into it.

Edith would do it up just right. She had the knack. Full but not cluttered. Homey but not sentimental. Contemporary, mostly Danish, but not screaming a motif. As tasteful as her furniture and furnishings were, not one piece ever carried a hint of "Be careful how you sit on me, touch me, use my surface." She would bring in many pieces from the house, and gradually flesh them out on the shopping excursions to the mall that The Fountains provided with their wheelchair-accessible mini-van every Monday, Wednesday and Friday.

"That's great that you like it so much, Ma. Let's take a look at the remaining two."

"We can stop here. I'm a very decisive person, and once I make up my mind…wasn't it you who said that if I'm not excited about a place, there's no reason to move? Well, I'm excited. What do you have to say about that?"

What made Edith so excited was the mirror, which covered the large wall of the living room from floor to ceiling. Andrew watched her watching it, thinking "visions of dance bars danced in her head." One conversation with Charles, some papers to sign, and the deed would be done.

Charles told her that she could take whatever she wanted. "Whatever will make you happy." Edith went through every item in every room, selecting pieces of furniture, clothing, linens, pictures and knick-knacks, repeating throughout "Not much how much do I need not much how much do I need" as a kind of mantra to avoid dragging too much past into too little future. When she had finished, Charles turned to her.

"What about the kitchen?"

He figured that she was saving this for last. It would certainly be the most daunting room for Edith to confront, what with the blender and Cuisinart and juicer and waffle iron and toaster and toaster oven and hundreds of pots and pans and trays and platters and bowls…and the twenty or so smaller drawers that were filled not only with utensils and small gadgets but also the accretions of sixty years of grocery shopping – twist 'ems, rubber bands, plastic bags, styrofoam trays, onion and garlic nets, plastic and metal lids, corners cut out from boxes of cereals, detergents, pastas, cookies to redeem prizes that were never redeemed.

Edith bypassed the kitchen toward the bathroom. "It's all yours. I'm never gonna use that crap. I don't intend to ever cook another thing for the rest of my life." She closed the bathroom door and peed.

And yet it was possible. Here she was, in a new life, away from the man with whom she'd lived a half a century. Here she was made up to the nines, a touch of perfume behind the lobes of her ears, whose holes, surprisingly, still allowed the posts of her pearl earrings to slip through after almost forty years of lobe nakedness. With the exception of her wedding and engagement rings, her hands were unadorned. They told stories of domestic drudgery carried out without latex gloves. The balls of her fingers were mildly eaten through, and filaments of black were etched in the fissures. Her nails were clipped short, unpolished. But the hands were steady. They did not look like the hands of an octogenarian.

Her mind, on the other hand, was not steady. It was trying to make sense of this moment, and she was being pulled in two directions. To open the front door, head down the corridor, enter the dance room, seat herself and wait for someone to ask her to join him on the floor, accept, and then place her hand on his shoulders to initiate: was this a celebration of liberation? Or was this a heinous act of betrayal? Alternately she felt pangs of acute longing and tenderness for Charles, and others of acute vindictiveness over his shortcomings and the undeserved misery they caused her. Love. Was it an outpouring of feeling? Was it a decision followed by an unspoken contract? Or was it an unsteady minuet between the two? Either way, Charles had failed her. Extending her arm toward the door knob, her hand remained steady, but there was a slight numbness from her wrist to her shoulder, and her head started to feel light. As her knees gave way, she grabbed onto the seat of the walker and dragged herself toward the emergency button on the living room wall. She tried to lift herself up to reach it, but her legs were like stone. She jiggled at the straps of her purse, which were snagged on the walker's brake mechanism. Once disengaged, she threw the purse toward the button. As the alarm went off, Edith let herself collapse onto the floor. Lying on her back, staring at the ceiling, waiting to be rescued, she was thinking: I will not stay here. Six months was a taste. But this is not where I want to die.

The diagnosis of colon cancer was not the reason Edith decided to suspend all medications and arrange for in-home hospice care. The diagnosis could have been gout, high blood pressure, emphysema (all of which she had) or any other condition, large or small, that required drugs and a further shrinking of what she called "lifestyle." The reason was that the colon cancer was her tenth condition, and Edith had long ago decided that at the number ten, maintenance would be excessive, against nature; at the number ten, the probing and prodding and poking would cease, and be replaced exclusively by pain management during her final wind-down. Andrew flew in from Paris to restore the house to order. Six months of his father's bachelor life had not transformed it into a complete disaster. However, the level of disarray was far beyond anything that Edith would have been able to tolerate – unmade bed, damp unfolded towels on bathroom and kitchen towel racks, filmy bathroom and kitchen sinks and faucets, and papers and paperwork everywhere. Andrew arranged to have the contents of

Edith's apartment transferred back to the house. They would slip back easily into their original locations. Charles was neither reluctant nor overjoyed to return to married life. "We've been married a very long time. It certainly deserves another shot." He insisted that things would be different, although he didn't explain in what way. He did take down the placard on the refrigerator door that Andrew had recently bought while he was in Las Vegas for a conference. The placard, a small thick piece of varnished walnut hanging from a black chain, read: "My soul has had enough chicken soup. Now it wants chocolate." Charles placed it in the back of his Classical CD drawer, returned to the kitchen and opened up the last can of Wolfgang Puck's Tomato Bisque with Basil. He rummaged the refrigerator for sour cream, but there wasn't any.

Edith had been home for one week. She spent most of her time in her bed, propped up by four pillows in an almost seated position. Even when she was dozing, there was a trace of a smile on her face. All voices coming from other rooms she called divine music. Other than that phrase – divine music – which escaped her lips like a steam valve, she hardly spoke. To look at her face, into her eyes, was to discern lucidity, a mind working overtime to fit pieces together, to come to conclusions and reckonings. There were no explosions, just continual eruptions of morphine-induced peace. Occasionally she said, as she had said all her life, even in her most volatile moments, that she had no regrets. Andrew and Sheila took turns keeping her company and bringing her light meals when she was awake. They sat beside her and filled her with stories about the details of their lives while she stroked their arms, hooked her finger around their fingers, caressed a cheek, a wisp of hair. There was little commentary on her part, although she did say to her son, "Don't think you've heard the last from me. I'll have much to say to you when I'm on the other side, and you'll hear it."

Charles busied himself around the house to avoid entering the room as much as possible. As consummate a provider as he was, he had never been the caregiver type. He didn't have the stomach for it. She did not ask for him either. When he did appear in the doorway, she would break into a half-smile and watch as he approached her. He was still as skinny as a rail, but his body seemed to have become a series of gentle arcs – bowed legs, stooped shoulders, craned neck. He bent over her to kiss her cheek, already thinking about when he could ease out and back into the living room. The last time he ventured to her side, she said to him, "I almost danced again. Can you imagine after all these years?"

Charles opened his eyes, which travelled the open-space living-dining-room- kitchen. So white, so bright, so uncluttered with the accrual of children's traces. With the exception of a several pictures on the walls, few objects were here that had once been in the split-level in Philadelphia. He felt satisfied with the look and the feel of his home, but he felt little attachment to it. Nothing burnished with his history, which, from the time he and Edith had moved here, had been without variation or milestone. It felt like one very long and unmomentous day. At Sheila's he would have his own very large room and bathroom – much like a studio apartment – on the ground floor. He would no longer have to cook or go grocery shopping by necessity, but only when time and mood prompted him. Sheila kept a beautiful home. But the air-conditioning was always too low (Sheila blamed it on her prolonged menopause and heat flashes). He didn't like her friends, especially the man she was seeing whom she insisted, too insistently, that she would never ever marry. Yes, he would think on it.

CHAPTER 5

"Those olives were really good. Kinda mushy but good. I liked them. 'Cala' what?" Ex helped Andrew clear the table and offered to wash the dishes. When the last of the last of them had been brought into the kitchen, Andrew turned away but only went as far as the corner of the dining area, where he could watch Ex from the shabby-chic serving table he'd picked up at a flea market. There he was, this young scantily clad stranger washing the dishes at Andrew's kitchen sink – head tilted to the left, pelvis rubbing up against the below-the-sink cabinet that held the copper cleaner, glass stove-top cleaner, faux granite counter-top cleaner and all of the other chemical products that Andrew had decided to pretend, like so many others, could forestall aging and decay of some of the objects surrounding him. Ex circled every plate methodically with the blue scrubby-sponge and placed them haphazardly in the simple dish rack. (During the renovation, Andrew had opted against a dishwasher, since, as one person living alone, it struck him as excessive.) As Ex transferred each item to the rack, his right knee took a slight inward bend that suggested a mildly feminine pose, even though the bend could also be a reaction of survival, intuited some time ago by his height, in order to prevent his head from bumping against objects that might be hovering above it. Ex washing the dishes was nothing less than a painting or a ballet, or a painting of a ballet. That such a banal and inescapable necessity after eating dinner – after all, dishes, pots, pans and utensils must be washed and placed in a dish rack to dry, if there is no dishwasher – (and such a sense of grief when Ex had finished and wiped his hands on the muted minty-colored terry-cloth dish towel hanging on the handle of the black oven) could be, in the posture of the doer, so exquisite and provoke such feeling, and the simultaneous awareness of feeling such feeling, created in Andrew a fierce competition between unbearable exhilaration – why doesn't each and every moment carry such weight? – and exquisite pain – why does it not? He retreated to the larger of the two sofas in the living room and considered putting on some music.

Ex called out from the kitchen, "Where should I put the dish towel? It's really wet."

"You can hang it back on the oven door."

Andrew knew that in a matter of seconds Ex would appear in the living room. And he did, as if this were a living room he entered many times a day.

"Nice."

Andrew looked at him, puzzled.

"This place. It feels nice. It makes me feel protected, safe."

Andrew smiled. "That was the idea."

"It was?"

"Yes, it was." Ex smiled. Andrew added, "For me."

Ex walked past him and headed to the front door. He reached toward the floor for his backpack. Waiting for Ex to sling it over his shoulder, and, on his way out, say something like "Thanks for everything," Andrew felt duped and devastated, and was prepared to say anything at all in order to prevent Ex from pushing open the screen door and slipping away, just now, forever.

Ex hooked his index finger through the loop at the top of the backpack and dragged it back to the living room. He sat on the far side of the sofa, unzipped the bag and started rummaging through its contents.

"Here it is." He extracted a crystal – long, translucent, many-faceted spearheads jutting out of a rough white base – and placed it on the mosaic coffee table in front of the sofa. "Burmese Citrine Cluster. It's for abundance and manifestation."

"It's beautiful."

"Thanks. I always keep it in my backpack, just in case."

Bobby McFerrin's *VOCAbuLarieS*. If Ex's crystal could produce sound, it would be the alchemized new language of *Vocabularies*. Andrew got up, inserted the CD, and sat back down. Ex had placed his feet on the coffee table, ankles crossed, lightly pushing aside a large book of Diane Arbus photographs.

"Non est ad astra mollis e terries via
None est mollis via, no no no
Emitte animo lucern veritatem
Non est mollis via, no no no
Et sicut vita fine ita
Cura cura kama cura cura kama…"

"Wow. That's really…"

"Shhh," Andrew whispered. He smiled softly and

placed his index finger on his lips. "Shhh."

Ex cupped his fingers and placed them behind his head, elbows out. He closed his eyes. He was at his most physically extended, until, eyes still closed, he stretched his arms upward, in what seemed like a gesture to pluck the sun out of the sky beyond the ceiling and place it delicately, and with thanks, into his mouth, like some god-sent lozenge. The mounds of hair glistened in the caverns of his armpits. As soon as Andrew imagined taking a few strands of that hair between his thumb and index finger, and twirling them until a droplet of sweat was slowly transferred to his fingertips, which he would then bring to his nostrils before slowly inserting into his mouth, he thought that this time it would be different, that Ex would not remain a static aesthetic, a silent intimate, fuel for his imaginarium. Andrew was convinced that he would break the barrier this time, cross over, come what may. Yes, he had forebodings but they carried virtually no weight, so potent was this awakened desire to be thrust into the maelstrom of human emotion and sensual tightenings and easings, and to not, oh no, not have him vanish, ever …

"Hey Hey say ladeo-ay
Time we took the words away
We're getting to that somewhere closer
That's hidden inside
Words only take you so far and leave you
Wondering just what it was you meant to
Say what you would say if you would let your
Heart just lead the way…"

The music ended, echoes of percussion drifting away to silence. Andrew and Ex turned toward each other, a faint smile on their faces. Andrew noticed that Ex's lips were thin. He resisted reaching over to embrace him so that he could fully concentrate on trying to silently will Ex to tilt toward him until his head rested on his shoulder or, better yet, his lap.

"I'm afraid I have to call this a night," he said. "I have some prep work to do for tomorrow morning."

Ex came to slowly. "Oh. Okay."

"Would you like a ride home?"

"That's okay. I don't mind walking." He bent over to grab his backpack, rose quickly and lumbered toward the front door. Andrew trailed behind.

Ex turned to him. "Let's do this again. I mean, if you want to."

"That would be nice." He pulled out his wallet and handed Ex a card. "Call whenever you'd like."

They continued toward the door. "Wait. You forgot your crystal."

"No I didn't. I left it there on purpose. I'll be back."

As Ex pushed through the screen door, Andrew reached up and tousled his hair. The creature strode down the driveway and erased himself into the night. Or perhaps, the night did not take him in, it was taken in by him, as if darkness were something he swallowed and fed off of.

CHAPTER 6

Charles drove to his son's house and let himself in, unannounced, to tell him that he was selling the house and moving in with Sheila. He had a key to both of his children's houses (they all had keys to each other's houses, which was only natural), but he took this to mean that he didn't have to ring the doorbell first, something that Andrew detested but didn't have the heart to tell him. Fortunately, Charles rarely went to Andrew's house on his own, satisfied by the phone calls and his son's regular visits, which were usually graced with a bag of specialty ready-made items – his favorite was the chunky gazpacho – that Andrew brought him from the only gourmet food shop in the area.

"Are you sure you want to do this? Now?"

"Son, I'm not sure of anything anymore. Sell it now. Sell it in a year. Don't sell it. I miss your mother. She calls out to me, you know. I want to go to her. But that place, where your mother is, terrifies me. It sounds crazy, I know."

"Do you want some coffee? Something to eat?"

"Coffee would be nice."

Andrew went to the kitchen counter to prepare the coffee. As he stood in front of the coffee machine, he bent one knee inward and wondered whether it looked effeminate. It felt awkward, but he held the pose as he spooned the coffee into the filter. He regretted not having asked Ex for his number, but at the time he didn't want the anxiety of "Should I call him" festering in the days to come. Now he found himself with the anxiety of "Will he call" pressing just as hard. It had begun as soon has he had stirred in bed that morning, trying to feel Ex's presence in whatever dreams he may have had. The coffee began to drip into the pot and he wondered why it was that his father's unannounced appearance, annoying as it was, felt like a victory, each and every time. It had something to do with need, of course. Not the need for approval that Andrew had sought from his father: since the time he began talking ("No, it's not 'I want eat', it's 'I want *to* eat'"); learning to swing a baseball bat ("Level, not tilted, or you'll never hit it"); playing the piano ("Only two mistakes that time"); driving a car ("You had plenty of time to turn left"); striving for academic excellence (in high school – "A 99? What did you get wrong?"; at university – "Magna Cum Laude. Isn't there one level higher?"). The proverbial prodigal son to everyone except the father to the son. No, it wasn't about approval. Perhaps it was about revenge or vindication, he thought as the coffee hit the two-cup marker etched on the coffee pot into which he'd poured water for four cups, in case he wanted ice coffee later in the day, which he never did, but he shuddered at the prospect of definitively eliminating possibilities; or in case

Ex should call, stop by, spend the afternoon/ evening/night and they could keep their glasses of ice coffee on the low-rise bamboo platform that jutted out into one side of the pool, while they immersed themselves naked. In his showing up unannounced, his father needed him in some way, and whatever triggered this need, it implied trust and, more critically after all, approval. Andrew, falling short despite his singular gifts, stripped of the possibility of ever being able to pat himself on the back for a job well done (it still could have been done better), demonstrating to his day-to-day world a soft but persistent rationality that seduced even the most mean-spirited, had won his father over. Yes, his father sought him out, needed him. And the need was at its most intense precisely when desire fueled by a twenty-three-year old was propelling Andrew's every inhalation and exhalation, as he thought, "Shit, Dad. Why couldn't you be Ex instead?"

"Do you want me to put your milk and sugar in, or should I bring everything to the table?"

"Go ahead. You know what I like."

"I miss Mom, too."

And he did. He claimed to friends that he found her more or less despicable as a human being – incapable of digesting a point of view that wasn't hers, of ever saying "I'm sorry" (even if she had much to apologize for), of ever saying "I don't know" (when in fact she knew very little). She was vulgar and crude, but she was his mother. He missed the mental space she took up – the routine of preparation before he saw her, the girding while he was with her, the decompression afterward – the lessons she never ceased to teach on how not to be, and the dancing motions she invoked to get through the cooking, the ironing, the folding of laundry, and all of the other rituals of her suburban life that her neighbors clearly did with greater ease and pleasure and sense of belonging and gratification. Mom. Who was she really, anyway? He was confounded by his need to hate her and forgive her.

"Do you want a snack with the coffee? We need to talk about moving you from your place to Sheila's. What goes, what doesn't go, what to do with what doesn't go, how to get what goes to Sheila's, how much time we have. All that fun stuff."

Charles replied, "The redwood beams are coming with me. Do you have any kind of cake? Andrew went to his desk, where he'd left his cell phone. Ex hadn't called. "Banana walnut."

"No zucchini?"

"Not today."

"I suppose I'll have a small slice then."

Andrew went back to the kitchen, pulled the paring knife with the black plastic handle out from the top drawer, and thought about holding it over his father's face and shouting things, for just a few minutes, like a madman. But unlike Edith, Charles didn't mean to provoke. Andrew brought two slices of cake to the table.

"You're going to have to be relentless about getting rid of things. You'll be going from a three-bedroom house into a room in Sheila's house."

"I'll have to build some shelving in her garage to store the redwood. Maybe up high so it's out of the way." "When is the closing?"

"I don't know. Soon. Your sister said she could seal the deal in a couple of weeks. You'll have to talk to her about the details."

"I will. I'll give her a call as soon as I leave."

"Aren't you coming with me to the urologist? Good cake, by the way."

Andrew was starting to spin inside. His body felt like a bed of leaves suddenly taken up by a funnel of wind. He knew how the conversation would unfold, with Sheila telling him to stop worrying, and assuring him that she could take care of everything – helping their father select what he was going to take, organizing the estate sale for everything that he wasn't going to take, finding and supervising the moving company, emptying the contents of the room that was going to be Charles's... -- and in the end taking care of nothing except to deposit her commission and greet her father with a beaming smile when he arrived. Andrew knew this, and also knew there was little that could be done about it. To offer to take care of everything from the outset would be to be met with his sister's "control freak" response; no, he would have to insinuate himself in increments, so that Sheila didn't notice (or would pretend not to notice) that she was playing no part in the transition except to supply the room, which wouldn't last anyway. Charles would inevitably migrate to the son.

"Can you go on your own this time? It's just a routine check-up and I'd like to start to organize the move if you don't mind."

Charles pressed the crumbs on his plate with his index finger and brought them to his mouth. "That's fine, son." He paused. "I guess I should be on my way."

They rose, walked to the front door and embraced each other.

"I love you."

"I love you too, Dad."

Andrew and Sheila had always been siblings first and foremost, and sometimes they had been more (friends, confidants, conspirators), but never less. Their twenty-three-month age difference didn't create any divides, except for a brief period when Sheila was entering adolescence and Andrew was not but was impatient to do so and consequently became a kind of combination of fawning parasite and spy as he prepared himself for that most hormone-fired of times with eagerness but also with sadness, somehow knowing (his male sexual fantasies just beginning to travel from the dark corridors toward the pinprick of light) that the draconian conformity required by adolescence – in each and every item of clothing you wore, in the way you positioned your legs when you sat in a chair, in the way you carried your books, in your handwriting style for love notes versus homework, in the geophysical location of your hair part, in your aptitude to calibrate the smart-aleck and the studious – would only come to him with enormous effort and a cinderblock-thick façade. So in that brief period, he followed his sister – who was pretty and smart enough and already had large breasts and had been practicing splits for two years before cheerleading tryouts, and therefore was a shoo-in for greatness – and studied her carefully, as if she were some secret fount that would reveal all. And she let him. In turn, it was understood that he was to be at her beck and call for services to be rendered in matters pertaining to the minutia of her self-concern: going to her bedroom when she called him after breakfast to help her zip up her skin-tight jeans or skirt as she lay down on her bed; quickly running the iron along her already straight (but not straight enough) hair each morning in the laundry room right before they left for school; storing her plastic vials of the forbidden blue and green eyeshadow and her large hoop earrings (all so cheap and whorish, their mother said) in his backpack so that he could slip them to her as soon as they reached the bus stop. Although these were all female accoutrements to the rite of passage, he observed and digested them nevertheless, since he was a boy who fantasized about boys. But it was her attitude that he was really trying to get at, that astonishing degree of self-involvement and its endless tiny components, which seemed so trivial but so essential, and that he suspected would never be within his grasp, since he was a boy who fantasized about boys and this secret fact would inevitably be detected by the jocks (particularly among those who also fantasized about boys) and then seep through the corridors like delicious leakage or deep dark sludge and he wouldn't have to worry at all about the rules and regulations and clauses and exemptions and amendments and addenda that made you "accepted" or not, since he would be banned from the entire system. But he didn't know any of this at the time. He just felt a sharp bearing-down, like some undiagnosed tumor.

"Beth told me that beer and raw eggs make your hair really shiny. Like Tahitian women," Sheila had told him the night before she was about to enter high school. "You have to soak your hair in it, put it in curlers and brush it out in the morning. You'll help me, right?"

"But your hair is already so thick and shiny."

"Beth's is thicker."

"Can we do it when *Bewitched* is over?"

"Sure."

After Samantha Stephens had twitched her nose for the last time and the credits started rolling down the twenty-six-inch screen of the Heathkit television set that their father had assembled in his workshop from a kit and had then encased into a walnut formica entertainment unit he'd built (on wheels so that their mother could move it to vacuum the gold and brown shag carpeting underneath), they left the rec room and headed upstairs to the kitchen, where Sheila grabbed two eggs and a bottle of Schlitz beer out of the refrigerator.

"Get the blue plastic bowl in the cabinet above the stove. And the whisk in the utensil drawer," she instructed her brother. He obliged. She beat the eggs and beer until they resembled eggnog.

"Boy does that stink," Andrew said. "Do you really want to go to school smelling like that?"

"Beth told me to dab some Fabergé Babe on my head right before I leave for school."

They took the concoction to the bathroom in the bedroom hallway and locked the door. Sheila placed the bowl in the sink, pulled her curlers out of the cabinet and set them on the vanity, wrapped a towel around her shoulders, put the toilet lid down and sat on it. "Okay. Put it in my hair."

"How?"

"I don't know. Just, you know, apply it."

Andrew looked at the bowl and plunged his hands into the foamy slime. He extracted them and quickly slapped them on top of his sister's head, sliding his slender fingers down her hair until the muck ran out. He plunged and slid again.

"Don't forget to wet the inside hair and get it into the scalp."

"I'll work it through when I get it all up there."

Once he overcame the smell and initial feel, he was enjoying himself. He liked playing with hair and did so (with Sheila's discarded Barbie doll and trolls) with the greatest of prudence lest, heaven forbid, he be caught. But here, locked in the bathroom with his sister and her thick hair and her permission, he was free to dabble and, finally, to try out Sheila's pink plastic curlers ("Curl under, not over. I don't want a flip"), whose diameters were so large that he could almost slip his hand through like a bracelet. He made seven neat columns of four curlers each, three on the left, three on the right and one centered in the back. She stood up from the toilet and looked at herself in the mirror, palming each curler with a beam of utter satisfaction.

"This is going to be amazing."

Andrew thought she looked ridiculous. He hadn't a clue as to what the male versions of these rituals would be when the time came, but even if he did, he was certain that he was eminently incapable of and uninterested in wanting to pursue any of them. When he attempted to consider and then be taken up by such things, in much the same way that he attempted to generate interest as he watched his father eagerly repairing some broken appliance or building yet another piece of furniture, his mind would make a U-turn back to his private stimuli – the photographs in The Family of Man (how often he returned to the pages of the Mongolian steppes and their desolation), the men's underwear section of the Sears Catalog, certain sentences he'd read in Narcissus and Goldmund or Point Counterpoint or The Stranger, the lyrics of Joni Mitchell, the blotches of sweat on the t-shirt of his neighbor Joey's hairy-chested father when he mowed the lawn on Sundays – and in these places he felt the fit, in these reliable sanctuaries where he was able to think the way he liked to think about things. Helping Sheila fit and fasten a tan hairnet around the jumbo curlers and imagining the torment she would have to undergo sleeping with such paraphernalia sprouting out all over her head, he understood that the male counterparts to these curlers, whatever they might be, were as distant to him as those Mongolian steppes (which he hoped to visit one day). And for the first time, he felt relieved. He might envy her for the cute boys she would date and go to first – or second – base with, but he would not envy the tragic compromise and settling-for that he was sure had to follow such a thin membrane of desire. He felt reassured, as if strength were finally gathering to lead him away from all that, which, deep down, he did not want. At the same time, he had no idea what he did want.

Sheila agreed to put off the closing for an extra month, after Andrew explained how complicated the transition was going to be. "I'll call my clients tomorrow and explain. They'll be fine about it."

Had the closing been delayed by an extra two months instead of one, their father could have avoided a double move and settled directly at Andrew's house. Three weeks after he arrived at Sheila's, his neuropathy flared up, preventing him from taking a shower on his own, and Sheila didn't have what it took to supervise him as he stood under the stream of water, naked, scrubbing his various body parts.

"I'm sorry, Andrew. I just can't," she told him as their father was getting into Andrew's car to transfer over.

"No need to apologize." He was sincere, but he bit his tongue as he said it, thinking of all the things she could have apologized for, or could have done in the first place so there would have been no need for her to make the apologies that she didn't make.

He closed the door once his father had seated himself and buckled his seat belt. Sheila walked over to her brother and embraced him. Her reading glasses fell off her head onto the driveway. Andrew picked them up. "Jesus, sis, how many times do you misplace those things or watch them fall off your head? You should get a chain."

"Too librarian. And they're the cheapo ones that you can get at the pharmacy. Believe it or not, I've had this pair for a few years."

"That's because I keep finding them for you."

"I'm so grateful that we're as close as we are, even if you are a royal pain in the ass."

Shapiro

CHAPTER 7

Andrew was in a virtual meeting with three representatives of international governmental organizations on three continents plowing through the agenda items – rationalization of resources, project exit strategies, harmonization of mandates and outputs, and disaggregated monitoring and evaluation data – when Ex texted him. His cell phone was in his pocket. The incoming message buzzed against his thigh.

"Hey. Any plans for tonight?"

He typed, "How about a swim, dinner, and..." but deleted the "and" and placed it after the word "swim" before sending it.

"Awesome. Around five okay?"

"Sounds good. See you tonight."

A simple barbecue would keep them outdoors, which was a safer place for Andrew, even if they went skinny-dipping. He needed to know what this boy was about, what Ex felt for or wanted from him, before daring to reach out and touch him un-innocently.

He arrived at 6:00.

"Sorry I'm late," he said as Andrew let him in. He dropped his backpack on the rattan chair in the front porch. "I had a couple of things to do." He looked worn. In fact, Andrew believed that he was wearing the same black shorts and t-shirt. His nails were dirty, his eyes bloodshot, and there were filaments of black between his toes. Andrew couldn't decide if he hadn't slept since they were last together, or whether he had just woken up after a sleep marathon.

"Where do you live, anyway?"

"Do you mind if I jump in the pool"?

"Go right ahead. I can get some juice."

"That would be great."

Ex stripped down and torpedoed underwater from one end of the pool to the other, back and forth four times until he leapt up in the middle of the pool and spun around. He then floated on his back. From the kitchen window, Andrew watched his firm stomach muscles rise and fall below the water level. Ex was breathing heavily, but his face was in a pose of complete relaxation. As Andrew dropped the ice cubes into the glass, he realized that he knew nothing about this creature except some vague ideas he had expressed about life in general, the bedazzled reaction he had to Andrew's house and his selection of music, and that he was beautiful. But where did he live? How did he live? How did he fill his days? And, the most pressing imperatives concerning the local youth: Was he up to no good? Which kinds? How often?

"Here you go." Ex swam over to the shallow end of the pool and took the glass.

"Thank you." He tilted the tall glass back, drank its contents without stopping, placed the glass on the pool's edge and torpedoed anew. "Come in this time," he said when he surfaced. Andrew stripped down and took the four steps. The water was warm. He could slide right in without flinching. He submerged himself and swam under water to the right corner at the far end of the pool, away from Ex. Ex followed suit, lifted himself up and sat at the edge of the pool next to and above Andrew, who looked up at him.

"So?"

Ex explained that he was temporarily staying on the sofa at a friend's house. He had come back to the area after dropping out of his first semester at university and camped out on the front porch of his parent's house, which was as much space in their house as he could convince them to let him have. "They don't get me."

Andrew wanted to ask him what it was they were supposed to get, but he refrained. He refrained from asking any other questions. His desire to know Ex better was matched by his desire to not know him at all, at least not the facts of him. They would trickle out in good time without the pressure of curiosity that could easily be misconstrued as interrogation. After a long pause, he replied, simply, "Ah."

Looking up at Ex was almost too much to bear. His face was less than a foot from Ex's thigh, which was cupped by Ex's fingers, his thumb slightly extended and buried in his pubic hair. He was hairy, and far from the age when the hair on the legs recedes above the sock line. His other hand was gripped around the edge of the pool, almost touching Andrew's. Andrew pushed off, twisted and swam under water to the other end.

They ate on the deck – barbecued burgers, white corn on the cob, coleslaw (exotic fare for Andrew after so many years abroad) – as the sun was setting. Ex deftly veered

away from the facts of his life and toward his ideas about
Life. When Andrew told him about some of the places
he'd lived, Ex told him he wanted him to take him to
Europe one day, to some city there that he knew, like
Paris. Why Paris? he asked. Ex said he loved hearing
French, that the sound of it felt like the kind of music he
wanted to compose. He said he couldn't explain it, and
Andrew told him there was no need, that he understood.
Ex looked at him, puzzled. "You compose music too?"
Andrew laughed and told him that he didn't, but that it
wasn't about composing music, that it was about – and
here he shifted the tone of his voice to something less soft
and more dramatic – "inchoate, roiling intensities"
(knowing full well that Ex wouldn't understand the
expression, but confident he would thrill over the new
words and understand the point). He asked him what he
would like to see in Paris. Ex told him he didn't know any
sights there. Andrew was tempted to tell him that
everything everywhere is a sight, but he held back. Instead,
he named a few – the Eiffel Tower ("Oh right, that's
there, isn't it"), the Arc de Triomphe ("What's that?"), the
Louvre ("How do you say that one again?") – and added
that they would spend one morning reading the dictionary
out loud in the Bois de Bologna. Ex asked why, not in a
confrontational way but in an excited way, by now
expecting a response that he could have faith in, cryptic as
it may be. Andrew told him that he couldn't think of
anything more luxurious that one could do, that that was
what moneyed, cultivated people did, even though, and
here's the secret, you didn't need either to do it. Ex liked
the idea. How Andrew wished he could whisk him off that
day, or the day after, while he was still an idea of a person.
Andrew no longer had a desire to travel, to wander about
and wonder at cities, museums, parks, monuments. But to

travel with Ex by his side, to watch him wander and wonder. "*On peut y réfléchir*," he said to him. Ex didn't ask what that meant. The sound satisfied him, fortified his trust and fueled what Andrew hoped one day, against all odds, would be his love for him. Or at least for them.

When it was dark, they returned inside to the living room. Ex lay on the sofa, head propped up on one armrest and feet and ankles dangling far over the other. He was wearing the same black nylon perforated running shorts, a black baseball cap (rim backwards) and sunglasses – completely oblivious to the photo-shoot perfection of every detail of the sprawl of him, even the slightly grimy soles of his feet which, since Andrew first met him, had never been inside of shoes. Certain features that are usually not part of extreme tallness lifted him out of that lanky, string-bean-like cuteness and thrust him unawares into a more robust and sexual terrain. His shoulders, which would normally be narrow on such a frame, were broad enough to create a tapering as his outline made its long journey to his waist; and his thighs, calves and ankles didn't have that stretched-out look of pulled taffy, but rather insisted on their fair share of form and sinuosity. He was relaxed. His hand slipped into his shorts. Andrew asked him when he last had sex. Ex felt obliged to respond (he wanted to be pushed further by Andrew, especially when he was lying on the sofa and a round of questions began), but the subject of sex was new and, as Andrew expected, a terrifying place for him to be, and perhaps especially with him. He slid through by saying that it depended on what Andrew means by sex. Andrew clarified: based on what *you* would mean by sex, you can answer. It has to be *right*, he replied. It's a *feeling*, he said. His struggle for sincerity was palpable, but his ambivalent desire to fend off the topic was stronger. Andrew wanted to stop, but he couldn't resist. "So tell me when you last had sex." He studied his face, but it was clear that Ex was not sifting through his memory to find that time, that place, that person, when that act of "sexing" last took place. He was shutting down, avoiding, as Andrew was hoping so tenuously to avoid, a slow seduction in the making. Andrew wondered whether Ex was afraid to say he was gay, or whether he was afraid to say he was straight. He got up from his chair, smacked the bottom of Ex's grimy left foot and said, "My turn tonight." He went off to the kitchen to wash the dishes, wondering how he would know more about Ex than the fact that he sleeps on the sofa of a friend. And how much more he wanted to know.

CHAPTER 8

The irregular pit-pat of light rain against his window woke Andrew up. It was still dark outside. He lifted his head and turned toward the clock on his night table: the soft blue digits read 5:30. He was tempted to let his head fall back onto the pillow and try to go back to sleep. But instead he rolled over on his back, kept his eyes open and listened to the rain, which usually came in decisive torrents in the afternoons, hardly ever in the mornings. The sound disoriented him, as did the fact, which announced itself as soon as he had stirred and reached over to feel the pillow next to him and make sure it really was fully fluffed, that he was in love. He remembered certain dream fragments – a nude woman with long brown hair, Ex's cock (longer and thicker than he'd remembered it by the pool's edge), dried leaves digging into his back, an ease of penetration (but whose?). He fitted and retrofitted but couldn't join these trailers of alternate reality into the coherence, the message, the meaningfulness, that he believed dreams were meant to layer onto the waking hours. He reached down to the crotch of his boxer shorts that he used as pajamas and felt a damp blotch on the right side that had worked its way up into the thick black elastic band.

As he prepared the day's portion of coffee and was creating his mental list of work commitments and their proper sequence in order to finish by 11 o'clock (six months ago, it was by 1:00, six months later there might be no work; he was rehearsing for an imminent early retirement), he added two non-work-related **items**: enumerate the steps to compress his father and possessions from a three-bedroom house to what was soon to be his new one-room quarters at Sheila's; and draft a text message to Ex inviting him to stay with him, perhaps nothing more than "Would you like to move into my place?", which might take him hours to craft and commit to a text window, but which he would then save, knowing that a simple click on "Send" was all it would take to potentially upend his life, if he chose to do so. (His father would upend his son's life in a month, but as yet Andrew was unaware of it.)

As soon as he had opened an Excel sheet, the phone rang. It was his sister.

"Morning bro."

"Hey. I was going to call you later."

"I'll bet you were. To go over everything, right? Well, Dad's room is all ready for him. I cleared out my stuff. I didn't realize how many dance dresses I had."

"Surprise surprise. Anyway, that's a good start."

"So let's get together today, if you're free. And I'm dying to show you my new hair color. I think I finally got it right. It hides the gray without announcing it. And the color seems perfectly natural."

Andrew envied Sheila's genius at maintaining young, healthy-looking hair, which was a mystery to him since she was a sucker for the endless possibilities of shades, highlights and streaks, and she experimented in kind, endlessly. Nevertheless, despite the occasional streak that was too unsubtle, the shade that was suspicious given the color of her naturally arched eyebrows that required no care, her hair didn't succumb, ever, to the brittle texture and filmy patina that seemed to come about in one's fifties, like so much else that, in one's fifties, seemed as if it had been lightly but indelibly dipped in ash. She persuaded her brother to make a number of conservative forays – with neutral hennas, coconut oils, aloe creams (he didn't dare enter into the world of the strictly chemical) – to "bring out the luster," but his hair remained steadfastly uneventful. Several years ago he had resolved to abandon his tenuous efforts, fearful that they would end up being the first in a series of overhauls – of the sagging eyebrows and eyelids, the emerging crevices in his already sallow cheeks (once considered sexy clefts, but at least he didn't have wrinkles, only crevices), the mysteriously thinning lips (where did the rest of the lip flesh disappear to?). He remembered Sheila's removal of a cabinet above her refrigerator so that she could buy a larger one with a water dispenser and ice-maker (both cubes and crushed) embedded in the freezer door. One thing led to another, and four months later she had renovated her entire ground floor. He bought a pair of cheap clippers and kept his hair buzzed uniformly short with the #3 attachment. Yet one more piece of the elements of attraction to be relinquished – to not be noticed by others – in the downward spiral of invisibility, or at least unnoticeableness.

He was impressed by what Sheila had done, or rather undone to the room that was to become her father's quarters. It had been stripped of everything except those items that she thought would be unconditionally essential for him – the queen-size bed with two lengths of contemporary geometric-design carpeting on either side (death by falling, inexcusable), a set of corner-unit bookshelves (white, unobtrusive, functional), bolsters on the large window seat that overlooked the small yard, and plenty of hangers in the clothes and walk-in closets in the small hallway leading to the bathroom.

As she walked her brother through the room and, like a tour guide, talked him through the pressing needs of the present that had caused her to alter the "historical" topology of this space, he understood that she was seeking out any and all approval that would absolve her from any and all other responsibilities insofar as further logistics were concerned. He acquiesced – "Perfect," he said, knowing his sister well enough to not waste his time or energy suggesting that she could do more. He couldn't abide her accusing him, explicitly or implicitly, of being "just like Dad." Casually counting the number of black and white plastic hangers in the walk-in closet, along with the wire and wooden ones hanging (clearly she had rifled through her own closets and yanked out whatever hangers weren't being used), he accepted the fact, unfair as it was, that his sister was now off the hook. (Had he known that his father would be living with him in a month, he could have spared her even this modicum of effort, but he didn't know.)

"By the way, your hair is great," he said. "You really got it this time," suspecting that she would continue refining and perfecting until her hair surrendered and broke off like an overworked straw broom, or until she died. "Let me check out the bathroom again." Before she could reply, he moved down the small corridor of closets and into what would soon be his father's bathroom. He would need to install a handrail in the shower and buy a shower chair before his father died. His father would die soon, but he would not allow him to die of falling. He looked in the mirror and pulled the flesh near his cheeks toward his ears. He calculated that at least ten years vanished with the smoothing out of those crevices – even if, he knew, those ten years wouldn't then be added onto his life-span. He released his fingers and watched the crevices reform.

"Andrew? What are you doing in there? I have some lunch for us. Leftover edamame salad and some empanadas from Blue Dolphin. They're good."

"Be out in a sec." He pulled his phone out from his pants pocket, navigated to his first and only draft in the Message window and, without rereading it, pushed the "Send" button.

He stopped at the beach after lunch and before going to his father's. Reaching the end of the sea grape tunnel and the vast stretch of sand to his left and right, he turned left, toward the unpeopled stretch and, further in the distance, the tikki bar. The fishermen would have long been gone with their catch of the day and made their rounds of the grocery stores and restaurants. As far as the eye could see, he couldn't make out a soul. He would be able to resist the temptation to arrive at the tikki bar as long as no indistinct figure presented itself at about that distance. He felt extra relief being at the beach at his usual hour, returning to a place that triggered another place in his mind that he was used to going to, where he could depend on finding a morsel of reliable happiness, which, he knew, love rarely proffered. At sixty, sameness of thought had become an aspiration, a comfort. At the same time, he wanted to be jarred, at least once more in the remaining time allotted to him. Beyond being altered in some subtle way or being even more conscious of the specifics of who he was. For the moment, however, he focused on pink shells below and pelicans in chevron flight above. There was nothing more to be done.

As he drove to his father's house from the beach, he had a clear idea of what would be going to his sister's house, what was to be displayed and tagged at an estate sale, what was to be tossed in the "For Free" box, and what was to be thrown out altogether. He also already knew a mover, and already knew a woman who would organize and manage the estate sale. In the end, he thought, it wasn't nearly as daunting as the prospect of his second bedroom inevitably being occupied by his father until he died, and his third bedroom possibly being occupied by a creature who had yet to spread his wings. But no text message had arrived, except an advertisement for an update to his Grindr app, which he'd forgotten that he had installed.

He let himself in. His father was in the garage, tinkering with wires. "Hello, boychik. Give me a second. Looking for extension wires for the speakers." He was standing next to a rack with at least thirty clamps of varying lengths pinched to the rod across the top and hanging like the boned remains of slaughtered animals. Next to the rack was a pegboard panel covering one entire wall of the garage. Here hung hangable tools and implements – brooms, hammers, saws, thick orange extension cords coiled on black spools – but no fewer than five of each. Andrew shuddered at the thought of having to go through each object, one by one, with his father, letting him ponder its history and usefulness in order to determine whether it was a keeper, a seller or a tosser. "That hammer? Oh that hammer was the one I used to…", "That Phillips head can really grab," "You made lanyards from those wires when you were little, remember?" (he didn't' remember) and on and on, room by room, drawer by drawer, shelf by shelf, object by object needing to be captured in a tiny story (and cohered into a complete and completed life) before being let go.

"You're sure you want to do this now?" he asked.

His father put down the wires. "Son, I'm not really in the mood to rehash this. I enjoyed living on my own when your mother and I separated. And I've enjoyed living on my own since she died. But I don't particularly care to die alone. Can we leave it at that?"

"I just thought that…"

His father interrupted him. "Isn't this supposed to be about what I think?"

"Sorry, Dad. I can come by for a few hours tomorrow if you want to get started sorting through things."

"Son, I can take care of it. I've already gone through the spare bedroom and the closets."

"I can come by at around noon, if that works…"

Again, his father interrupted him. "I can take care of it. Let me say it another way. I want to take care of it."

"Sure thing, Dad."

"Do me a flavor and get out of my hair. You have better things to do than to dote on an old man who doesn't want to be doted on. Leave me with my things. Now git boy."

"I'll talk to you later."

"As opposed to sooner, right? Now git. I love you, but you can be a royal pain in the ass."

"Like father, like son. I love you too, Dad."

When Andrew arrived home, he went directly down the hallway to the two spare bedrooms. One was quite small, with a single bed, and the other was the largest of the three (Andrew had chosen the middle-size bedroom because its two windows looked out on the backyard and not the street). The large bedroom would be his father's, when the time came. In it, there was plenty of space for the desk that his father had made out of a no-longer-used teak head- and footboard of a bed, his navy green leather reading chair that could tilt back and lock into the desired position by turning a black knob on the side of the chair, and one of his two flat-screen televisions. It wasn't as large as the room he would have at Sheila's, and the bathroom was across the hall and not "en suite," but Charles was not one to barricade himself up in rooms unless he was building something, which he hadn't done for years, even though he spoke passionately about various projects that he "intended" to begin "in due course": the dining room table for Andrew, very long and very narrow, to accommodate the space in front of the picture window overlooking the pool; an entertainment unit for Sheila, to house all of the media devices she had bought and rarely used but had assumed that she would one day, once she turned into the kind of person who used such devices; and several other projects that hadn't even seen the light of a preliminary sketch before he died six months after moving in with his daughter, and five months after moving in with his son. He wasn't a compulsive talker, but he liked the presence of others and the background sounds they made – the clearing of a throat, the rustling of a piece of paper, the closing of a drawer, the clink of a glass being set down on a counter or table – as they went about the business of being busy. The small bedroom would therefore be Ex's, unless, of course....Andrew hurled the rest of the thought to a faraway place and went to the kitchen to cobble together a light dinner, stopping by his desk to deposit his phone, out of earshot, and wondering how to break the news of this new possible presence – this creature, this specimen – to his father (who would assume that his son's paternal instinct was at last latching onto a healthy outlet) and to his sister (who would sniff out the erotic, the inherent aroma of pedophilia that, despite her show of hipness, was always at the core of her considerations of homosexuality).

"Irresponsible. Outrageous. Revolting. When are you going to settle down already!" That's what his mother would have said, not relenting until he became the doctor or lawyer with a wife and children and a fine home in the suburbs that she was belligerent about having known all along was his true destiny. Edith would brandish this sword against her favorite child, and her favorite object of contempt, from the moment he had had his first thought that his mother couldn't attribute to her love, her care, her control. Andrew had learned to dull that blade years before his mother died. He considered it his most responsible act.

He opened the freezer door and noticed a Tupperware container of meat sauce that he'd made several weeks ago. Pasta would be easy, satisfying, topped with some parmigiano reggiano freshly grated off the block that was sealed with a small grater in a zip-lock bag on the top shelf of the fridge, and accompanied by the bag of mixed organic greens in the crisper. In twenty minutes, dinner would be ready, even though he was in no hurry. A handful of empty evening hours were waiting for him.

The frozen meat sauce rotated in the microwave, the pot of water for the pasta began its pre-boil rumble. As he was pouring the greens into a small ceramic bowl wondering whether he should eat them plain or add a few vegetables (the tomatoes and the red pepper would have to be used within a day, or thrown out), he remembered his mother's jarred spaghetti sauce (the brand varied, depending on whatever was on sale or she had a coupon for) and the dense heads of iceberg lettuce that she would cleave and hack furiously into ragged postage-stamp-sized bits. He missed her. She was his mother and he missed her voice, her rage, her hawk-like protectiveness over her brood, especially her son, and the reactions that only she could provoke in him. Where did they go? Where did she go? Sheila insisted that she was watching from above, and kibbitzing with their grandmother from above, and that she could sometimes feel her presence so strongly that she took it as a tangible sign, like when the photo of her wearing a dress (a dress!) in front of a Florida resort hotel fell off the wall when she was dusting several months ago and thinking unkind thoughts of her. Andrew didn't feel these presences, and he couldn't conjure them now as he eased a fistful of fettucine into the pot of boiling water and remembered her jarred spaghetti sauce and iceberg lettuce. But didn't she warn him that she wasn't through with him? So where was she, he thought. What he also thought as the stiff pasta slowly withered under the force of the wet heat was how much he would soon miss his father, although in a very different way, and how much he would hate him for having the audacity to force him to simultaneously be an orphan and the patriarch the moment after he took his last breath.

The pasta was ready. He turned off the stove. The rumble of the boiling water subsided and there was silence, which Andrew hastened to put an end to by vigorously shaking the pasta in the colander, since that silence, at that moment, had the desolate quality of a pre-winter early dusk and an old person living alone preparing his simple, solitary meal. He brought his dinner to the dining room table, a large rectangle of glass positioned in front of an even larger picture window that looked out onto the even larger pool and surrounding strata of tropical vegetation. He forked up his first mouthful of pasta. As children, he and his sister played the "twirling game" whenever their mother served up spaghetti for dinner. They'd choose some long and complicated word and with each twirl of the fork would have to name the next letter of the word without missing a beat. Andrew's favorite winning word was antidisestablishmentarianism. Looking out the picture window into his yard and beginning to twirl that first forkful, he found himself playing a variation of the game: Name the Vegetation by Strata. At the upper level, Christmas, areca and majesty palms and tangerine, pomegranate and mango trees and a jacaranda (providing random canopies against the sun and heat); at mid-level, birds of paradise, firecrackers, yellow cassia, hibiscus, crotons and ixora; at ground level, oleander, flax lily, desert rose, bromeliads, boston and macho ferns; and jasmine and lavender and fuchsia bougainvillea spilling over the rear and side fences of the back yard – all the while sensing glass, waning light, profusions of color. He finished the game, not quite satisfied that he had named everything but confident that during his mental off-hours he would come up with some mnemonic device to not miss any of them the next time (as he did when he had bought his first car, a royal blue

Oldsmobile Omega, and cantillated "Moneygumkeyscombcigarettes" each time he left the house to make sure he hadn't forgotten what he considered his essentials; although a mnemonic device didn't come into play when, at his father's funeral six months later, he recalled the flax lily and the crotons along the left side of his pool as he stood over the deep rectangular pit that the coffin was about to be lowered into by some highly sophisticated mechanical device that his father would surely have been impressed by). He reached for the sea salt grinder. Next to it lay the Burmese Citrine Cluster, resembling a large chunk of glistening, opaque salt. He didn't remember moving it from the coffee table. In fact, he was sure he hadn't. He licked his finger, rubbed it lightly against the crystal and put his finger in his mouth. It didn't taste like salt, but he imagined it tasting like Ex, in some recess of his body where sweat formed and steeped. In one of the neighboring yards, a weed-whacker started up. Andrew welcomed the break in the silence, although it didn't make him feel less old or alone.

CHAPTER 9

"When?"

The one-word text arrived three days later, shortly before midnight.

"Fuck. Fuck fuck fuck," Andrew sputtered, infuriated by Ex's three-day disappearing act broken by one floating and decontextualized adverb sent at an hour when people who text are drunk or drugged or desperate or in some other mindless or irresponsible state. "When" – How dare he! A single hand can't clap, but a single text-message word that reaches only the eye and not the ear – devoid of tell-tale tones and inflections, the positioning of the eyes and lips as it is released, the fidgeting hand or downward tilt of the head or swaying back and forth of the legs – one word that appears only in a text window with nothing preceding it and nothing following it except proper punctuation, holds a thunderous force of ambiguity. To be easily excluded were "Wow. I'll think about it" or "Thanks, but I don't think so" or "No." "When" meant "Yes." He was infuriated again as he considered the

"When" as "It's about time you asked" or "I'm very busy; just give me a date and time and I'll let you know if that's better than the other offers I've put out" or "Thank God. I'm about to be on the street." He tried to imagine Ex saying the word, but he couldn't locate the intention that propelled it. How and what could he respond?

At midnight, when he was usually sound asleep, he took a shower; rather, he stood under the shower nozzle, remained perfectly still, and let the hottest possible water spray over him for fifteen minutes. He decided how to respond – in kind, but using four words: "Call me. We'll talk." He also decided to send it in the morning, so that the anticipation of a middle-of-the-night reply would be removed from any of the possible things that might keep him awake.

It was a wakefulness filled with a parade of interrogatives and vexing images of cohabitation that he couldn't subdue – of domestic uncertainties (Does he cook? Is he tidy? Will he invite friends over and be up all night yakking over loud music about things that they don't yet understand and that he no longer cares about? Does he know how to be alone in company? Have I learned how to be alone in company?) and of sexual uncertainties (Will my bedroom be our bedroom? Will he slip into my bed from time to time? Will he shut off the sexual valve as soon as he has accomplished his mission of finding a home?). He was terrified to get out of bed, switch on a light. The darkness made all of it unreal, and this particular unreality felt safe. Unable to see his bed (and the extra set of pillows purchased and positioned for the exclusive purpose of symmetry), he could imagine anything, rearrange it, make it work, make it disappear. If he turned on the light, the bed, the closet, the chest of drawers, the unmatching nighttables, would call for resolution. And so he thrashed about in the dark until some undetermined hour when he must have fallen asleep, since at a certain point when the sun had already appeared between the slats of his white plantation shutters, he had the distinct sensation of being aware of the soft morning light, the blanket knotted around his legs and the two extra pillows stuffed between them...of waking up out of sleep. He got up, went to the kitchen to prepare the coffee, and walked out the front door to fetch the newspaper. When he returned inside and poured his first cup of coffee, he texted: "Call me. We'll talk."

CHAPTER 10

The countdown toward the end of the father-daughter cohabitation began only three days later, with two phone calls. The first was an early-morning call from his sister.

"I asked him what he wanted for breakfast and you know what he said? He said 'Just a simple veggie omelet.' Can you believe it? Like at 7:30 in the morning I'm going to start chopping up a bunch of veggies to make him an omelet. And what the fuck are simple veggies? What the fuck is a *complex* veggie?"

"Did you make one?"

"Like hell. I pulled out three boxes of dry cereal and told him to pick one. What does he think I am, a short-order cook? As if I have nothing better to do than whip up a goddam simple veggie omelet."

"Let me guess. Raisin Bran."

"Nope. Wheat Chex."

"Close." He then told her had taken in a roommate.

"Right. And Ryan Gosling asked me to marry him last night while I was trimming Dad's nose hairs."

"Well, I'm on the verge of."

"Can we talk about this later? I'm backed up with work from the buffet breakfast."

"Okay. Call when it works for you." He hung up.

The second was a late-morning call from his father.

"I'm wearing a sweater. It's 85 degrees outside and I'm wearing a sweater in this house. She keeps the thermostat at 69. Says it's a menopause thing. She's got the thermostat on the second floor. She spends all her time up there. She doesn't get that hot air rises, which means that down below, where I am, the temperature is probably hovering at the freezing point. I can almost see my breath."

"I'll talk to her."

"Waste of time. No getting around the menopause thing. I didn't move to Florida to wear a sweater in July. She wants to kill me. Freeze me to death."

"Dad."

"Remember that episode from the Twilight Zone? Or was it Alfred Hitchcock? Anyway, remember the episode when the woman murders her husband by clubbing him to death with a frozen leg of lamb and then serves it up to the police officer who comes to investigate? Do you remember? Did you see that one? Now that I think about it, would I have let you see that one?"

"Dad."

"I'm kidding, son. But this could be the death of me."

"Apropos of nothing, I have a roommate."

"Hang on. Sheila's calling down to me for the nth time. Frankly, I could do without all of her concern." He hung up.

Andrew cursed them both as he spread cream cheese on his toasted, pre-packaged frozen bagel, thinking about the bagel store at 105th and Broadway that drew a line of white-collar types on the sidewalk by 6:45 a.m. as they waited for the door to open and release the heady scent of trays and trays of piping hot bagels (sesame seed, poppy seed, onion, whole wheat, plain, garlic, and "everything") being carried directly from the oven and then tilted into huge wicker baskets that looked like primitive baby basinets. Instead, here he was, as he was on many mornings, undoing a twist-em from a frozen plastic bag and squeezing his hand into the bag like it was some kind of alien glove in order to get at the top bagel, pry it off the second bagel, and dust off the frost before putting it in the toaster oven...the operation was a sad affair, especially for a bagel that lacked yeasty texture and flavor and wreaked of freezer-burn. It was dry, tired, stripped of its sense of purpose. To be living in New York again. A modest one-bedroom apartment on the Upper West Side. No ocean, except of people, and of films that would never arrive in the multiplexes in his area. Finding the off-beat gem of a this and that to go to, or not to go to but at least knowing it was there to go to – which it wasn't there to go to in his area. When the desire to return to the States had reached a point when he knew he'd have to either succumb or live forever with this festering plea, he calculated and recalculated, manipulating the numbers in radical ways to make them accommodate a modest one-bedroom co-op anywhere in Manhattan below 125th Street, east or west side. The result was always the same: thousands and thousands of dollars, and light years, away from the possible; a hard fact which he softened by imagining the house, the yard, the swimming pool, the ocean within walking distance, and family nearby, if he settled in this area. A decent trade-off, to be sure. There had been moments when he ruminated over unearthing some hovel in some as yet unpioneered neighborhood of Brooklyn, the edgy paradise-wasteland. Perhaps that would have been preferable to this tropical paradise-wasteland. He hadn't had one of those moments since he met Ex, who was here and not on the Upper West Side or in some unpioneered neighborhood of Brooklyn (and who, had he been "there," could have gone almost as unnoticed as Andrew was everywhere, at his age). He bit into the bagel. Its hard edges scraped at the roof of his mouth like a snow plow on asphalt. He'd managed to pitch the subject of Ex at his father and his sister in one morning, but they didn't flinch. Ball one. Fuck. He'd have to pitch again. Maybe "roommate" was outside the striking zone. Young friend? Boyfriend? Surrogate son? Lover? Life partner? Companion? Project? What did he want Ex to be for him? What was Ex for him now? His index finger scooped up a crumble of the not-so-creamy cream cheese that had fallen off the bagel and onto the plate. He brought it to his mouth, smeared it on his lips like chap-stick and circled his tongue counter-clockwise until the cream cheese was gone. It had been warmed by the toasted bagel and felt slickery and dense. He was still hungry.

He wanted more of Ex, even if, he thought, he might not need to be with him all the time, merely in just enough doses to create his imaginary Ex, the version he wanted to spend every moment with. He might be too rich a dish to feast upon in large portions. Small tastes of him could take hours/days to digest, and while there was the delight of immediate pleasure to be had in the being with him, when every nerve ending, ever fiber, every heart string, every brain cell came clamoring to electrifying life, it might be the after-being-with-him that offered up the long and lingering aftertaste of enchantment and warning, which could be turned this way and that, pushed toward or away from some source of heat (love-erotic-desire-intellectual musing) until the urge to both lose and find himself was at peace, for an instant like no others. And then it could begin again.

He opted for a couple of slices of canteloupe. Not that he really wanted canteloupe, but the half-melon in the fridge had to be finished by the end of the day, or else pitched. If he ate half of the half now, he figured, he'd only have a quarter to worry about later, perhaps as a snack or, if need be, as an unsatisfying dessert after dinner.

He scooped the seeds out of the melon directly into the trash bin. His phone rang.

"Sorry about that, son. Had to give Sheila my dirty laundry. She was doing a load."

"Everything going more or less okay?"

"More or less."

"Tell me the 'more' part, if you don't mind. We can save the 'less' part for another time."

From Charles's accounting of matters, there wasn't much in the way of "more" – meals prepared, laundry done, house kept in order (except for his room, which she informed him at the outset that she would not enter under any circumstances unless he were to press the bellhop device that she had placed on his nighttable for emergencies), the usual wife-role duties that he expected women to perform as a kind of genetic predisposition and imperative and for which he therefore felt no particular need to express more than a blip of gratitude, in the form of an occasional and flat "Thanks, dear," as if it were a monosyllabic space-filler, without so much as turning his head in her general direction. This came as no surprise to Andrew. After all, his father had married at the normal age of twenty-four, in the 1950s, when "Leave it to Beaver" and "The Donna Reed Show" had solidified and codified what would be termed in the infinitely more evolved 1990s the gendered division of labor. It couldn't be otherwise in his swath and history of reality, and Sheila was a fool and an ass to think that her own tailor-made sense of modernity and feminism, evolved out of her desire to be desired by a man who would serve her and lack the gumption to leave her, could, and should, have the power to obliterate the entirely cogent and air-tight, if perverse, sociology of a generation that had pioneered the concept, dream and utopia of suburbia. She never considered that her mother, whose abject misery and contempt had infected her animus like some irrepressible cancer, was one of many victims of the construct (how many housewives stored bottles of cooking sherry at the back of the cabinet above the refrigerator?) but that it couldn't be otherwise if one chose to live in those green manicured deserts. Yes, a man of her father's age and circumstances expected an omelet for breakfast, or pancakes, or French toast, or whatever his heart desired, especially if each morning for more than thirty-five years his wife had asked him, dutifully, "What would you like for breakfast?" before he set off dutifully for work, smooch at the door, until he could retire (which, he had figured from his first day on the job, would make sense after forty years and two months of service). Sheila didn't think about these things.

"Son, would you mind if I stop by later today? I think my hernia is acting up. I'd like you to take a look. I can't ask your sister. Can't have her looking down in those parts."

Andrew wondered if he would have made the omelet. "Sure, Dad. Any time after two should be fine. Just give a call before you leave." He also wondered if he would find a way to bring up the "roommate" thing again before, during, or after his father's groin inspection. It would probably have to wait.

Ex did call him, shortly after the hernia inspection, which looked serious. A swelling the size of a golf ball, and corresponding discomfort, had erupted on the left side of his father's groin, next to his penis, which Andrew noticed had not been spared from looking old. It was shrunken, drawn into itself, as if ashamed of no longer being able to stand erect and proudly and confidently plunge into spaces that begged for some kind of brief, irresistible and mutual transcendence. Andrew made an appointment for his father to see the family doctor the next morning, and also made a point to study his own penis as soon as his father left.

"I can come by later this afternoon. Like at five or six, if that's okay," Ex said.

"You're welcome to stay for dinner."

"That would be great."

To be sure, Ex ate enough. His body was taut and toned without being chiseled or bulked up; his skin was healthy and vigorous. His leg and chest hair glistened. Andrew imagined passing his hand along the dense but baby-fine hair that runs up his arm, and felt a jolt of tenderness and pain. He felt Ex's destiny laid out before him and wanted to warn him about the inevitable erosion of his breathtaking beauty and stature (and the demotion from supreme to lesser divinity), about the first day when no one notices it because it is no longer pronounced enough to notice, and how the entire free-spirit/saint thing starts to no longer work. But there was still plenty of time.

Yet Ex ate as if he hadn't eaten in days. It wasn't merely the voraciousness of a young, active body requiring constant and abundant nourishment; there was something desperate about the way Ex shoveled down the dinners that Andrew prepared, as if he didn't know where his next meal would be coming from, or perhaps out of some pathological need to feel full or filled – yet another detail among so many that Andrew looked forward to, or wanted to avoid, understanding.

The hernia had swelled, but what was worse, his father's feet were cold and blue.

"I'm calling the doctor," Andrew said. "This is no joke. Why do you wait until things reach this point before mentioning them?"

"Because it's manageable. You can't understand. You're not eighty-five."

Dr. Kundumadathil told them to come in right away. "He's Indian but nice. And so intelligent," was how Andrew's mother had characterized him to her son when she and Charles had decided to take him on as their primary physician. Andrew had let the remark slide, as he had with so many of her other unpremeditated racial slurs.

The doctor agreed. The hernia was serious, but the feet were more serious. "We need to take care of your feet right away or you risk gangrene and possible amputation. Sorry to be so blunt, but this is urgent. I'll schedule an angioplasty for the left foot as soon as possible. We'll see how it takes, and then take care of the right foot." Andrew asked him what an angioplasty was and learned that it was a kind of roto-rootering of the main veins leading to the feet, to allow the blood to reach them more quickly and more freely. "For the hernia, for the time being you can pick up a special set of underwear to hold it in until we take care of the feet. I'll call you this afternoon with the details, once I've set up the appointment for the angioplasty."

Andrew and his father headed to the parking lot. Charles collapsed into the passenger seat. "It never lets up.

Do yourself a favor, son. Don't live this long. Of all the advice I've given you in sixty years, hear me out on this one."

Andrew's hand automatically went toward the radio dial but he pulled it back. Silence was in order. Fact: An eighty-five-year-old man will die soon, as it could be for a seventeen-year-old (and here the thought of Ginny Darcy, his high-school class Homecoming Queen and National Merit Scholar – the "girl who had everything" – who asphyxiated herself the summer after graduation with long gulps of carbon monoxide as she sat in the closed car of her parents' closed garage. They had forbidden her to date the basketball center who was bound for vocational school – Chad, was his name; or was it Chet? – and whom she thought she was in love with. So she killed herself instead.). Unfair in the degrading descent toward it, the onslaught of breakdowns and stunning indignities that lead one to embrace the end, not out of sublime acceptance but out of sheer despair and desperation. Turning left onto the highway, he tried to feel signs – a joint ache, a whisper of rheumatism... He was disappointed. He wanted to begin to understand, to know, already. He was fifty-six, his closely cropped beard was white, his skin no longer taut. He had his morbid list of "I'll never agains" – do back handsprings, party until sunrise, trek in the Himalayas, lose himself in love. Losses, never-mores, mini-deaths. But they were nothing compared to the sight of his father right now, silent and brittle and hunched and shrunken.

He pulled into his father's driveway and turned off the ignition. "Son, would you mind helping me out of the car?"

"Sure, Dad."

Shapiro

CHAPTER 11

Four cement quadrants, each just large enough for a medium-size car, had been poured in the 1950s to create Andrew's driveway. Most of the driveways in the neighborhood were similarly conceived, although some had been remodeled with pavers and others re-formed into semi-circles. The front two slabs had a few historical oil stains that resembled Rorschach panels, and a ragged hairline crack ran from the single-car garage down to the dead-end street. Small weeds poked out in the seams between the slabs. The weeds were too small and the seams too narrow for his fingers to reach in and dig deep enough to pull them out by the roots. Each week he yanked their upper halves, and they grew back, a little fuller and a little more stubborn. He enjoyed the predictability of their tenacity. They were like children, defying the greater power while pleading for limits that they could then defy again.

At the end of the driveway was a simple black mailbox affixed to a four-by-four wood post. Something about the mailbox warmed him. It felt so quintessentially American suburban, especially the red arm on its side that he eagerly raised into a salute position when he had mail for the postwoman to pick up. He had glued a large white Helvetica 4, 5 and 7 to the armless side of the box and made a kidney-shaped cactus garden around thick weathered post, defining the space with white pebbles and a border of white paving stones. Here and there, white and lavender vinca sprouted out from among the pebbles and cacti. He hadn't planted them and he didn't pull them out. They made him wonder what a weed actually was. Besides, something about the way they disrupted the garden's thematic coherence gave him a tingling sense of insubordination, although against what or whom he wasn't certain.

The front door was open. Pre-dusk neighborhood sounds filtered through the screen door of the front porch into the living room – a woodpecker tormenting his next-door-neighbor's dead oak tree, a squirrel or opossum provoking frond friction as it leaped from Bismarck palm to Bismarck palm, a child's "Kowabunga!" preceding the splash of a cannonball into a pool, and, above all, the whirr of lawn sprinklers. For two splendid minutes, it returned to him, almost verbatim: Knoxville: Summer, 1915 – "…*and the sounds therefore were pitched much alike; pointed by the snorting start of a new hose; decorated by some man playful with the nozzle; left empty, like God by the sparrow's fall, when any single one of them desists: and all, though near alike, of various pitch; and in this unison. These sweet pale streamings in the light lift out their pallors and their voices all together, mothers hushing their children, the hushing unnaturally prolonged, the men gentle and silent and each snail-like withdrawn into the quietude of what he singly is doing, the urination of huge children stood loosely military against an invisible wall, and gentle happy and peaceful, tasting the mean goodness of their living like the last of their suppers in their mouths..."* Written about sixty years ago, by a man writing about an evening forty years before that. And here they were, now and still, gloriously and whirringly alive.

But it faded out as soon as he straightened the set of coasters on the coffee table, which led to the fluffing up of the two sofa pillows and other such busy-ness, which he confined to the front of the living room where he could keep an eye on the driveway to see when (in a car? on foot?) and how (with the ceremonious gait of a guest arriving at a formal gathering? the unconcerned air of a child returning home after the usual pre-dinner round of soccer in the field with his neighborhood buds?) Ex would appear.

His thoughts ran amok – the unpleasantness of the kiss he had finally managed to plant on his junior prom date, the fictitious-girlfriend talk with certain male colleagues in bars after work in Paris, the penises in the locker room after high school gym class – and no amount of rearranging objects on tables or removing dust motes on shelves with a tongue-moistened thumb could slow or pare them down. Until Ex appeared. He lumbered up the driveway, flip-flops in his right hand, backpack slung over one shoulder, looking toward the sky as if the world were oh-so- secondary a place, and reached the screen door. He entered without knocking.

"Hey."

"Hey,"

As comfortable as Andrew had felt with him on the few evenings they had spent together, which was in part what convinced him that asking him to move in was not total insanity, he now felt only total insanity, as if he were about to mainline an uncontrolled, and perhaps uncontrollable, substance into his aging veins. He wished that he, like his sister, could slip smoothly into an attitude of convenient but irresponsible fatalism in these rare moments of cliff-jumping, but the only thing that fit him snugly was sheer panic.

"Mind if I swim?"

"Not at all. I'll get you some juice."

Those few precious minutes when Ex stripped down and dove into the pool while Andrew poured juice had already become a refrain that laid the reassuring bedrock for what would follow, whatever it might be. He paused at the kitchen window and watched Ex's head slowly emerge from the water, face up and eyes closed, drinking in the diffuse rays of the setting sun, shaking his glistening mane, so unaware of the cover-boy model that he could be. Ex opened his mouth into an oval, and Andrew could only imagine that he was letting out a robust "Ahhhh" and wonder whether he was feeling as transported as he was – and if so, for how long it could possibly last.

They ate dinner – leftover salmon and a salad; a bottle of pinot grigio – under the pergola on the deck by the pool. It hadn't occurred to Ex to get dressed after he had hoisted himself out of the pool and perfunctorily dried himself off on the green and white striped towel that Andrew had brought to him along with the juice. (Later, in the bathroom, it hadn't occurred to him to stop poking inside his left nostril with his finger when Andrew walked in.) Was it about strategic seduction or just one more display of his ingenuousness and a certain animal instinct that has not been domesticated, Andrew thought. During the meal, Andrew braced himself to possibly interrogate Ex about who he was. He had to know certain things, he thought, if only to grant himself a modest portion of having a sense of being able to manage things, decide things, control things. But there was a competing urge: to accept having haphazardly stumbled upon an improbable someone who would change everything forever.

"Something is missing," he said, and went to the living room space, where he picked up the crystal and placed it on the table, slightly off center, next to the large disposable salt and pepper mills.

Who would Ex be? He was continually on the verge of beginning to ask the series of preliminary questions – Where do you live? How do you make a living? Who and where are your parents? – but each halting attempt was met by Ex nervously clearing his throat, followed by silence.

"This is awesome," Ex said, his mouth brimming with arugula and leaking a droplet of balsamic vinaigrette onto the corner of his mouth. Andrew waited to see if Ex's tongue would slip out, snake-like, to grab the droplet; he noticed that Ex's lips were thin. He was alarmed. They seemed to betray the fullness and openness of this creature, as though a precocious tightness and antipathy were taking root and vying to predominate. Ex did not lick off the vinaigrette. He raised his hand to the corner of his mouth and quickly dabbed it with his index finger. His hand, and presumably the other one as well, was not educated, but this was an imperfection that Andrew welcomed. The short nails, the chafed fingertips with traces of grime in the cracks, signified a primitive contact with things of this earth – of sand, soil, lawn mowers, chain saws, spades, mufflers, carburetors – of the potential to not only soar above the world but also to sink into and tinker with its unsublime elements and appurtenances.

"You don't mind the slightly bitter taste?"

"No, it's great. Amazing mouth feel. How do you know all this stuff?"

Andrew fell in love with him again. Ex's unwitting

ability to make him see how many ways there were to prevent sameness of thought in the remaining time allotted to him drew Andrew to him like a tiny filament to a mother magnet.

"I worked in high-end restaurants when I was in university and a few years afterward when I was trying to figure out how to make a living without having to go to an office every day. I loved my mother's food, but something about it told me there must be a better way. You know, everything was in boxes and jars and packets."

"You'll have to teach me."

And he fell in love with him again, this towering inferno who, without knowing, acknowledged, embraced, honored, the peculiarities and wonders of others, of life, of the life of others. Each moment, he seemed to have been born at that moment, taking in the mass of unfamiliarity with unfrightened curiosity and a reassuring sense of the overall benevolence and marvel of things. But his lips were nefarious. How could Andrew not have noticed before?

"Feel free to finish it off. No need to leave room for dessert. I don't do dessert – except for an occasional sorbet or a really good chocolate something."

"Sorbet?"

"Sherbet? You know what that is?"

"Sure."

"Same thing."

"Ah."

"Let's have it in the dining room so it doesn't melt. And then I don't have to carry everything out here."

What Andrew learned over leftovers, two glasses of wine, and a few questions tendered with hesitation, were the following: For an unspecified period of time (Andrew didn't ask for how long), Ex has been crashing on the sofa of a friend until he finds more permanent accommodations; he is in between (unspecified but most likely minimum-wage) jobs (Andrew didn't ask what jobs); he has interrupted his studies (he did volunteer to let slip his major – "undeclared" – but Andrew didn't ask why he had interrupted, even though Ex's apparent struggle to unleash the word "interrupted" suggested a not-so-pleasant history that would need to be chiseled at); he isn't on good terms with his parents or three brothers and (on one more level of inquiry) hasn't spoken to them since they moved out of state a year ago (Andrew resisted pushing this potential gold mine further; hopefully there would be time); and he wants to write lyrics, and direct music videos in which he sings and dances to the lyrics and melodies he creates (Andrew had no interest in pursuing the "artiste" dimension yet, as it smacked of the cause of, and vessel for, all of Ex's disaffection). He poured a third glass of wine, which he didn't drink.

And then there was what Andrew perceived over leftovers and two glasses of wine: a young man who was expressing an entrenched impermanence, not the metaphysical kind with which all of humankind is blessed or cursed, but the daily-grind kind, which can take us one step forward and two steps back and one step sideways until we are dizzy. Or lost. Or until we drift into the entrenched permanence of drift. Ex was able to express an idea beyond the fact of the idea. His ability to form thoughts, and to craft sentences to capture the thoughts, was beyond his years, and he knew how to steer away from thoughts about which he didn't know enough to make it seem like he knew enough. Yet Andrew could also feel a pressure to Ex's thoughts, as if they were being horded through a persistent checkpoint of blame, directed at circumstances or at others, and never at himself, before being cleared for expression. Not unusual in itself for a twenty-three-year-old, but it contrasted so radically – like his lips – with his thoughtfulness, with what seemed like an earnest desire (and need) to get at things, to find some soft anchor in all the harsh chaos that he attributed to everyone and everything outside of himself. Clearly troubled. And clearly trouble, and clearly taken by his own beauty (no blind peacock was he!), which he assiduously watched reflecting itself in the dining room window as he spoke or listened to Andrew while primping a strand of hair, testing an expression, working a look.

Ex offered to help clear the table and wash the dishes. Andrew was feeling tiny one-way warning blips, as if a diode had been connected from this strapping youth to this waning man in order to be recharged, perils notwithstanding.

"It can wait. Come sit on the sofa. I have something I want you to listen to."

Madradeus. *O espirito da paz.* Visceral, urgent, soothing. Andrew sat on the three-seater sofa.

"Where should I sit?"

"Where do you want to sit?"

"Close to you." Andrew patted the middle bolster. As soon as Ex sat down, he pivoted to the right, lifted his legs, let them dangle from the ankles over the armrest, and laid his head in Andrew's lap. "Is this okay?"

"Yes."

"I want this."

"What?"

"This. It's a sanctuary. Can I really move in?"

"Yes. But let me think. Just be still for a moment." He dared to rake his hand slowly and lovingly through Ex's hair. "There's the matter of my father. Charles. You'll call him Zee."

Ex lay still in Andrew's lap for more than an hour. Andrew sifted through Ex's hair for more than an hour. When the last track of Madredeus – *Ajuda* – had finished, Andrew said, "You can spend the night tonight, if you'd like."

"I'd like to. But I didn't bring anything with me."

"What do you need?"

"I guess I don't need anything, except something to sleep in."

Andrew lifted Ex's head up. "I think I may have one thing that will fit you." He disappeared down the hallway and returned with a cream-colored kurta. "Here. This should work. I got it in Rajasthan. In India. It's made of silk. I think you'll like it."

Ex stood up, undid the towel and let it slip to the floor. Andrew handed him the kurta. Ex slipped it over his head. As it softly tumbled down over his body like a slow-motion wave, his body began to tremble and his voice to emit light gasps. By the time the kurta had reached his knees, he was fully erect.

"My God, I feel so strange. I feel so soft. So feminine."

Andrew look at him intently.

"I don't know what's happening. Can we go lie down together?"

Andrew led him down the dark hallway to the bedroom. Ex lay down on the bed, on his side, curved inward. "Hold me."

Andrew lay down on the bed and molded himself behind Ex. Ex reached behind gently for one of Andrew's arms and slowly pulled it around him, guiding Andrew's hand to his sternum and then pressing at the same time that he managed to create a hair's breadth of space between their bodies.

"I want to sleep like this," he said. "Can we?"

Andrew let his lips arrive as far as the baby hair on Ex's neck. "Yes. Be Still. Sleep."

CHAPTER 12

Mrsa. Andrew had never heard of it until he saw its four letters printed on his father's scrip and thought the acronym, with its lower-case letters, was some kind of honorific.

Methicillin, amoxicillin, penicillin, oxacillin, anything ending with a "cillin" was rendered powerless under Mrsa, which was bellicose, invincible in its will to vanquish and flourish. It was innocuous, until it wasn't, a barely mentioned microbe lying ruthlessly in wait to seize the day, the rest of days, as it had with Charles, as soon as the scalpel had made its tiny incision on his inner thigh to begin the angioplasty the day after his visit with the doctor. Immediately after the long procedure, the bluish tint to his feet gave way to a flush and healthy pink. The blood was coursing through again. Charles was so relieved that he didn't think twice about the small pimple that appeared by the incision. A natural swelling that would recede. It didn't. By the next day it had risen like a plump and warm freshly baked mini-doughnut, complete with hole, and he had a fever.

"Andrew," he called from his son's second bedroom, where he had spent the night, "Could you come a take a look at this?" Andrew arrived at the threshold to find his father sitting up in bed, naked from the waist down, legs spread open shamelessly as he pulled on the skin around the doughnut with one hand and held a magnifying glass in the other to get a better look. He was wearing a sweater from his tennis days and shivering. It was seventy-six degrees in the house. "The oddest-looking thing."

Andrew touched his father's forehead. It was burning. "Let me get a thermometer."

"That's okay, son. It's just a slight chill. My skin is so paper-thin I get cold easily. I'm starving."

Andrew returned from the bathroom with a digital thermometer. "I'm just curious, Dad. Tongue up and out. In you go."

The thermometer beeped after eight seconds. Andrew extracted it. "Jesus, Dad. A hundred and four. Slight chill my ass. Hoist up your pajama bottoms. I hate to say this, but we need to get you to the emergency room."

Charles didn't put up a fight. As he bent over to pull up his underpants and pajama bottoms simultaneously, the stubborn tuft of top hair that some men of his age still had and was usually left to grow to lengths that these same men had never before allowed them to, and who then proceeded to perform the comb-over (who were they kidding?), defied its unnatural part over the left ear and arrived almost to the back of the lower mandible. The tuft looked like something that had been fished out of a clogged drain. "Fuck."

"Can you get yourself up and walk to the car?"

"Look at those pink feet. You're damn right I can walk." Andrew trailed him closely, on the ready to clasp an elbow or shoulder at the first sign of unsteadiness.

Charles was released from the emergency room with two more prescriptions – a cocktail of antibiotics that might not do the trick (the doctors themselves had told him this) but was the first move in a game plan of experimenting with combinations and permutations of antibiotics, which was the least – and most – they could do in dark Mrsa territory. In any event, some kind of pill was *de rigueur*, the tiny embodiment of primitive magic and technological sophistication that was the justification and reward for any medical visit that gave a name to an inherently obscene and mysterious condition in order to cure it or exacerbate it.

He was wheeled out to Reception, where Sheila was waiting with a gift that was to accompany him permanently, along with his blood-thinner, cholesterol-lowerer, blood-pressure stabilizer, white blood cell booster, and other capsules and pills and tablets that had found their way into his survival kit over the years: a new and deluxe walker, not Edith's walker, which he used informally, but his very own. "Just make sure he doesn't think I'm the one who came up with the idea," Sheila said when her brother had called her and asked her to rent a walker from the medical supply store and bring it to the hospital. "If he thinks I suggested it, he'll never use it."

"Don't exaggerate, sis."

"Android, I have news for you. We have two fathers. One is yours, and one is mine. They just happen to share the same body."

Charles saw the contraption and bristled.

"Dad, they won't let you leave the hospital unless you use it," Andrew said, looking at his sister for a sign of complicity. Their father stiffened, as if he had entered into a state of living rigor mortis. He glared at the contraption, the arch enemy compared to pills, which were popped into the mouth, disappeared and did their good deeds and secondary harms invisibly and thus could be ignored. A walker was a brutal apparatus. It enabled its users, who quickly became dependent on it, to go about their business (which was more about biding time than any other business – and how it showed on their faces and their shufflings), as soon as they clasped the brake handles and relented to the new mobility. Charles couldn't abide it, this stain of enfeebledness for which he could feel no responsibility, and therefore no power to cure, and that carried no redemption with it, only humiliation, degradation and defeat.

"Dad."

"Fuck." He clutched the brakes, shifting them up and down with an aggression that can only be unleashed by intimacy of one kind or another, and the power plays that vie for supremacy in such a vulnerable state. Finally, wrists tired from the furious squeezing and releasing, he loosened his grip and the brakes opened. "Let's get out of here. But I'm warning you. If you buy a little basket to hook on the front so that I can tote around my meds and Depends, I'll disown the both of you."

Sheila wheeled him toward the parking lot. "My car is to the right."

"I'm to the left. Let's take him to my car. He can stay with me for now."

She didn't pretend to object. She was most likely even waiting for him to offer. "It's probably best. It's a crazy time for me now. So many new clients. Snowbird season. All of those northerners descending and thinking that they can still pick up a McMansion for a hundred grand. Wait'll you hear this one. I have this one couple, from Michigan..."

And here it came, on schedule, the crazy period, the out-of-towners client tale – couples from somewhere in the Midwest or New Jersey or Canada – who had stopped the clock at 2008, the peak of the housing crisis, when prices were so low that a token down payment could purchase a dream, and who insisted that there were still deals to be had. Over and over again she had to wean them away from their outrageous hopes to a sober reality, a process that had been rendered tedious by repetition, especially since the result was more often than not a no sale, after hours and hours of researching and showing houses in an effort to enlighten these clients that time marches on, things change, one must adapt, accept, sketch new horizons. And over and over again, she unloaded client sagas onto her brother, anticipating a reaction of keen interest that would enable her to believe that this business of brown-nosing to sell houses to a perilously unfiltered clientele was, when all was said and done, reasonable, purposeful. At the very least, she could count on her brother to listen patiently and give an opinion about her strategy or her plight. She needed that from him, and had grown to expect it from him. Even though he was gay, he was still a male. And for her, validation from that half of the species was worth its psychological weight in gold.

Andrew would have liked to say, "It's a crazy time for me too," but since Sheila had never in more than twenty-five years inquired, "What is it exactly that you do?" there was no point. Andrew didn't take the initiative to talk about his work with anyone, even when the topic of conversation provided the perfect – or mildly imperfect – opportunity. He took it for granted that it would at most be politely tolerated by anyone except by him or by those in his line of work (with whom he detested talking "shop," especially after hours). Each time that he was tempted to relate one of his "sagas," he thought of friends who were clueless enough to spend an evening showing photos or selfies of a family vacation ("Will you just look at Dylan on the ferris wheel? He actually has his thumb in his mouth! And those overalls. Aren't they just the cutest?"), and refrained from resorting to a segue into the "I", especially with his sister, certain that in not refraining, she (like so many others) could then rearrange him for use.

Turning left in the parking lot, toward his car, he said, "When I need a break, I'll let you know" and realized that Ex would indeed have to take the smallest – what he thought of as the third – of the three bedrooms, when and if a separate bedroom might be required. As small as the third bedroom was, it happened to be the only one with a double closet, where in the left side Andrew stored the vacuum cleaner, the linens, his winter clothes, a few boxes of photos to eventually (but probably never) arrange into photo albums, and other bits and pieces that didn't figure into daily use. He decided that it wasn't necessary to move them.

"Call me if you need me," she said, heading to her car with a spring in her step that made him angry. He knew that she knew, knowing him for as long and as well as she did, that he would not call her if he needed her. She could remain kind, generous, and free from familial responsibility. In the meantime, she had left her glasses on the walker's fold-out seat.

The sun had passed its zenith by about twenty degrees, and its bottom rays were accentuating, like eye-liner, the top of a thick lid of charcoal clouds forming in the west. At this late afternoon hour, heat and light were strong but no longer hurt, and to the east, over the ocean, pelicans were gliding effortlessly above the skyline of scattered low-rise condos. If there were going to be a downpour, it wouldn't be for another couple of hours.

Andrew glanced at his father in the passenger seat. "Let's stop at the beach."

"Don't think I'll get very far in the sand with the walker."

"We can stop at the beach that has the boardwalk and sit there and watch. It's on the way to the house. C'mon, Dad."

The parking lot was full, except for a few spaces for the disabled that were delineated with bright blue stripes. "Paydirt," said Charles. "I probably qualify for handicapped parking. I'll need to get one of those tags. Son, open up the trunk. But I'll get out of the car myself, and I'll get the bloody walker myself." He paused. "What's the word I'm thinking of? Solicitous? Hell, I need to do more crossword puzzles. Anyway, whatever it is, please don't be that."

By the time Andrew had found a parking place, his father had already climbed the four steps and seated himself on a bench on the boardwalk, which was a misnomer. The weathered wooden planks had not been laid out with strolling in mind – the entire length of the boardwalk was only about one block – but simply as a lookout point for those who wanted to commune with the ocean, or kind of "hang" in nature, without having to commit entirely by stepping onto the beach and getting all sandy. This modest arrangement of planks, the only of its kind for a twenty-mile stretch, coupled with an ample parking lot, quickly drew commercial speculation like ants to sugar, and within a few years a series of food chains ranging in stature from Starbucks to Wendy's had claimed the swath of the dunes as their own, offering an array of products in paper and styrofoam containers that spilled over the too-many (but never enough) blue plastic waste bins that had been mounted on either side of each of the twelve or so benches along the modest strip. It was anything but serene and contemplative but, Andrew thought, who knew how long it had been since Charles had glimpsed the striation of sand-ocean-sky? It might do him good.

As he lowered himself beside his father, Andrew said, "About this roommate."

The fins of two dolphins broke the surface of the ocean about fifty feet out, the only intrusion in an infinity of sky and water. Andrew focused on a spot another fifty feet to the right, waiting to see if they would expose themselves again, on their journey to wherever it was they were going. There was something playful about that sudden appearance, as if they were still young and could hope that they would get around to everything they had dreamed of, eventually. He looked at his father, and at his own hands (still youngish, but), and recognized that most things don't happen in the end, and that as time runs out, one needs to choose carefully – which movies to see, which books to read, which conversations to engage in. Which follies to succumb to in a last-ditch effort to believe that things can still happen.

"Tell me."

Tell him. Tell him how at fifteen years old the forty-two minutes you spent sitting in the front row of Mr. Atchinson's English class that junior year day after day burnished every thought you had with unbearable angst and bliss from the first day you walked into his class and saw him standing next to his desk until halfway through the following year, when your affair with him ended, and how you lived for those moments when the weather was warmer and he came to school in a short-sleeve shirt and you waited as he finished writing something up high on the blackboard, praying to the gods that as he turned around his arm remained elevated enough so that you could gape into the tunnel created between the bottom of the sleeve and the bottom of his upper arm and catch a glimpse of the hair in his armpits, and how that rare split-second sighting set you reeling in an ecstasy that made everything make instant sense and be right, even though you had no sense at all of what was going on; how, toward the end of the school year, you devised any pretext in order to remain behind in class with him, talk to him, miss your bus and pray to the gods that he would offer you a ride home and that somehow, eventually, you would find yourself in his arms, smelling his neck, waiting for his lips to touch yours and his tongue to slowly enter your mouth. And somehow, it did happen, and continued to happen, soft and easy, through the summer and into the following school year, until you had another encounter with another man in the back of his shop that was next to the store where you worked part-time after school, and after that second encounter, that second taste, you fell out of first-love and were hungry for other man tastes and smells, which would come and go, punctuated by a foray into a relationship here and there, but which never stopped, until this strange and exquisite reversal with the twenty-three-year-old Ex. The roommate.

Tell him how Cal, the thirty-one-year-old man with whom you lived kept his grip on you, an eighteen-year-old, for two years because after four attempts the pain of anal intercourse finally gave way to an unspeakable pleasure that you were sure only Cal knew how to get at, and that that was enough, and how he and Mom were right to constantly question you about this relationship of yours with such a handsome but dim older man but that even if you had understood that it was this deep and raw penetration that seduced you into putting up with all the rest for two years, how could you have possibly explained that to them; and how, when things with Cal started to go bland and then sour, and you found the courage to betray him by allowing another man inside you and that other man provoked the same unspeakable pleasure way deep inside, it was suddenly so easy to leave him for no one — and he expected and dreaded that the same fate awaited him with Ex, if it came to that, but in reverse.

Tell him how your three-year relationship with Louis, your first peer (he was actually one year younger) and first Jewish lover, was so good and so healthy and so loving because Louis had told you on your first date that he was HIV-positive, which put an external expiration date (at that time) of two years maximum on his life and thus on the relationship and also added an intense care-giving quality that was your particular specialty and proclivity, and so for two years maximum you could commit to making it work beautifully; and how when he died (after one year), something shut down, like a trap door of a cage held open precariously by a wooden stick angled into the ground, and it felt permanent, something having to do with the desire and ability to merge friendship and love and sex into one male body and instead you went about seeking these things separately, in separate people, which you have done in the twenty-odd years since Louis died; and how, when Ex appeared, you were unexpectedly struck by a slight draft of air that wasn't cage-stale and realized that the trap door was opening and that you would let Ex enter, or let yourself out.

He told his father. He told him that he was taking in a young man from the area whose parents had relocated and who had decided to stay in the area, that this young man was smart but a bit lost, and needed some guidance, and that the house was plenty big enough for all of them. He told his father, "You'll like him."

"Do you mind if we head back? I'm not supposed to be in the sun too long because of the chemo. When does move in?"

Andrew took his father's upper arm and helped him up. "Soon."

Shapiro

CHAPTER 13

His father was napping, and Andrew walked around the house as if he was on a dry run of a guided tour: Entranceway, check. Living area, perhaps reverse the sofa that has armrests with the futon that doesn't so that Dad can lie down with his head propped up on something solid when he wants to watch television or listen to music, rather than rely on the two flimsy toss pillows that I bought to understand this mania for toss pillows on sofas (but I still don't get the point). Check. Kitchen, my take-charge turf and domain that will never be tampered with by Dad or by Ex as long as I provide (and I will; my compulsion to nourish can't resist) three meals a day. Check. The two bathrooms, the three bedrooms. Stop. Not ready for these intimate zones. To be determined. In the meantime, they are clean, set up, welcoming, I can easily…

Stop. Enough. He sat down on what he hoped would not become Ex's bed and clasped his hands around the side of his head, pushing tightly as if to squeeze himself back to his senses and grasp the nonsense of his private urges, whatever they were. And whatever they were, how to proceed? He reaches but misses; he grabs something, but it is only and always an approximation of "it," somewhere in this vast space between his eighty-five-year-old father and this twenty-three-year-old creature, vying against each other, it seems, to convince him to relinquish or to insist upon the idea that something inexplicably on target and transformative and right could be had, and had to be had. Otherwise what was the point of all these hours and days and years? Where were the colors on this gorgeous arc? Where was he in all of this? Who was he in any of this?

He lay down on the bed and inhaled the pillow, waiting to be comforted by the smell of laundry detergent or the effulgent traces of some imaginary head that had tossed and turned on it one night, but knowing that such comfort would not be forthcoming since no one had used the third bedroom and consequently the pillowcase had not been washed of late and had a musky smell. Until now, it had been purely decorative, unused, extraneous matter. He heard his father grumbling in the second bedroom, which shared a wall, and began to sob into the pillowcase, turning a segment of its celery green stripes to something darker, less cheerful, like sage.

When will he call? It, the next move, had to come from him, from Ex. Andrew knew that he had to resist to the death making another move. He knew that Ex could not be made to understand that he, the lost boy, had the upper hand. Such power in a twenty-three-year old could only be reckless. Yes, Ex had to be made to understand that there was a difference in years that demanded deference, deserved it, that this cloudburst of generosity was to be treated with gratitude and a touch of fear, and not with hubris and a sense of entitlement. There was only one way. Andrew knew that he had to wait, and to care for his dying father all the while, keeping his cell phone pressed against him as tightly as the bandages around his father's infected incision wound.

Sheila dropped by in the late morning, between clients. She brought a pot of chicken soup and a Tupperware container filled with already cooked fine egg noodles.

"Thought you might want to have this around."

"Thanks, sis."

"How's Dad?"

"He's okay. Settling in. I was going to take him for a walk around the neighborhood. Why don't you join us."

"I'd really love to, but I'm meeting a client in twenty minutes. But I wanted to stop in to give you this and to see how he was doing."

"He's probably up if you want to go into his room."

Sheila went down the hall while Andrew put the food in the fridge. One less meal to think about. By the time he had finished pouring a cup of coffee, the two of them had appeared in the dining area.

"Here he is. All decked out and ready to do the 'hood." He cringed at this announcement, as if their father were a small child, and as if she had been the one to get him dressed.

"Anyone want some coffee?"

"I really have to run. I'll talk to you later." She gave her father a peck on the cheek. "Bye, handsome."

Charles looked at Andrew. "I'll have some, thanks son." Andrew held his gaze and in those few seconds a complete conversation and understanding about Sheila silently took place. No need for commentary.

"We can take a walk whenever you feel like it. I only have a little bit of work to take care of, but I can do it any time today."

"Can you pass me the newspaper? And why are your eyes so red?"

Andrew shrugged his shoulders and went out the back door onto the deck. The potted flowers flanking the pilasters of the pergola needed watering, especially the jasmine, which had begun its slow climb toward the lattice-work roof of the pergola that Andrew hoped it would cover within a few months. He cursed himself for having planted the jasmine in a large expensive pot. He should have planted it directly in the ground, where its roots could have dug down and spread and arrived at the water table. How stupid of him to place such a wild thing in captivity for the sake of his own personal aesthetic. But it was too late, unless he wanted to break the pot, disentangle the jasmine and relocate it to the pilaster closest to the dirt perimeter. The plant probably wouldn't survive it.

They took their walk around the neighborhood, which consisted of four streets, each two blocks long. Andrew hadn't realized how many dogs there were, but the grating noise of the walker's wheels against the streets caused barking of all kinds – from killer growls to hysterical yapping – to break out in almost every house. Occasionally he could make out a face peering out from a curtain or vertical blind or plantation shutter. Charles seemed to be oblivious to the sounds, focused as he was on keeping the walker going at a steady clip, head slightly downward and hands on the ready by the brakes. He was good for thirty minutes, after which he told Andrew that he was ready to head back.

"And to think that only a few months ago I was playing tennis twice a week."

"You'll get back to it. Just be patient."

"Patience is not one of my virtues. And neither is excessive optimism. Let's face it, son. I'm fucking eighty-five years old."

"Yes you are, Dad. And you have a fucking fifty-six-year-old son. How's that grab you?"

"Right by the dysfunctional balls."

Andrew gently took his father by the upper arm. "So tell me, Dad. What do you do? Resist? Give in?"

"Vacillate."

"That doesn't sound terrific."

"If you have any better ideas, I'm all ears. At least those still work."

"I'll think about it."

"I forgot to tell you. Good news. Well good news for me. Maybe not so good for you. In today's obits, everyone who died was younger than me. There's my modest portion of optimism."

They headed back toward the house. Andrew eased his hand from his father's upper arm and let it drop back down to his side.

A week went by. A routine was established. The Mrsa was neither worse nor better, which was as much as could be expected from the combination of antibiotics that Dr. Kumu said would keep things under control temporarily, after which they would try another combination of antibiotics to temporarily outsmart the bacteria. Andrew's father was sweet, undemanding, unobtrusive, and often good company. He took the edge off of Andrew's edginess: Ex hadn't called. He had expected some sign of life, even a "Hey, I'm in the area and thought I'd drop by with the Tupperware box I borrowed," some miniscule sign of Ex's desire for him. It didn't come. *When will he call* gave way to *Will he call*, and as each day went by, Andrew's torment was subdued by horrific concern. He was afraid. Ex lacked concreteness, his insights were muddled, his head was in the clouds and his feet weren't far beneath. Maybe something had happened other than the flightiness of youth. One morning as his father was checking the obits, he Googled the local obits for the week. No one under forty-five had died, except one fifty-six-year-old, whose cause of death was given as "complications from surgery." Mrsa, no doubt. He then decided to check the county arrest records. He typed in Ex's first name. Several "Alex"s appeared under yesterday's records and Andrew's heart raced as he clicked on the mugshots for each of them. One was black, one was white, both were not Ex. He tried the records from the day before yesterday. No Alex appeared. Three days ago, one Alex, who was possibly a woman but clearly not Ex. Four days ago, two more Alexes. Both white, both male. The first mugshot was of an older man. Bald. Scruffy. Mean. Domestic violence. The second was of a younger man, lean, taut, pale, almost expressionless except for something feral that bolted out of his eyes and razor-thin lips. Case number 05-2014-CF-040589-AXXX-XX, "possession of heroin, resisting officer obstruct, possession of drug paraphernalia." The unruly luxuriant hair crowning the face was Ex's.

Andrew couldn't help but add to the pain of his intoxication of Ex in the present the pain of imagining Ex's future, this strapping youth who thought of himself as a cool vagabond, refusing to accept the slow onset of fatigue from his wanderings, even if they had never taken him beyond a five-mile radius; denying the slow creep of desire for a destination – a treacherous traditional fate to which he arrogantly felt immune in his insistence that he would always be happy and morally correct by scraping together enough money for the next meal, by sleeping on a bench under a Bismarck palm by a lake in a local park, somewhere, and an occasional night spent in luxurious sleep in a house like Andrew's. And the security of prison. Let him rot there.

But, Andrew continued, perhaps Ex was just beginning to weaken, to yearn for a tad of safety and security – *It's time for dinner; Drive safely; Call me tomorrow.* In spite of himself and his youth, such stanzas were maybe becoming less vexatious and more kindly, and Ex was fighting to the death against these very pulls that would cause him to decamp, return, decamp, return, until…

Ex's personal possessions, including his cell phone, would have been taken from him and stored in a zip-lock bag. To whom would he have made the one phone call allowed him? Andrew imagined him waiting as desperately for him to call as he had been waiting for Ex to call him, his young body being scrutinized like fresh meat by the other inmates, his utter helplessness and fear at being thrust into such a snake pit. Andrew put his cell phone on the table near his father and walked over to his desk. He quietly uncradled the landline and called his cell phone. When it rang, he walked back over to the table and picked up.

"Hello? Yes. I see. I should be able to. Let me take care of some things and I'll get back to you before noon. Sure thing."

He turned to his father. "Dad, it looks like I may need to go out of town for a couple of days. Work stuff. Would you mind going back to Sheila's for a day or two?"

"It's not a problem for me, if your sister'll have me. Everything okay?"

"Sure."

"You're shaking."

"So I am. Must be the coffee." He knew his father didn't believe him. But he also knew his father wouldn't pursue it. And his father didn't.

"So what's with this stone sculpture and what's with this roommate you mentioned?"

"The stone sculpture is a crystal and the roommate will be arriving soon."

"Okay."

"Dad, I need to get my shit together."

Charles looked at his son and then resumed reading the newspaper, fondling the crystal with his left hand as he turned the pages with his right.

PART II - NOW

"…My head and my heart are drunk, and my steps follow the dictates of that darker god whose pleasure it is to trample man's reason and dignity underfoot…." Thomas Mann

Shapiro

CHAPTER 14

The coastal highway, A1A, will get you there. It's not the most direct route, as it cuts too far east and adds almost another twenty minutes to the fifty-minute drive. But at that hour over the ocean, the pre-dawn light spectacle casting pinks and blues and yellows onto one half of our still-sleeping orb as if giving it yet another chance to come through, peacefully, will be the perfect antidote to his mounting unease as the car arrives at the intersection where it must veer away from the coastline and its full horizon and head toward the interior – a place of scrub and swamp and roadkill (opossum, alligator, raccoon, turtle), a trailer or pre-fab sprouting up here and there like mold from such desolate fecundity, and an occasional prisoner, freshly released and tossed out, walking down the dark dank street with a small backpack containing the sum of his material life and heading toward…toward…. – until the car reaches the county prison complex. There is nothing subtle about this forbidden landscape. It is the stuff of the sinister half of fairy tales, where brambles and thickets and dragons must be hacked and cleaved in order to arrive at the destination – a stronghold where the beloved, compleat with cascades of hair, is being held in captivity.

This particular destination is not a stone turret with a postage-stamp-sized window at the top and the faint sound of patient, hopeful lamentation echoing out to lure the pre-destined hero. No hackings or thrashings are necessary. Barbed wire announces the arrival, behind which has been constructed an entire complex of cruelly functional structures meant only to deprive its inhabitants of any possible hope they may have had for a life other than the one they had had before being escorted here; meant only to feed their conviction that the "system" has always been, and will always be, their implacable enemy, to be fought against any odds. Long live anarchy.

There is even a website, with photos and narrative that perversely touts this particular penitentiary as a veritable Club Med. *"The main jail opened in 1986 with beds for 386 inmates. Today, the Jail Complex routinely houses over 1,500 inmates daily. The Jail Complex consists of a Booking area, Housing areas, Medical Ward, Laundry facility, Courtroom, Visiting areas, Recreation area, and office/support areas. In addition to the maximum security main jail, there are three tents housing inmates (with a fourth tent to open at a later date), a Women's Jail, and a mental health/medical facility."* Hurry while accommodations last! Ex probably didn't make a reservation, but here he was, the tall white mouse trapped inside this airless, windowless labyrinth.

Andrew pulls into the parking lot. He grips the stick to push it up into "Park." He hesitates. Shifting to the "P" will change his life forever. Shifting down into "R" and backing out of his parking space to leave the empty parking lot and return home (this time taking the faster, uglier route) will collapse this episode into a tight pleat that never need be stretched open. Fabled prince? Reality's fool? The padded pummel of the stick shift vibrates in his fist.

"Can I help you?" she inquires, bending over so that her face is framed by his window. It is a fat face, heavily and carelessly made up (crumbs of navy blue mascara stuck in her eyelashes, which could be false, excess lipstick spilling over into the capillaries around her mouth), and capped by a bleached blonde mullet.

"I'm here to see an inmate," he says, feeling guilty of a crime hidden behind this simple truth.

"Up that ramp over there. Y'have ID? Any weapons?"

He shows her his driver's license. No weapons."

"Up that ramp over there. They'll process you."

"Thank you, ma'am."

"Don't forget to put your car in Park. Don't want no accidents in the parking lot. We got enough on our hands."

"Sure thing."

"Just up that ramp over there."

He watches her toddle off to one of the low brick buildings surrounded by barbed wire and concrete sidewalks (for taking strolls?) in between. The merest trace of nature has no place here — not a tree, shrub, blade of grass, weed. Anything that had to do with what this place once was has been purged to construct, in its purest, sparest form, what it has become — a storage facility for masses of alleged malignancy trapped in human bodies. No one, but no one, he thinks, should spend even one minute of their time here, let alone a few days, years, a lifetime. It is all too clear to him that any possibility of a "re" — -form, -habilitation, -newal, -adjustment, -programming — is out of the question in this kennel. Ex must be extracted. Andrew puts the car in Park and turns off the ignition.

He isn't led, as he had expected, into a room with friends or family or "associates" of those trapped inside, and then seated on banquettes facing their loved one behind a thick pane of plexiglass. Instead, he is taken into a small room lined with study carrels, much like a library but without books. He is assigned to a carrel and told that the instructions for all communication with inmates are taped to the computer in the carrel and that he will have fifteen minutes to speak into the computer screen as soon as the tiny overhead bulb flashes red. He reads the instructions and turns on the computer. When the screen produces an image after several seconds of blackness and munching sounds, he can see the room that he had imagined he would have been taken to, the one where he would have been seated across from Ex, his face close to his, their hands eventually pressed against the plexiglass when their time was up, the torment of deciding whether to look back one time before Ex was escorted out of sight into the recesses of that place. But it is not as he had imagined. When Ex is seated behind the plexiglass, and his attempt at a smile cedes to a stream of tears and a stuttering "I'm a good person, really I am," Andrew will have to take it in in black and white on the fifteen-inch computer monitor, and to talk and listen to him with a set of cheap disposable earbuds of the kind that are distributed on airplanes for passengers in economy to pass the time watching some innocuous piece of entertainment, rendered flat and tinny by tiny screen and earbuds, instead of making demands on the flight attendants. To make matters worse and more unreal, he has to turn off the device when the red light begins to flash again. A simple but mandatory click, and all is gone. As he stands up to leave, he isn't even sure whether he has spoken with Ex. He must get him out, if only to prove to himself that he really is inside.

Is he really a good person? He wants his mother back, just for five minutes. She would know. Although she strove to hate, her hate required effort and exquisite discernment, and Andrew had quickly learned how to peel away that obdurate and calloused epidermal layer to get at that subcutaneous, pulpy stuff wherein lay what felt like the stuff of truth.

"What do you think, Mom"? he says aloud in the car. "What kind of fool am I this time?" He looks in the rearview mirror, hoping, this time, that she won't fail him, that she will issue, as she had promised when she said to him on her deathbed, "You think you're finished with me."

He sees her. She is wearing an old stained white t-shirt of her husband's, the Sergio Tacchini logo so faded it looks like just another stain, and a pair of large green shorts with an elastic waist. She has just put them on but she already looks dirty. Her thick black hair, with streaks of gray, is short and shapeless. She takes the scissors to it each day to cut off any strands that stick out. She is about to mow the lawn when she hears her son ask her. She wheels the lawn mower out of the garage, positions it on the driveway next to the piece of lawn where she prefers to begin her mowing, walks to the lawn and sits down.

Son, I have so much to say that the temptation is to say nothing. But that isn't my style. I y'am what I y'am. I say it like it is. But where I am now, I don't know what "it" is. I love mowing the lawn. I walk back and forth. That's nice. Good exercise. Good for the circulation. And look at my legs. Still young. And good for the mind, too. I have to concentrate enough on maneuvering the mower so that I can't think too much, but I don't have to maneuver so much that I can't think at all. Except under the maple tree. Damn those giant roots sticking out of the ground. And sometimes under the peach tree too, when too much rotted fruit has fallen and I'm afraid that the pits will go flying out from under the mower blades and hit me in the eye. I could wear your father's workshop goggles, I suppose. But how the hell could I find them in his mess? I tried to convince him to buy a bag mower. But you know him. And anyway, if I wore the goggles, I wouldn't be able to see. I mean really see, if you know what I mean. So I take my chances.

You are a good person, my son. You used to get so annoyed when I called you my savior. But you are a savior. Your instinct is to save. Once you even brought home a dead field mouse that you'd found in the garage and you were so sure that you could pet it back to life. You must have stroked its disgusting little back for hours. How many times did I make you wash your hands after that? And with that horrible lye soap I kept in the utility room. I never did know whether you were crying over the mouse or that soap.

Is that young man a good person? I'm laughing right now, and I'll tell you why. And I can only say something like this to you because you are my son, my savior, and because of where I am now. I don't know him well enough to hate him, so I can't say. But that said, I have much to say. I always do. I'll try to get to the point. I really do need to mow the lawn before it gets too hot. But you know me.

After Bubby's husband died, she started dating other men. But after a date or two she would turn them down. Your grandmother had quite a line-up of suitors. There was one man, Vlad, who was a cut above the rest. He had depth, he wasn't just looking for someone to take care of him, you know cook for him, clean for him, yield to him, if you know what I mean. Plus he was very handsome. She went out with him about five times, which was a record for her. I was thirteen at the time, but I could imagine him being my new father. I could imagine having dinner with him every night and even maybe having him kiss me on the cheek before I went to bed. But in the end, he met the same fate as the others. You wanna know why? Because his eyebrows were too bushy. They made her nervous.

Now your father's eyebrows are pretty bushy too, aren't they? But Bubby adored him. She treated him like a son. You go figure.

You have my eyebrows. Full but not bushy, and with a natural arch. If you were a woman, you'd only have to tweeze them once every few weeks. They are perfect eyebrows for a man. It's a shame you started to lose your hair so young. You can blame that on your father's father, the bastard. Not just for his hair. But you've met the son of a bitch. You know. Incredible that your father turned out to be such a mensch. But still, no bargain to live with.

He tries to be a good person. He wants to want to be a good person. What can I say? Handsome he is, in a goyishe way. Smart, he is. Good? That's a tough word. It means so many things. What do you think he meant by good? Tell me.

You know, the first time your sister got drunk, I think she was fifteen, a normal age to get drunk for the first time. She tripped and banged her head against a table and had to go to the emergency room to get stitches. So we found out right away. But what drove me out of my mind was that her schmuck of a boyfriend at the time — remember, T.J. or B.J. or T.R? — was with her and when he saw blood dripping from her head the asshole fled. And not only that, but she still pined for him. And that time when she snuck up and got her ears pierced against our wishes, the stupid kid came home with giant hoop earrings in her ears that her boyfriend at the time — some other schmuck — had shoplifted for her. So we knew right away. But she was, and still is, such a good person. Anyway, back to him and heroin. Was he like your sister and got caught the first time? Or was he doing it so much that getting caught was inevitable? What do you think, son? What does your gut tell you? If he were five-foot-six and weighed 170 pounds, what would you think, son? You've got fifty-six years under your belt. What've you got to show for it?

All of your girlfriends were so ugly. I remember thinking that that was why you were gay. If only you would go out with a pretty girl...isn't that silly? But all of your boyfriends were so handsome.

Some were smart, some weren't so smart. Some were kind, some weren't so kind. But all of them were handsome. Your father was very handsome at that age too. Not drop-dead handsome. But pixie-cute handsome, with this ear-to-ear grin that made me melt every time. I think that's why I stayed with him until the end, except of course that episode at The Fountains. Oy that grin. But doesn't he have thin lips? Did you lose some weight?

I see that look on your face. I've got news for you. I ditch the t-shirt after I finish the lawn. I found another one in the back of the bottom drawer. But I may go at the pyracantha first. What a mistake it was to plant it next to the retaining wall. Gorgeous berries, but all those thorns! They could kill you. Live and learn.

Remember when you were cleaning out my night table after I passed and you found some trashy paperback inside with a scrap of paper that I was using as a bookmark and you opened the book to where the bookmark had been placed and saw written on the scrap of paper in my chicken-scratch handwriting "Most people are shit"? Well, most people are. But I'm sure that doesn't surprise you, coming from me. But one thing I want to make very clear. There is good shit and there is bad shit among the majority of people who are shit. And then there are a few people who aren't shit at all. They're good to the core, in their core, even if they end up doing not so good or even horrible things. How can you tell? How can you know? What can I say? How do we know anything? Do we know anything? Anyway, one thing I do know is that this lawn needs a major haircut, and I need some exercise. Don't worry. I'll watch out for the pits. Never been hit by one in my life. The odds are pretty good. I think.

As he pulls into reverse to make his way out of the parking lot and to the nearby hotel that he has reserved for two nights as a kind of decompression chamber between the time when he pays bond to yank Ex out of jail and when he must gird himself to inevitably invite him and his belongings into his home (what else at this point?), Andrew sees the full-faced guard approaching him. But she stoops in front of the window of another car that has pulled into the lot — a mid-60s "look at me" red Mustang convertible that has all the trappings of being destined to be retrofitted to be a pricey and enviable classic, except that its driver has the aspect of someone who bought the car when it came out on the market without any fanfare (just the next year's model) and whose only thought was to keep it going. The woman assumes the same position in front of the window, and Andrew can faintly discern the same interrogation taking place. This is what consumes most of her working hours, he thinks, as he watches her stoop down to ask the litany of questions that she's been trained to ask in order to receive her minimum wage, or slightly more if she has successfully stooped and interrogated for a period of time that demonstrates reliability. He wonders how many children she has, what her husband and home are like, what she prepares for her brood for dinner, what words make up the content of her mind as she goes about doing what she has to do.

Before driving to this place, he'd opted for a "suite" — bedroom, bathroom, living room, kitchenette. Consummately characterless, but at least with more than one articulated space, for breathing purposes, to give him and Ex the possibility of having segments of solitude in their company, if need be. The bed and sofa have no concave dips from a squalid history, the caulking around the bathtub is whitish and relatively smooth, the kitchen cabinets whose walnut-style veneer hides their particle-board interiors are squared and level, and nothing living appears to be leaping from the carpeting (low-plush neutral beige, with a stain here and there) or corners of the mattress, which is where any leaping has the habit of taking place (Sheila shared this wisdom with him many years ago, when he began travelling regularly for business). In this space, they will have a one- or two-day cohabitation (he can't know beforehand), before Andrew invites Ex to move into his home, a proposal that Ex will not be able to not accept, even though, Andrew wonders as he does a free-fall onto the firm mattress, whether Ex's acceptance, and possible enthusiasm, will be the outpouring of anything more than a mere a lack of alternative. He closes his eyes and almost immediately falls asleep, before he can set the alarm to make sure he is awake before lunchtime, when he intends to pay bail, head to the parking lot to face the full-faced lady again, and liberate the creature and his belongings, and before he can try to coax his mother into appearing again to give him a straight answer, dammit.

The door to the empty waiting room opens and Ex appears, with a weariness as deeply infiltrated as cold biting into the marrow of an Arctic traveler.

Andrew rises from the back-row banquette, goes over to him, takes him by the arm and leads him to the bright, humid outdoors. Ex's arm hangs, lifeless. The palm trees on the far side of the parking lot are swaying in the breeze.

"Come," he says.

They drive to the hotel in silence. When the prison complex disappears from view and the desolate scrub and lean-tos give way to a setting that is greener and more promising, Andrew presses buttons on his control panel to lower the front windows and let in fresher air, a fresher scent, and with them a sense of hope for Ex, for them. Ex keeps his gaze straight ahead, without moving his eyes, as if they have been emptied of the ability to see, to take in, to feed and to be fueled.

Once arrived at their hotel room, Andrew leads him directly to the bathroom, where on the sink he lays out two of the four white towels and adjusts the shower water so that it is warm enough for steam to quickly amass in the cubicle.

"Take off your clothes and get under. Wash it off."

Andrew returns to the bedroom, lowers the blinds, turns back the soft white blanket and top sheet, and sits on the corner of the bed, waiting.

"Hi." Ex emerges from the bathroom wrapped in one of the towels and holding the other, hair still dripping, and sits on the bed.

"Give me the towel." Before Ex can fully give the towel to him, Andrew intercepts it midway, brings it to Ex's head and begins to lightly dry his hair. "There. Now lie down. Sleep it off."

Ex pushes back and lies down at the far end of the bed. "Will you lie down with me?"

"I'll be here. Near you."

Ex turns on his side, facing away from the window, away from Andrew. Andrew moves onto the bed, positioning himself so that pieces of Ex – lower vertebrae, back of left calf – are touching him and he begins to run his hand along the length of Ex's back, gently and in a circular motion, as if he were smoothing out a piece of freshly laundered linen. Moving his hand upward along Ex's back, he allows it to arrive at the side of his neck, and then to the side of his face, where he lets his index finger travel over Ex's closed eyelid and up across his eyebrow. He cups his hand over Ex's eye, bends around, and kisses his forehead, holding his lips there until Ex's breathing becomes regular. He covers him up to the shoulders with the blanket and sits in the armchair in the corner of the room, beside the double-paned window that looks out onto silent traffic.

From there, he studies this young man buffeted by thick pillows and blankets and soft light filtering through the blinds, a white-suffused embodiment of innocence, and tries not to dwell on imagining his future, their future, since none of the possible outcomes could possibly include him. Nevertheless, he can't stem the flow of what-will-come-of this-boy fragments: hand-to-mouthing it with a series of random jobs that point away from career, as he gradually congeals into one of those (too many, alas) people who believe themselves to be experts in everything they do and think, who derive their abundant expertise from cool but spurious websites and take pleasure in pronouncing with supreme authority and arrogance all of the conspiracy theories and alternative realities that enable them to avoid dealing with things as they are, all the while releasing ignorance in torrents – not knowing that Rome is a city and not a country, saying "explanation mark" instead of "exclamation mark," "git" for "get," and never using a past participle when it calls for use. He recognizes Ex as his illusion, or delusion, since he first appeared on that stretch of beach and Andrew felt immediately punch-drunk when he sighted him – that towering, luminous ideal. But he also expected those moments, those terrifying ones, when the intensity and passion begin to flatten, the edges to feel smoother and less edgy, and when the towering luminous Ideal reverts to the clueless boy that he is, and will continue to be long after time has chiseled away at his aura. He sits in the armchair, motionless, watching this living painting on the other side of the small room, struggling simultaneously to beckon and repel these, and other, things, as he thrashes about, immobile, to keep afloat and to desire Ex – and to desire to be desired by Ex. His neck muscles relax, his chin drops onto his upper breastbone and soon he too falls asleep, upright in the chair as traffic goes by without a sound.

CHAPTER 15

The incision is the size of a pin-prick, and around it is a tiny swelling and redness, like the very beginnings of an anthill. It, in itself, doesn't bother Charles in the least. It doesn't itch, doesn't hurt, doesn't graze against his shorts. But the idea of it – this fecund micro-colony of bacteria feeding off a speck of his flesh and spreading the word like the most zealous of televangelists, drives him to distraction. He stares at it, curses it, infuriated that such smallness can be responsible for such largeness of havoc. And occasionally he squeezes it, imagining it to be nothing more than a relative of a whitehead whose contents need only be evacuated from the pressure of his two thumbs and then wiped off with isopropyl alcohol or Stridex. But nothing comes out. His personal imagery is wrong, the hypothesized imagery of the scientific literature that he has Googled for hours on end is wrong. There is no cure. He will not die of his cancer, his pre-leukemia, or any of the other large conditions that his aging body has accommodated but managed to hold at bay. No, he will die from a dot on his thigh that was created in order to prevent him from dying from a larger drama that was so much more in the order of things and that, subsequently, he may have had the possibility of resigning himself to with a dab of grace or resignation. But this, no. Not this.

He looks around his room. It is chock full of the objects of his life – the desk he built out of Sheila's old head- and foot-board, his pictures on the wall (art) and on the shelf (family) of the bookcase he built, his green leather reading chair, the reading lamp that he'd bought after two years of researching reading lamps, even his pillows and blanket – but he is not at home. It is warm here, comfortable, he lives with his daughter, whom he has known since the day she was born. But he is not at home. He feels this warm, comforting place as the cruelly unhistoried waystation before the end, where he and his artifacts have been deposited in a caring, thoughtful way, but deposited nonetheless. He looks at his arm. The skin is scaly and blotched with what he remembered being called liver spots back in the day. It looks useless, clearly no longer in a position to carry out its function of working with all of his other body parts to keep this organism vibrant and abuzz. The hair that used to adorn his thighs has long since disappeared. It is the skin of a man who is reaching the end of the line. The last place he wants to be is in this waystation. But he doesn't know where he'd rather be, other than some place where the anthill and his scaly, blotched skin and his other larger conditions would succumb to a more forceful sense of "I am alive, dammit."

Sheila calls out to him in a voice whose tinge of shrillness makes him know that despite her good intentions she'd rather not have him here. He knows that, and he doesn't hold it against her. Who would want to care for such a decaying thing for any reason other than a sense of family devotion? For the carer, that may be enough. For the caree, on the other hand, it is little but a reminder of his superfluousness. Breakfast is ready. He is not hungry. He doesn't remember the last time he felt hunger. Not for food, anyway. He is angry at his body and wants to punish it by not feeding it, by pushing the plate away in an act of despairing intransigence. At the same time, he doesn't want to be the cantankerous and moody old man who causes people to have more than a tinge of impatience in their voice when they attempt to placate people of his age in a caring way. He gets up from his chair. He will eat what she puts before him. And he will remember to compliment her on it and to thank her. It's the least he can do. She is a disappointment to him, he knows this, but she is a good person. She means well. She tries. A brain surgeon she wouldn't have been. But still. He would like to give her credit for her accomplishments, but she was simply lucky in those, by no means strategic, he thinks. She didn't create a career track as much as fall into a mediocre job, after falling into many mediocre jobs, that happened to lead to a career that happened to give her a respectable wage. And her husbands were nothing to be proud of. On the contrary. At best they were bland, and at worst violent *shikkers*. She settled too soon for whatever came along and would do, terrified (but why?) that nothing would ever come along again. She seemed happy, though. That is important. But still, he wonders as he watches her shuffle up the stairs, fifty-eight years to make so much more of herself, her life, and she didn't, and now, at this age, wouldn't. He hopes that Jason, his only grandson, will make something more of himself. He is a man and therefore has the obligation to, and more opportunities to, he thinks, even though he has his doubts, what with Sheila and Jason's father, who was one of the bland ones, not the violent one, thank God. He should call him. It's been awhile. He'll do that today.

Eggs, bacon, toast and orange juice. He is relieved that it isn't a bowl of cereal. It would be hard to compliment her for pouring out a bowl of cereal. The eggs are sunny-side up. The whites have a thin layer of clear mucus floating on the amoeba shape that the two eggs have taken on. (Sheila used a large pan, allowing the eggs to go free-form, rather than using her small copper-bottomed skillet, which would have forced them into a perfect circle.) He would have preferred over-lightly, the way Edith made them (sliding the eggs from the pan onto a plate, putting the pan on top of the plate, upside down, and then flipping, so as to lessen the risk breaking the yolks and having them harden, which would prevent Charles from dipping his toast into the yellow pool with the pleasure of a child finger-painting), but doesn't say anything. He can sop up the mucus with his toast. He breaks open the yolks and smears them together with the mucus over the top of the eggs. Next to his glass of juice, she has placed his weekly med box. It is pale blue, with seven compartments, each compartment labeled with one large-print letter for each day of the week (except Thursday, which has "Th," and Saturday, which has "Sa"; he appreciates the logic behind the exceptions). He has developed a system for filling the box, taking inventory of his stock, ordering well in advance, and taking his pills at the designated times. No one need interfere in this nasty business. It was thoughtful of her to place the box near his juice. He is offended. But she means well.

"Thanks, sweetheart. It's delicious."

"Sure thing, Dad."

For a moment, he feels for her, can almost taste her

pain. Her hair is beautiful, as thick and glossy as when she was a junior varsity cheerleader (she didn't make the varsity cuts; he had tried to convince himself that it was because she was Jewish, although not too deep down he had assumed that it was because, once again, she couldn't make the cut) but kept at a modest above-the-shoulder length. A sensible length for a woman her age. She has always been so very attractive. Not beautiful, but so very attractive. He wonders whether her attractiveness incites the sensual in men and, if it does, why she ended up with the men she ended up with. But she is his daughter; he can't feel her in that way, and wouldn't allow himself to even if he could.

"I'll be out most of the day," she tells him. "Out-of-towners expecting me to find them the house of their dreams at a price that didn't exist even twenty years ago. I hate these days when all I do is educate clients. I don't get paid for educating them. I only get paid if I sell them something."

"Do what you have to do. I'll be fine." He's not sure whether he is happy that she'll be out for the day or whether he'd prefer her presence in the house, as each carries its burden and both have the capacity to make him feel more estranged. He offers to clear the table and take care of the dirty dishes (after which he'll give Jason a call. It's been a while). She thanks him and heads upstairs, where her bedroom and her office are. (She only comes downstairs for meals, having relinquished the living room when he moved in, preferring to watch television in the privacy of her upstairs quarters and leaving the giant screen in the living room to him in the evenings. Sometimes he can hear that they are watching the same show.)

What can he expect from her when all is said and

done? He didn't treat her badly, but he should have mustered the energy to praise her more. With her, he was apt to scout out fault, perhaps because she was his first child and he was terrified of her coming out wrong, like the time he assembled his first television set from a kit. Thousands and thousands of pieces and an instruction manual the size of a phone book, and when the last piece had been meticulously soldered in, the family gathered around the six-month endeavor, the set turned on, and then nothing. He shooed everyone out, and the hissing and cursing went on beyond the closed workshop door for two straight days until, finally, he emerged, beaming, and convened the family into the workshop once again, this time to see The Flintstones – in color – appear on the screen. Perhaps he shouldn't have micro-managed her so much, making her feel inadequate as a consequence of that very micro-management. He could have been lighter, looser. He was so young, so wanting other things in addition to the buoyancy and weight of fatherhood, things that didn't agree with fatherhood, as Edith had chastised him for over and over. They should have waited, but Edith was so eager to begin a family once they had bought the suburban home, with all of those big clean empty bedrooms to fill and in an optimum school district, that he couldn't refuse her, especially since he had nothing to offer her as a temporary substitute, and neither did she, having only worked at her mother's grocery store after she'd graduated high school in the inner city. That he wasn't ready was something he didn't truly understood until the incessant nightly wailing began (Sheila was a colicky baby), even though Edith was the one to get up and drag herself to the nursery, as he lay on his half of the bed, half-asleep, thinking, "What have I done?"

His wife was beautiful once, and for quite some time

too, until she let things slip, after Andrew was born. He can barely remember the beautiful version of his wife as he circles the remaining corner of his toast around the plate to get up the last of the liquid yolk. It was so long ago. He hears Sheila coming down the steps. She is still beautiful, he thinks, as he watches her take each step carefully, in the way that older people do, even though by her clothes and by her hair one would think she could skip down them without a care in the world, and again he feels the flat texture of her scrap of happiness, which, at her age (as she goes down the stairs) will not be able to accommodate anything too new, too radical, to enlarge it, just as he cannot expand his threshold for tolerating things that fall in the range of average, as he feels his daughter does.

"Heading out now."

"Have a good day. I think I'll call Jason at some point."

"Give him my love," she says as she is halfway out the door. He wonders when she last spoke to Jason, how often they speak, and what they might talk about. He thinks of her as a "checklisty" person, one who zips though the "What's new" kind of interrogation (most likely as she is simultaneously washing the dishes or preparing dinner) and then believes her job to be done. He is relieved when he hears the door shut behind her. He doesn't relish thinking about her the way he does, but he can't help himself.

He stacks the plates, gathers the utensils into his left fist and carries them to the sink. Quickly he is able to determine that nothing needs to be pushed into the garbage disposal; a simple rinse and placement into the dishwasher will do the trick. The plates are square, but with rounded edges that curl up ever so slightly. Very tasteful, he thinks, clearly purchased with thought, and so utterly in contrast to his son's round black plates, which he isn't sure whether he likes or not, although something about the blood from Andrew's notoriously thick rib-eye steaks (he insists on cooking them no further than medium rare) that accrues on glazed black strikes him as the most inviting way to consider blood as something to relish. Andrew does have a way, no doubt (the glasses will come last, since they need to go on the top rack of the dishwasher and don't need to be rinsed), which he responds to. And this concerns him. Is it a gay taste that he is responding to? Or simply some other kind of taste that resonates? No matter. He has, and always will, think formulaically. He has accepted this ever since he told his son, after Andrew had uttered what for him were three of the most difficult words for him to hear in sequence – I am gay – "There is something fundamentally natural between a man and a woman. They are two pieces of a grand puzzle that fit in a unity that, for those of a religious bent, is called Divine." He will never be able to not believe this. But, strangely, he has always gotten along with Andrew's boyfriends. He pours the liquid Cascade into the small compartment of the inside door of the dishwasher and snaps shut the lid. Both of his children, he thinks, deserve to find the right person. But at fifty-six and fifty-eight? He closes the dishwasher door, pushes the "Normal load" button and waits for the whirring noise that will assure him that the cycle has begun, will continue until the end, and everything inside will come out sparkling, spotless.

CHAPTER 16

They spend the rest of the day, and one night, in the hotel. When Andrew wakes up in the chair, he looks over at Ex. He hasn't changed position, but Andrew can see a slow, regular rising and falling of the sheets, and is reassured that an essential restorative process is taking place, that neurons, ions, blood cells and the trillions of other of elements to his chemical self are realigning, purging themselves of this and, perhaps what's more, whatever other traumas this beautiful, yearning young man may have been harboring for however many years. His facial muscles don't flinch, his lean, taut body is splayed on the bed (at this, Andrew snickers as he realizes that Ex is in the shape of an "X" and fantasticates about the day when Ex will confess to him why certain people call him Ex) in a position of vulnerability and trust, and is reassured that his decision to let him become part of his home, his routine and order of things, perhaps even his bedroom, may not, after all, be the *coup de grace* of a man severely afflicted by his own mortality. He remembers that he should call his sister and let her know that Dad can come back to his place tomorrow (or perhaps the day after) and hopes that Sheila is treating their father kindly. He deserves it, if for no other reason than because he is dying.

The still-life is brought to life by the barely perceptible shifting of Ex's leg upward toward his chin, erasing the "X" and creating a domino effect of willful breathing, a scratching of the muscle under his testicles, an abrupt intake of air through his nostrils. Andrew waits for him to wake up, but all subsides and the deep curative sleep continues for another two hours. When the stillness is interrupted at more frequent intervals, he orders room service for a late lunch: soups, sandwiches, cakes and coffee.

Ex has already awakened and is just starting to sit up in bed when there is a knock at the door. The porter wheels in a cart laden with items covered variously by metal lids and linen napkins folded into sailboats, a pitcher of coffee, and a bud vase holding a red rose. Andrew indicates the left side of the bed and gives the porter a tip.

"Wow." Ex sits up, rubs his eyes and brushes his hair back from his face with both hands.

"Where would you like to eat? On the balcony?"

"There's a balcony? Oh, good morning."

"It's afternoon. The balcony isn't much, but there's fresh air. Lunch isn't much either. There's soup and you can choose between a turkey club or a roast beef on rye. And there's plenty of coffee."

"I'm not into coffee so much."

"Balcony or here?"

Ex's eyes are fixed toward the wall in front of him but is not focusing on the print of Van Gogh's *Sunflowers* or anything else on or near the wall that Andrew can discern. There is no intention in whatever it is he is looking at, if he is looking at anything at all. He is dazed, glazed over, somewhere far from present.

"I can just wheel the tray over the bed. No need to get up."

"That makes me feel kinda weird. Like I'm either a hospital patient or some kind of royalty."

"Get over it. It's just soup and a sandwich."

A sour-sweet smell permeates the room. It is not coming from the sealed foods. And it is not the disinfectant stench of assorted industrial cleaning products used to sanitize hotel linens, mattresses, carpeting or bathrooms in vast quantities and that emanate a distinct Lysol-derived odor as if to reassure clients that, by virtue of the vile odor, the room is bacteria-free from top to bottom. The odor is irresistible, and Andrew can't place it as he continues to breathe it in deeply. He wheels the tray over the bed and begins removing the various covers with the exaggeration of a magician.

Ex picks up a tablespoon and indifferently dips it into one of the bowls of soup, which has a tomato base and chunks of irregularly chopped and sliced vegetables vying for surface space. He then goes for the turkey club, its three layers fastened in place by two unfrilled toothpicks. Andrew can sense his discomfort eating in bed, but there are no surfaces in the room – other than a desk against the far wall – where he could eat. He could have said the balcony, Andrew thinks, which has a small bistro table and two chairs. Nevertheless, he tries to eat. He is clearly not hungry, but probably wants to have food in his mouth as often as possible in order to not say much, if anything. He has nothing, or everything, to say. He says he wishes there were more mayonnaise or lettuce on the sandwich. It's true. The sandwiches are a bit dry. But if he wants to get up to get a glass of water from the bathroom tap, he'll have to get over his self-consciousness about being naked and his extreme awkwardness about the whole set-up in general, Andrew thinks. At the same time, he wouldn't dare ask Andrew to fetch him a glass either. That would seem too imperious, even for Ex. Who is he, after all? Royalty, certainly not.

The direct light coming in from the balcony is harsh and unpleasant. Early afternoon rays of the punishing summer sun are penetrating the sliding glass doors into half of the room. But it is good to see a snippet of the world – mostly sky, a thin but dense layer of palms and pines below, and, at ground level, the hotel parking lot and a sad little fenced-in swimming pool surrounded by unoccupied chaise lounges. Does anyone ever swim in these small roadside pools, Andrew asks himself as he watches Ex eat without enthusiasm and wonders whether he should have chosen one of the hot dishes instead, something heartier and less snack-like. He doesn't want to be here, but he is not ready to bring Ex into his home. And there is nowhere else for them at this point. Of all the things he could say, and they are many, there is only one small question that is pressing: who are you?

"Would you mind if I ate later? I think I want to sleep some more."

Andrew nods his head.

Ex lowers himself back down, rolls onto his left side, facing toward the window and away from Andrew, and curls into a C. "Would you lie down next to me, behind me?"

Andrew wheels the tray to the left of one of the matching night tables (and when are they ever unmatching, he asks himself as the wheels hit the baseboard). He gets onto the bed and slowly molds himself against the back of Ex, the top of one foot pressing lightly again the sole of one of Ex's, his kneecap fitting inside the back of Ex's bent knee, his arm placed around Ex's until his hand rests against Ex's sternum, his nose brushing against Ex's neck, right where the hairline fades to smooth. The odor has located itself. It is everywhere on Ex, coming everywhere from Ex. And going everywhere. Not just the room, but elsewhere, seeping even into his past – onto his father, whom he napped with every Saturday when he was five and six years old and whom he couldn't wait to nap with because of that very gamey Dad smell and the thin boxer shorts that separated the flesh of father from the flesh of son; in the school locker room, after the fifty-minute period of gym that he dreaded except for the delicious reward of the locker room with its myriad heady smells being released from the flesh of boys who had sweated out their deepest selves exerting themselves like savages in football, baseball, basketball, wrestling, it didn't matter, what counted was the smell; behind the zipper of the first zipper he unzipped that was not his own, when he was sixteen, on his knees, in the back of a parking lot where a good-looking man had motioned him over to him as he groped himself hoping he had chosen well (and he had). It is all there, at the bottom of Ex's hairline and the crest of his shoulder, and, he thinks, even more potent and pungent in places where air rarely reaches and dilutes, which he would be able to reach simply by sliding his face downward toward that source of bleach-vanilla-cream-mucus-rotting-meat-maleness that reduces him to pure animal instinct, devoid of brain, of the annoyance of thought and reflection, and triggers a drive to possess that is infinitely sharper than any amount of sunlight refracted through any size of magnifying glass. Pheromones?

But he also catches a sharp whiff of danger that he is not willing to risk. Not here. Not now. He slips out of bed and goes to the balcony. The air is heavy, but reeks of vegetations and cars. He can see the roof of the prison complex in the distance. It is safer here on the balcony. When Ex wakes up, he will insist that they take a walk on the beach, away from confined spaces whose centerpiece is unresolved, unwashed youth. He breathes deeply. Yes, that is what he will do. His father will be coming back from Sheila's soon. Introductions will need to be made, a domestic rhythm tested and modified, through however many subtle iterations, until it works. The sun is cruel at this hour. Sweat is leaking through every pore and he longs for central air-conditioning. But he doesn't dare to go back into the room and contaminate it with the odors of a man who, he can't deny, must carry to a barely discernible degree at the very least the redolence of decay. He will, however, slip in to grab a cup, pour himself some coffee, add cream and sugar, and return to the balcony. He pushes the sliding glass door and wonders how all of this can possibly work.

CHAPTER 17

The non-committal weather forecasts in the morning run the gamut and therefore cancel each other out. It's understandable. Hurricanes are unpredictable from mile to mile. In the span of a half-hour, the pronouncements range from Tropical Storm (i.e., a lot of rain and inconvenience, get out the special umbrella that you paid more than five dollars for, if you have one) to Category 3 (i.e., if you are a seasoned Floridian, hunker down with bottled water, canned food, candles and batteries, and wait it out; if you are new to this, evacuate), and a few stations that need to up their ratings very soon or *arrivederci* and dare to mesmerize their viewing public with a Category 5 (get out). It is his sister who has called him in the early evening (Ex is still sleeping, and will do so until the morning) to warn him. He doesn't know what to make of it. He is not a seasoned Floridian, and Sheila tries, when she can, to begin any phone conversation with something dramatic – in this case "A hurricane is coming!" – before the opening grabber devolves into what, after all, barely registers on the dander-upping or feather-ruffling registers.

Wasn't it only a few days ago, he remembers, that she'd called him and shouted "I've had it!," which was soon deflated into her having found ants for the second time marching along the splashboard in her kitchen (caused by the improperly sealed sweetened granola in the cupboard next to the sink). Besides, she is also alarmist by design, he has suspected for years, preferring to bring her life into relief by pronouncing some kind of doom-like event that will thwart her aspirations, whose realizations are always just around that dark, menacing corner.

He doesn't know what to make of her phone call. Too many motives come immediately to mind – Take Dad off my hands, Don't come back yet, Pick both of us up and drive us to safety, Stay away – although there is a possibility, however slight, that there is no motive, that it is merely a good-will desire to share information. He can't bring himself to believe this.

"Oh-kaaaay," he says to her, lingering on the second syllable as if it were a half-thought for her to pounce on and finish off, and thus reveal herself.

"You should either get back as soon as you can to pick up Dad or, if you can't, then just stay where you are until this blows over."

"I was planning on being back by noon tomorrow. Will that work?"

"It should."

"Should I plan to pick him up and evacuate or pick him up to take him back to my place? And what about you?"

And here, she revealed herself. "Well, I supposed you can start by taking him back to your place, and then stay glued to the weather station and on the ready. I'll be fine. I'm used to this. I have a bunch of friends on the mainland who can take me in."

"Okay, sis. You know better than me."

Why he refuses to confront her, now and every other time she does something so thinly veiled as empathy, is beyond him, he thinks as he hangs up the phone and looks through the balcony doors at Ex, who is still sleeping (he has started to shift from time to time, about a half hour ago, although Andrew doesn't know whether it has to do with dream interference or sleep saturation, or something else). He hears it coming, prepares himself, and lets her get away with it always. He could be a wimp who avoids confrontation at any expense, or he could be someone who is discriminating, who confronts when there is something mutually substantial to potentially be gained. (He did slap Jorge around in public once, ending with a punch in his face and stomach, when Jorge refused to explain why he couldn't take their relationship to the next step after four months of a plateaued intensity; and God knows how he tried to talk through dissatisfactions and frustrations with Cal and Louis, although, he realizes as he thinks back, he himself wasn't so sure about where he wanted things to go – did he really want them, or was he *trying* to want them and furious at them for not making the decision for him?) What about his sister, though? She was easy, she didn't prickle at criticism, if it was dished out in small gentle doses. Peace in the family, whatever gunk must be swallowed? The long habit of getting along? Sheer cowardice?

In the morning at the hotel, still beachside but on a section of ocean that laps near a prison an hour away from his house, there are no signs of meteorological doom. Not even meteorological gloom. The morning sky is a soft blue, a few non-threatening clouds hover toward the west; two tiny ones, like charcoal briquettes, hang overhead. A summer morning like any other, except that by the end of the day his father will be back in his house. And so will this young man, who is still sleeping.

He glances back through the glass doors at Ex's languorous length and then steps toward the balcony to look out toward and away from, hoping for some flash of convergence where things will be made to be understood, and this wantonness that enables old, persistent and failed ways of pleading for connection to either vanish or be fully quenched. But nothing comes except an embarrassing feeling of contrivance, a mere desired desire, the enemy of desire. One of the black briquettes unleashes a small fury of rain. He turns his shoulder away from all that he had come to the balcony to feel and goes back inside.

Enough. Time to slip out of his own company, he thinks as he rouses Ex gently, rubbing a hand on his shoulder, along his neck and up through his hair. Ex turns over on his back, his indolent flickering lids opening as he stretches his arms toward the headboard and his lips arc upward in a smile.

"Good morning. Is it morning? Where am I?"

"Good morning. We are in Florida, and a hurricane may be on its way. We need to get moving."

Ex sits upright. "Where are we going?"

At this, Andrew laughs. He needs to pee. It is a relief to be in the bathroom relieving himself. *Where are they going?* He laughs again, shakes off the drops, goes back to the room and explains to Ex that he will drop him off at his house ("You do live somewhere, don't you?"), he will then pick up his father and re-install him in his house, and they will then listen to the weather forecasts to see how to proceed. However the hurricane plays out, he adds, Ex can move his belongings ("No furniture, please") as soon as possible ("You do have a car, don't you?") so that the three of them can evacuate, or co-habitat, depending on weather patterns.

Ex listens to Andrew with the intensity of someone who is hearing a foreigner speak a language that he has studied in high school for a year or two and for which he has gotten good grades – but still.

"Okay," he says.

"Are you okay?"

"Yep."

"Okay. You may want to think about getting up. There's some coffee in the pitcher. I can't promise how hot it'll be. But you don't like coffee very much anyway." Ex makes a motion to rise but settles back. "Can you come over here for a sec?"

As Andrew approaches him, Ex extends his arms toward him. The sweat on the hair of his armpits reflects the light pouring in from the sliding glass doors, and Andrew, getting nearer, wonders where this phenomenon came from, and why?

Ex embraces him tightly, as if he wants something deep inside Andrew to cross over into something deep inside himself. He places his mouth so very close, but not touching, the curved cartilage of Andrew's ear. "Where did you come from?"

CHAPTER 18

The final verdict is tropical storm, maximum. They will stay. He resents Sheila for having cut his "business trip" short. At the same time, he can't imagine how he would have passed much more time in that room, with its depressed furniture and furnishings, its parenthesis of a balcony, and the unassailable stench of disinfectant/pesticide.

Charles, he can tell, is happy to be back for the afternoon. (He will move his father permanently in a day or two.) He moves about with comfort here, easing onto and off of chairs and sofas as if he has a long history with each. Andrew has moved a cantilevered coffee table from the third bedroom into the living room and designated it as his father's "hoarding station." Here Charles can keep his small barbells, junk mail, magazines, coupons, and any other domestic detritus that he has difficulty parting with ("You never know,"), although Andrew expects to be gathering such items regularly as they spread through the house like hardy chunks of dust. No matter.

Andrew moves about his father with comfort, which wasn't always this way. Up until adolescence, he was afraid of him. It wasn't a fear born of anticipating judgement or punishment or violence. It resided somewhere far deeper than a hand threatening to use the belt (which he never did) or a voice reaching the volume and pitch of bowling ball making a strike (which it never did). His father was a mild man. But he was a man. A man's man. He had hordes of tools, he teed off on Saturdays with other men, he was an aerospace engineer (Andrew never did know, or really care, what that was). He did what men do to make babies. As a boy, Andrew felt a pricking absence of man factors in himself. His father's mere presence, walking through the den, eating dinner, paying bills at his desk each week, was like a constant menacing whisper to Andrew that something inside himself was missing, that he was in some way, and hugely, made wrong. He avoided being alone with his father, terrified that such comaraderie would inevitably reveal the missing or gravely damaged part, even though he had no idea what that part might be or look like. His father didn't goad him on to play baseball or to help build or repair something in the workshop. He didn't talk sports or talk tough. Nevertheless, Andrew felt unbearable pressure in his presence: either his father was completely aware of the "secret" his son possessed; or he was clueless, and it was up to Andrew to keep him that way, even if he had no idea what kind of secret it was that he needed to keep under wraps. Whichever it was, the goal was the same: Being in the sole company of his father was something to be avoided at all costs.

The two-day father-son crabbing trip every summer was the most dreaded event of Andrew's childhood, a dread that was doubled by that fact that they were joined each time by Charles's boss, Frank, and Frank's son,

Glenn. Glenn was just a few years older than Andrew, but enough to seem "mature." He was handsome, with smooth mocha-colored skin, dark wavy hair and green eyes. His lips were smooth, too. Almost shiny, and with a purple hue. The ride to the ocean was three long hours, and Andrew didn't sleep the night before, trying to make a list of all the possible topics he could talk to his father about in the car to pass the time. In the end, as they drove off at 5:30 in the morning, he took the easy way out: he feigned sleep after fifteen minutes. They would meet Frank and Glenn at the dock, carry all their gear – a cooler filled with canned beverages and sandwiches prepared by the mothers, bushel baskets to store the crabs, and a box of bait, nets and rods – to the small rickety outboard motorboat and push off. Frank started the motor by pulling hard on a string like a lawnmower. He and Charles took turns navigating. The men drank beer, the boys had Cokes, and they peed in the empties. As soon as they dropped anchor, about a half hour out, Andrew set about the task of crabbing with a fury. His father had made the rods out of old paint stirrers and thirty feet of cord, which was wrapped around each stirrer, covering the length of wood two thirds of the way up, leaving enough bare wood to grip. One end of the cord was attached to the stirrer with his father's industrial staple gun. The other end had a lead weight tied to it, whose size and shape reminded him of a photograph of Elizabeth Taylor's drop earrings that he had once seen in some magazine in the waiting room of the dentist's office. (When he turned the page of the magazine to arrive at her high-school graduation photograph, he thought that she was the most beautiful woman in the world, and thought that this thought offered a ray of hope, until he remembered how often he looked at the men's underwear section of the Sears catalogue when his parents weren't home.)

Andrew tied a large chunk of raw, bloodied bait to the weighted end of the cord, and dropped it onto the surface of the ocean, watching it penetrate that distinct edge and disappear under the murky water as he slowly turned the stirrer to unwind the cord. He then bent over and kept his eyes fixed on the water, never raising himself up until he felt a bite. It was the only way for him not to participate in the conversation and risk giving himself away, or to have to figure out how to avert his glance – when one of the others (especially Glenn, whose dick head would surely share that same shade of purple as his lips) would pick up an empty, spread his legs, pull down his zipper and extract his man penis to full view, in order to pee – so that no one could possibly know of the secret he carried within him that was so secret that even he didn't know what it was.

As much as he dreaded the two-day crabbing expeditions, he cherished the few days after when, in his bed at night, he would think about the other men peeing in cans and feel a sensation that was so stirring that, in those moments, he couldn't believe it was wrong or bad. It felt too good, especially when he touched himself down there. On the return home, regardless of how many crabs they caught – sometimes sixty, sometimes a dozen – his father praised him for his concentration. This pleased Andrew to no end. It signified that his father remained clueless, and that this thing made wrong or that was missing could remain safely in abeyance, and maybe even go away.

Comfort with his father arrived in the throes of adolescence, when the beauty and the power of words arrived, competing with the by-now unavoidable beauty and power of the male body. Both were inchoate and needed each other desperately, if both were to survive.

When Andrew realized what the wet spots on his pajamas were in the morning (it was his friend Kyle who had first mentioned the term "nocturnal emission"), and remembered that his dreams, of men, provoked these wet spots, it was as if some unidentifiable fruit had ripened to the point where it needed to be picked and bitten into. But the fruit needed a name: Apple. Pear. Or something less evident and neutral. He needed words to understand it. On several occasions, his mother had urged him to read *The Well of Loneliness*. He bought it and read it. Then, in the bookstore in the local mall, his radar zeroed in on *Confessions of a Mask*; and upward and onward. Words described it, gave it a shape, a smell, a feel, erections, and he could return to those words on those pages over and over again, to find comfort, arousal, communion, courage, hope. In the process he fell in love with words generally. And that passion, adolescent but steadfast, magically dissolved his fear of his father, who, he understood, was a man of words. His father became a joy to be with. He could spend hours with him. He could even imagine living with him.

"I'm going to lie down for a while."

"Sure, Dad. I'll wake you up in an hour or so. Give you time to get the juices flowing before I take you back to sis."

Despite the forecasts, the sun occasionally pokes out from the clouds, which are lying low in the sky and pushing the air down so that it can be felt. It is soothing, like warm damp gauze placed delicately on the eyelids. There will be no rain. Andrew listens to his father shuffle down the hallway to his bedroom and feels a dread that surpasses the dread he felt of being alone with his father as a child: the dread of his father's material absence from his life and – with the exception of his ashes scattered in the ocean (he has requested this, and has had it notarized, as an addendum to his will) – from the face of the earth. As soon as he hears the bedroom door close gently, his thoughts alight on something that, he realizes, he has completely forgotten about for an hour: Ex. He decides not to call him. It will happen when and how, and if, it happens. Instead, he sits down at his desk in front of his computer. He wants to see if he can find the photographs of Elizabeth Taylor.

It does happen, two days later, while his father is visiting Sheila. He is watering the potted plants on the front porch (which need watering almost every day if there is more than six hours of direct sunlight) and can see a car coming down the road. It could be Ex's car, he thinks, realizing that he has looked up at every sound of a car to see if it is Ex's. This car, an old non-descript burgundy Dodge, has a neglected, battered look that seems fitting. The roof has boxes strapped to it. The trunk door is open wide, held steady with elastic cord. The rear passenger windows are blocked by other boxes. The car turns into the driveway and pulls up behind Andrew's convertible. Ex extends his arm out the window and waves. "Is this a good spot to park?"

"Let me help you."

After depositing the first round of boxes on the floor of the small bedroom, Andrew turns to him. "This is it. Your room, your space." He has no idea what he should say next. It seems impossible, preposterous, that his sanctuary is now occupied by an eighty-five-year-old dying man whom he knows so well that he is almost a habit, and a twenty-three-year-old who has rapidly succeeded in becoming habit-forming. He proceeds to the safety zone

174

of logistics, explaining to Ex that he can keep the room in any order or disarray that he wants but if it's the latter to not let the disarray creep. And if there is anything here he doesn't need or want – the sheets, the blanket, the linens, whatever – to let him know. He is congenial, matter of fact, terrified. Ex goes to him and holds him tightly, burrowing his face in his neck. Neither says anything. Andrew feels dampness on his neck but doesn't know if it is sweat (and if so, whose? His? Ex's?) or tears.

"Let's get the rest in in case it rains."

As Ex gathers the last of the loose items from the car, Andrew goes to the kitchen and pours two tall glasses of juice (his own spiked with vodka) and places them on the mosaic coffee table where the crystal had originally been placed but which he'd moved to the nighttable of his own bedroom when his father arrived back and asked, "What the hell is that thing?" He sits on the sofa where he hopes that Ex will also end up sitting.

Ex appears in the living room after depositing the last of his belongings.

"Sit. Relax. Have some juice."

Ex picks up a glass and sits on the divan perpendicular to the sofa.

"Everything okay"? Andrew asks.

"Way okay."

"Good. I'm going to get some work done. Feel your way around a bit. Make yourself at home."

"Is this really home?"

"Pool towels are in the bamboo cabinet next to the back door if you want to swim. Help yourself."

Ex quickly downs the juice and places the glass back on the coffee table next to where the crystal used to be. The pressure of his fingers against the glass puts the tips of his nails in relief. They are clipped and clean. As he sits back,

175

the bottom of his gym shorts opens up to reveal a glimpse of his left testicle.

"Off I go. By the way, it will be interesting to understand what you want me to be for you." Andrew smiles, picks up the glasses and heads for the kitchen. "Let me know if you need anything."

Ex opens the back door to the deck. Before he goes outside, he turns and says, "When are you going to ask me why I was arrested? And other stuff about me?"

"I'll think about it." Andrew has thought about it. A lot. When the heavy-set woman crowded her face into his car window in the prison parking lot, he decided to try not to ask Ex about why he was arrested and other stuff. He has decided that he wants to know who Ex is from the moment he has entered this house until the day, and the day will surely come, when he leaves this house. Ex without context, without the tedious bricks and mortar which, unlike his father, Andrew has no proclivity for assembling in order for all the pieces to fit together and then – voila – it works. In fact, he suspects, he may be after something more radical: to throw himself wildly off kilter and see if he can assemble himself in a new way. In any event, he decides, Ex's past, however little he knows about it, will somehow entirely inform his present. It's merely a question of time and of him being acutely attentive. Not just to his beauty, although his beauty along with the radiant promise of his youth seem to be nourishment enough for now, as he watches Ex, naked once again, dive into the pool and burst out of the surface of the water as if he were ripping through the womb, ready and eager to be born.

Ex, too, moves about with comfort here, he sees, but it is a comfort that Andrew doesn't particularly relish, smacking as it does of a sense of entitlement that has not been earned, a familiarity that is brash and unwarranted. There is brokenness here. How could there not be, what with thirty days and nights spent in prison at the very least, or from whatever other events, large and small, in his life that gradually coalesced and conspired to produce a solid, steely pair of handcuffs locking his wrists behind his back as he was carted off by officers of the law who were putting in their hours and probably didn't care in the least whether this young man would be redeemed, rehabilitated, or rot. Yes, he will think about it and many other things. But he needs at least one, or perhaps many, days in which to create a kind of cocoon here, in his home, where he and Ex can develop the beginnings of a movement and a language of their own, before his father arrives. He calls Sheila, fully prepared to hear, before she agrees, the litany of sacrifices she will have to make in order to keep their father at her house for a while. He calls her. She doesn't fail him. Dear sis.

He lays out a simple dinner from the meager offerings in the fridge – salad fixings (he has to poke and pick from among the wilted greens), cold cuts, cheeses – and motions to Ex from the picture window to come in. The initial minute of silence at the table is broken by Ex as driplets of water form on the back strands of hair and fall from their tiny weight onto his neck like glass beads.

"Thank you."

"For what?"

"For this. For everything. I've been trying to think of what to say, but I don't know where to start."

"A thank-you is a good place." He raises his glass and motions Ex to do the same. "Cheers. Here's to."

Ex takes a gulp of wine and looks over the spread on

the table. "It all looks so good. Would you be angry if I said I wasn't hungry? I feel like I just need to sleep some more."

"Come." Andrew rises from his chair and walks ahead of Ex down the hall until he arrives a few feet away from the bedrooms. He stops and turns. "You can lead the way."

Ex continues down the hall and stops at the first bedroom, the small one, his. He looks inside and then continues on.

"Where are you going?"

"I was hoping to sleep in your room."

"And why is that?"

"I'm not sure."

"What makes you not sure?"

"I'm not sure."

"Let me ask you something. What is it that you want me to be for you?"

"Sorry, but I'm not sure about that either."

Andrew reaches up, places a hand on each of Ex's shoulders and turns him about-face. "Why don't you sleep in your room tonight?"

"Will you lie down next to me?"

"Let me clear the table and then I'll come back and lie down next to you." He accompanies Ex into the bedroom and pulls back the blanket and top sheet. Ex removes his shorts (pulling them down to his knees with his hands and then using his feet to scrunch them down below his ankles and kick them off, thinking nothing of leaving them where they land, damp and crumpled on the floor) and climbs into bed with the languor of someone who is above having a care in the world. Andrew pulls the blanket up to his shoulders. "I'll be back later." He strokes Ex's hair and lets his hand travel down so that it brushes softly against the lashes of his right eye and the stubble on his cheek and chin. He closes the door on his way out, leaving just a hairline crack between the door and its frame, at the moment just before the door creaks.

He takes his time clearing the table and decides to also put things back into the fridge (except his plate of food, barely touched, which he leaves on the dining room table to finish later, perhaps) and to wash the few dishes that need to be washed. Rather than place them in the dish rack, he hand-dries them and restacks them back in cabinets and drawers. He surveys the kitchen, dining and living areas. All things material have been restored to a degree of order that enables him to abandon their demands and succumb to more impulsive desires. However, he hesitates, and finishes his dinner before venturing into Ex's room, where, he hopes, he will find him sound asleep. Before sitting down to eat, he goes to the picture window and looks out toward the pool and deck. Ex's towel is not to be seen. He steps outside. To his immediate left, the towel is there, abandoned in a heap on the curve of the pool molding, along with the empty glass of wine. He picks up the towel and without putting his face into it and inhaling hangs it on the outdoor rack by the outdoor shower, and goes back inside, empty glass in hand, muttering with a half-smile, "A piece of work."

He rolls up a slice of the pastrami as if he were making a cigarette, and takes a bite, expecting a tug of resistance, like biting into a bathing cap. Instead it breaks right off, is not too salty and has just the right nip of garlic and pepper, a taste that will linger in his mouth for several hours after he has finished. He doesn't mind kissing men whose mouths taste of something — wine, garlic, barbecued chicken — and he doesn't mind the lingering taste of something in his own mouth, although he assumes it will be unpleasant to someone else, as if his "bad breath" means breath that exudes anything but toothpaste or mouthwash or nothing.

Taking another bite of the pastrami, he thinks back to when he had ordered a pastrami on rye on the Saturday that his high school English teacher, Mr. Atchison, had taken him to a deli in a nearby town for dinner in order to head down a path of conversation that he'd hoped would help Andrew come out. When they took a walk in the park afterward and sat down in an isolated wooded area, where Andrew was terrified of the kiss he could feel was about to happen, he thought about his breath. If only he could steal away and gargle with something. But here he was, stuck, and his teacher would begin to kiss him and immediately withdraw his tongue in horror at his adorable student's bad breath. He wanted to run, but Mr. Atchison's face was so close to his own as they talked that he could smell the marvelous and perfect breath of his teacher – mustardy and with something else coming from much deeper within – and he liked it, and liked it even more when, after a year of waiting and hoping, his beloved teacher's tongue was inside his mouth, taking it over. How could Mr. Atchison have done it? How did he know, during that kiss and the many that followed for months afterward (along with the blowjobs and the anal intercourse and the conversations and the walks), that all of it – until his student inevitably discovered the same possibility with a boy his own age (which he did after six months) – would be okay? Andrew rolled up another piece of pastrami. He respected Mr. Atchison more than anyone he had met. His parents, had they known, would have had the teacher arrested.

He rolls a final slice of meat. He will not brush his teeth or rinse with mouthwash before he goes into Ex's room. There will be no kisses tonight. It is too soon. He is willing to be many things for Ex, but not a potentially combustible experiment. No first-, second- or third-degree burns of the heart for him. For Ex, possibly. He is young. But not for a senior-citizen evolution of a young man, whose various types of aged protective membranes are no longer supple or regenerative (although his father did locate a suppleness for radical change that enabled him to let his mother walk out at age eighty-five, and at that he wonders if the separation would have been permanent had Edith not fallen in the bathroom). He reaches for a slice of Monterey Jack; it is insipid (and whether his father would have latched on to another woman, given how much time he spent – within days after Edith had moved out – stalking the lumber aisle of Lowe's in search of some woman who looked utterly helpless amidst the endless shelves of pine, cedar, treated and untreated planks, panels and fence segments, and, if not married her, at least allowed his sexual and domestic needs to be taken care of by her by setting up house with her. But his mother fell and things took a different turn). He doesn't finish the slice of cheese but doesn't throw out the package that contains the remaining pre-sliced squares that the wrapper indicates "Best used by" today. Ex may like it.

The sun is beginning to set, stealing away the intensity and harshness of color and heat that make it difficult for Andrew to stay outdoors for long, as much as he would want to. He pours himself more wine and tip-toes, glass in hand, down the hallway. Without having to open the door and risk making it creak and cause Ex to stir or wake up, he peers through the hairline opening. Ex is on his side, curled into his usual crescent, sound asleep. He thinks he can make out a wet spot on the pillow, where dream saliva has trickled out from the side of Ex's mouth, which is slightly opened even though he is breathing through his nose. Andrew is overcome by a sense of outright lovingness, which he can permit himself to have now that he has seen that Ex is in a state of sleep that can signify nothing other than that he feels safe, protected, cared for. Andrew feels this too, and nothing more needs to be done with or for Ex tonight. He goes to the deck with his glass of topped-up wine and watches night set in, eager to get into his own bed, knowing that down the hall, two doors to the left (the first door is to the bedroom of his father, who will be returning soon, he reminds himself), is a species of universe, making its rotations and revolutions and orders and chaoses but, for the moment, is inanimate and still. He finishes his wine, brushes his teeth, strips down, gets into bed and quickly falls asleep.

When the light of dawn begins to rise, a pale blue/pink that he has forgotten to fend off by pulling the cords of his shutters to assure that the slats are at a severe diagonal, he feels Ex wrapped around him tightly. Normally his inclination is to leap out of bed as soon as he awakens, but now he has a drunken desire to hold tight and get his breathing in unison with the rhythm of Ex's slow and regular ins and outs of breath. Ex will be famished, he thinks. He will make a big breakfast – freshly squeezed grapefruit juice, eggs, bacon, toast – while Ex showers. But for now, and despite himself, he is motionless as he feels their bodies rise and fall in unison, spies on Ex's dreams, and takes in the uncensored scent of him ploughing through his dreamscapes, whatever they may be.

CHAPTER 19

Andrew breaks into a forced smile as his arms make an effort to fan out from his sides. "Welcome back, Dad."

Sheila has called her brother, with no notice or explanation, to say she is on her way and in a hurry. She drops their father off in the driveway, with his walker and duffle bag, and pulls back out. Andrew doesn't read anything into what for him is such a heartless but unsurprising gesture. He knows his sister, especially when it comes to clients versus family. Family is a given, an unconditional and rather bland attachment, and so can survive and forgive neglect or any other breach of consideration.

"Great to be back, son." Charles looks fit, rested. His hair is neatly combed, he is wearing a tennis shirt that Andrew has never seen before, and his socks are extremely white. He leaves his walker at the entrance, removes his sneakers and walks toward the living space. "And who do we have here?"

"Dad, this is the young man I was telling you about. Alex."

"Nice to meet you, young man."

"Nice to meet you too, sir."

"Please, call me Zee."

"Zee?"

"Yes. It's short for 'zayda,' which means grandfather in Yiddish. I'm sure you still have your grandfathers, but kids your age, all of them who get to know me, just call me Zee. Even if they're not Jewish. You're not Jewish are you?"

"Zee. Okay. No, I'm not."

"I didn't think so." He waits to see if Ex will react to this mild provocation, but Ex's expression – weak nervous smile, eyes darting from Charles to Andrew and back but always avoiding their eyes – remains unchanged.

"Would you mind moving to the sofa? You're sitting in my dad's favorite chair."

"Oh gosh, I'm so sorry."

"Stay there, young man. I can sit on a sofa too. So tell me, what do you do?"

"Well, I make music."

"You make music. I make music too. In the bathroom, while I'm sleeping, and every time I eat nuts. But I love nuts, so my audience has to put up with my music. Do you like classical?"

"I haven't listened to much classical. I'm more into pop advocacy."

"That's a new one for me. You'll have to explain it to me one day. Can I play something for you?"

Andrew knows that the test is about to begin. Rachmaninoff's Third, which Ex will be subjected to while his father proffers commentary in order to determine whether the young man has rich marrow. "I'm afraid you're stuck, Ex. Think of it as a rite of passage not to be taken too seriously." Ex has a supplicating look on his face. "Just sit back and enjoy. I'll fix us all something to eat. And Dad, I'll dig your med box out of your bag, if you don't mind."

"Dig away."

Andrew leaves them and goes to the entrance to rifle through the duffle bag. Next to it, beside the front door, lay his Birkenstocks (lined up), Ex's flip-flops (overlapping each other like an upside-down "V") and his father's bulbous white Nikes that resemble small yachts (one on top of Ex's flip-flop and the other on its own a foot away). There they are. Six shoes. He has an urge to line them up but instead pulls out his cell phone and takes a picture of them. Something about their asymmetry, their diverse geographies of isolation and mingling, is worth having another look at, at some other time.

Now we are three. This simple fact, which repeatedly gallops through his head with a gladiator-like fury as he tucks his phone back in his right pocket and surveys the living area (from his vantage point, it is unpeopled, as it had been for the two years up until his father ended up living with him), makes him already nostalgic for the habit of his solitude and the great and wonderful silence he may have lost. At the same time, he is thrilling at the prospect of a habit blown to smithereens. He studies a small picture on the far wall, by his desk, that he picked up in Burkina Faso. He has traveled a lot, lived in different places and set up roots that didn't have enough time to grow thick and deep. He has met people along the way, special people, important people, the kinds of people who could form a personal community or family, had he stayed long enough in the places where he'd met them. But he didn't, and instead toted his memories of them, and the feelings they provoked, along the way, like keepsakes or knick-knacks for the heart, to be brought out and polished from time to time in order for a ray of light to occasionally cause them to glisten, catch his eye, and make him remember how special, how important they were for a brief time, and how they could have continued being so, if he had simply stayed put. What was he after, after all?

Ex will be held hostage by Charles and Rachmaninoff for at least another half hour. He considers joining them but, for the sake of solidifying at least two sides to this extremely scalene triangle in the making, keeps away. They will need their own *pas de deux* if this is to work, whatever "this" is. He always wondered why all tables weren't made with three legs, which would eliminate all possibility of wobbling. There must be a reason that he is not aware of. He was never great in math. Very good, but not great.

The commercial part of the symphony begins – the one that has figured into so many soundtracks and muzaks that Ex, being a product of his time, will have heard it before, and will connect. Andrew slips down the hall and opens the door to Ex's room. Even if there is a creak, no one will hear it. The boxes are still stacked, a legal tablet and pen are on the bed, and discarded clothing – mostly perforated nylon gym shorts of different colors – is strewn about the floor like tumbleweed. How he would like to pick up the shorts and hold them to his face; or, alternatively, approach the legal pad and see what is written on it. But there is time. He scoffs at the platitude and instead decides that it is simply too early for him to get caught doing such a thing. Once he and Ex have a bit of history established, should Ex walk in on him smelling his shorts or reading from his tablet it could be a source for laughter, or even sex or conversation. But at this point in their timeline, it would create only distance. He closes the door until the hairline crack remains and heads back down the hall to the kitchen where, as he cobbles together dinner, he will be able to hear whatever, if anything, his father and his...his (what is he?) ... and Ex may be saying to each other. If only he could see them, however. But should he make himself visible to them, the risks are many and great. Ex could quietly beseech him to join in and save him. His father could throw him a glance that says, "Hopeless." Or, they could be entirely engaged and Andrew's presence breaks the spell. The platitude — there is time — repeats itself like some cruel intonation of the brevity and speed of a life. Is there time? Standing in front of the open refrigerator door, a single tear escapes as he realizes that his father will die soon and Ex will move on, as he should. Wiping the tear from his cheek, he can feel the deep crease that up until then had only been evident (to him, anyway) in the mirror on those mornings when he hadn't slept well. He remembers that there are four ribeye steaks, individually wrapped, in the freezer. He pulls out three of them, paints them with a mixture of soy sauce, minced garlic and grated ginger that forms a kind of lacquer where it touches the frozen surface of the meat, and slides them under the broiler, which he will turn on when the *Finale: alla breve* begins. They are extra thick and will produce a pond of blood on the serving plate that is mouth-watering, unless Ex prefers his steaks well done.

There is a passion, an awakening, that is pressing on him, and for which he understands perfectly well that time is short. He even doubts whether there is any time at all. And this passion, this awakening, he will not banish it for the sake of prudence, although he will be prudent in letting it manifest itself, if that is even possible. Still, he can't help but wonder as he rinses the baby spinach that he will steam whether all older generations cannot escape the curse of seeming old. He knows that, as close to his father as he is, Charles is still a creature who can have had only an unvibrant life, one carried out in black and white, like all of the photos and films that have documented such lives. And here he is, his son, born in the Polaroid and Technicolor era. How much of a difference does that make to Ex's generation? Is it only about color? Or is there some unbridgeable gap between any two generations – the younger one, which thinks it has a monopoly on intensity of feeling, truth of thought and outbursts of discovery, and the preceding one, the "older" one, which has been merely a conduit for the real thing?

The final movement has started. "Dinner will be ready in about twenty minutes," he calls out. He wonders if they've heard him.

The venerable Sergei must have worked his magic. Andrew watches and listens to the sounds of his father and Ex talking and listening to each other uninterruptedly while he forks out side dishes, spoons some of the pond of blood back onto the meat, replenishes glasses, passes the sea salt and peppercorns housed in large disposable grinders, slices more bread. He feels like a spy with special clearance, and their conversation seems uncensored in his presence. He is envious of his father, who, lacking the burn of desire for this boy, is able to glide along from one subject to another as if he were a tourist who had three hours to sightsee a major city. However, as Ex begins to feel more in his skin at the table, Andrew notices slight shifts. When Ex starts talking, he keeps going. It is not the typical nervousness of the many for whom the onset of silence signifies failure of some kind. Something about his eyes, the way they seem caught in the web of some internal matter (when they are not watching himself reflected in the picture window, taking himself in, as he talks), indicates that he is not only under the spell of his own discourse, but that he has gone beyond testing it and has instead taken the step to proclaim it, to this man who is more than sixty years his senior. Moreover, when Ex is listening, he is physically restless – one hand massaging the other, the fingers on one hand raking his hair, lips tightly poised and revved up, waiting to pounce rather than understand. Charles isn't privy to the engine that prompts these shifts, which to Andrew are so strong as to be almost violent. And why would Dad be, Andrew asks himself, since his father's investment in Ex at this point is minimal (he is not looking for "signs" of anything, beyond Ex's degree of interest in classical music), and since an old, dying man probably considers the musings of a young man to be as heartfelt but harmless as a young man considers the musings of an old, dying man to be out of date and sweet, if not somewhat pathetic. That's the way it is. Nevertheless, Andrew senses an obdurate and narcissistic quality in Ex that he finds troublesome and irritating, something to not underestimate and let fade from the radar. As he begins to clear the table, he wonders where his place is in all of this.

"Anybody want some ice cream or sorbet? I've got coffee, chocolate chocolate chip, and mango.

Ex looks at Andrew with an expression of surprise, as if his host has just then magically appeared, like some capricious rabbit pulled out of a hat. "I'll have some chocolate chocolate chip, please."

"Dad?"

"Tempting, but I'll pass. Son, you could reach over and pass me my meds? It's that time."

Andrew and Ex reach for the box at the same time.

Andrew has grabbed the "S" for Sunday, while Ex has grabbed the "F" for Friday at the other end. They look at each other. Andrew's resolute eyes are tempered by a strategic smile; Ex's resolute eyes are accompanied by no such strategy. He pulls lightly so that Andrew loses his grip.

"Here you go, Zee."

Charles snaps open the appropriate lid (he has never confused his days of the week) and extracts the five pills from inside the tiny translucent baby-blue compartment.

"What are they for?"

"What *aren't* they for? Oy, there's the cholesterol, there's the blood pressure, there's the blood thinner, and I forget what the other two are for. They are new additions. They must be for my new condition, the one that's going to do me in. A fate worse than life." He tosses all of them into his mouth at once, takes a large gulp of water and swallows. "There. Better living through chemicals. Or so they say."

As Andrew scoops out the ice cream, he can hear Ex telling his father about when he chipped a tooth and broke an arm playing basketball. When his father laughs at the end of the story, Andrew wishes that both of them were not there. Navigating these two seas is making his head and stomach turn and churn on themselves. He puts the bowl away that he was going to use to give himself a small portion of sorbet. The threesome at the table has lost its appeal.

"Here you go, Ex. CC chip. If you want more, let me know."

"Hang on a sec. I'm confused. Is it Alex or is it Ex?"

"Whatever you want," Ex replies.

"I started with Alex. I'll stick with that. It has substance."

"Thanks, sir."

"Did you say 'Sir'?"

"Sorry. I meant Zee."

"Accepted. But don't do it again. 'Sir' reminds me how old I am. And with that, young men, I'm going to my room to do my exercises so that I don't die tonight, and then I'll lie down and sleep. That's the plan, anyway. 'Night all." He rises from his chair. "I'll get the walker on my way to the bedroom, Andrew." He shuffles to the entrance to fetch his walker. "Do you mind if I leave my shoes here?"

"That's fine, Dad. 'Night."

The ice has been broken, chipped away at rather. They have started moving about in, and choreographing, a shared domestic world, individually, collectively, and in the three permutations of "2." When his father leaves, Andrew takes the seat at a right angle to Ex, who is eating his ice cream at the chair that faces the picture window and its view of the pool. It is dark outside. The window is clean, and the reflection is strong. Ex is studying himself. Andrew bounces back from Ex and the reflection of Ex, both of them (Andrew and Ex) watching how he flexes and relaxes his biceps as he brings a spoon of ice cream to his mouth, how he tightens and releases his jaw in between bites, how he draws in his cheeks when his mouth his empty. He watches as Ex even experiments with different smiles and intensities of other facial expressions, as if he were trying to uncover his optimum seductive self. Troublesome indeed.

"Your dad is awesome. He knows so much about so much."

"He's a great guy."

"You're really lucky."

Without saying it, and without trying to show it, Andrew takes issue with the word "lucky." It precludes any sense of responsibility from all parties. His father wasn't instantly a great guy, or a great father. That would have been lucky, and luck of such caliber doesn't happen. It's smaller, more piecemeal. Charles has always known a lot about a lot. It has been in his nature (as far as Andrew can remember) to acquire knowledge, facts, odds and ends of interesting items to think about, talk about, insist upon, make harsh judgements based on. But still, at times, when parents and children were under one roof seated around the round dinner table (expandable to oval by inserting a perfectly matched formica leaf that was stored in Charles's workshop) encircled by six black leatherette swivel chairs, his father gave it all up to have a hearty burping contest with his son, especially after a few consecutive gulps of the flavored generic soda – grape, black cherry Wishniak, vanilla – that Edith served in flip-top cans at dinner, hoping that her children wouldn't seek it out elsewhere if they could have it at home (she succeeded with her son, who never touched the stuff when he moved out; and was partially successful with Sheila, who kept and drank twenty-four-packs of Diet Coke but nothing else flavored and carbonated). Yes, his father had much at his disposal to initiate a conversation, and he was thoughtful about the words he chose, which made listening easy. But as Andrew grew older, he grew bored with the regular calibration of his father's thoughts and the words he assigned to them, the paucity of their scope and their refusal to enter into places beyond real things that had happened to happen. By the time he was sixteen, Andrew was sated with the abundance of his father's information and starving for some other kind of outpouring that could be anchored to the concrete but extended beyond it and could make his body (and his father's, if he had his way completely) shake and incite tempests of shouting to be regretted later, or of introspection that could be fed on later, when the family disbanded from the formica table and went their separate ways in the various rooms of the house. And this did happen from time to time, and Andrew and his father would regroup and have reckonings, rooted in the words they chose with care. Partial reckonings, but beautiful ones, enough for Andrew to sense that his father was capable of inquiring as well as acquiring, of being a man of feeling, finally. No, luck had nothing to do with it. It was a much-deserved reward for work, intention and courage.

Ex can't know any of this, so Andrew thinks to ask him, "What's your dad like?" But he refrains. He is not sure at this point how interested he is in what Ex's father is like, or how much he cares, especially if Ex uses the question as a sharp implement to puncture some stubborn swelling (much like the expresser Andrew used as a teenager to pop his whiteheads, waiting for them to detonate onto the bathroom mirror and restore him to some semblance of attractiveness) and let ooze out all of the parental travesties and injustices that have gone into making him all of the things he has hoped to evolve out of being, whatever they might be; or that have prevented him from evolving into the being he aspires to, whatever that may be. No, he is not in the mood right now, doesn't have the patience, and doesn't remember the last time he had the patience for or interest in subjecting himself to such ruthless and facile parental blame, although it must have been before he'd sat on the edge of his mother's bed as she lay dying, softened (for the three weeks before she actually died) by morphine and the small teddy bear she clutched at her belly, and in that supine stillness when she said that her son's voice was music to her ears he remembered what it was like to feel love for her and was ashamed by the unsparing harshness he had heaped upon her for all those decades (even if she had been an eager sparring partner), and he forgave her, and stroked his forgiveness into her arms and face as she lay there, alert enough to understand, he hoped, and to let him know that she forgave him too by a mere flick of a finger or tic of a lip – and then she managed to say in a strained whisper that she wasn't finished with him. So for the moment he does not ask, and instead gets up from his chair and walks out to the deck (stopping by the wall to switch on the pool light, which doesn't interfere with the night sky and its display of stars), hoping that Ex will take it upon himself to clear the table and wash the dishes, slowly warming to the demands of this new domestic constellation that need to be met if it is to continue to glimmer. Ex in the kitchen, his father in a bedroom. All under one roof. That is fine. Company in solitude. Very fine.

CHAPTER 20

He awakens to company. Ex is sleeping beside him in bed, on his back, with one leg crossed over Andrew's thigh and the other bent at the knee, upright, with his foot flat against the mattress.

The top sheet covers him from the base of his breastbone, where his chest hair forms a thicket, to the bottom of his calves, just where the hair begins to thin out at the ankles. (Andrew no longer has hair on his ankles. For years he attributed it to wearing elastic socks; but he hasn't worn socks for two years, and the hair hasn't grown back.) He has no recollection of Ex slipping into his room, onto his bed and under the top sheet. How long has he been here?

He eases out from under the warm, thick leg and peers into the hallway. His father's door is closed. It is quiet. He nudges Ex on the shoulder and brings his mouth next to his ear. "Ex, you need to go back to your room now."

"But I…"

"You need to back to your room. My father can't know about this."

"Doesn't your father know about you?"

"Yes, he does. But he doesn't know about *us*. I don't know about us. We'll talk about this later." He pokes at Ex on his neck until he rouses himself unsteadily and staggers out of the room and down the hall, his morning erection springing up and down with life. Andrew hears the door to the small bedroom click close. It doesn't make the usual creaking sound that Andrew keeps telling himself he'll fix by spraying some lubricant on the hinges but never does. The expectation of that creaking sound that Andrew is sitting up in bed waiting to hear but that doesn't arrive unsettles him. Disrupting that unanticipated silence, and retrospectively the silence that accompanied Ex's slipping into Andrew's bed, is not a noise, but a word: stealth, a word that Andrew is not particularly fond of.

It is a work day. He has reports to make progress on that are expected by the end of the week. But they are in good shape and don't require full brain capacity. His father will expect breakfast and lunch, and in between meals he will interrupt occasionally (regardless of where in the house Andrew is, his father will speak to him as if he is within earshot), but this is a small annoyance among many small annoyances (the emails, the phone ringing, the dirt accruing along the top edges of the floor molding), and a predictable one at that. And Ex? What is his day like? What are his days like? Does he go to school? To work? Why and when will he enter and exit the house today? Will he slip in and out, like he did in his bed at who knows what hour of the night, or will he announce his comings and goings? Is stealth a modus operandus or exceptional?

It isn't until after lunch and his father is out for a walk that he hears a toilet flush in the hall bathroom. Charles strangely had nothing much to say at breakfast about Ex other than "Sweet kid," to which Andrew gratefully replied, "Yes he is" and the conversation took a turn to the logistics of a number of doctors' appointments his father has in the coming days. Andrew hears Ex's footsteps but keeps his head steady on his work.

"Hey."

He swivels his chair counter-clockwise to the three o'clock position and then turns his head so that his eyes have to shift all the way to the right to look into Ex's. "Good morning. I mean, good afternoon." Ex is "dressed" – gym shorts (clearly no underwear) and a loose-fitting tee-shirt – and holding a skateboard. His hair is damp and he has two (or more)-day stubble.

What he will not allow under any circumstances to come out of his mouth, even though the question is searing, is: Where are you off to? He looks at Ex and holds his smile.

"I'm going for a skate and a run. I need to work off some toxins."

The forbidden query is superseded by another: When will you be back? He swallows it like a horse pill and says, "Sounds good."

"Later."

"See you."

He turns back to his work, not knowing whether to preen himself for being strong or flail himself for being such a fool – or to chastise himself for putting himself in a position to have to decide between two such absurdities at his age. He goes back to his document, where he knows what needs to be said and how it needs to be said. "The marginalization of rural women, particularly in remote areas of developing countries," he types, and he feels anchored.

Charles has gone to bed long before Ex turns up. Throughout the day, his father's only mention of Ex has been one "Where is the young boy?," to which Andrew responds, "At work. I forget what he does, and what his hours are." When he does hear the front door open, he is sitting on the sofa reading by the light of the sleek black floor lamp that his father had bought him as a house-warming gift. Ex's footsteps are heavy and purposeful. When he sees Andrew sitting on the sofa, he marches up to him, bends over, grabs his head, and shoves his tongue into Andrew's mouth. Before Andrew can register what is happening, Ex has taken back his tongue and sauntered off to the deck, where he strips down and dives into the pool. Andrew can taste Ex's sweat around his mouth. It is salty, with a slight metallic tang to it.

After twenty minutes of trying to read, he hears the sound of water being transported through the pipes inside the wall next to the picture window to the nozzle of the outdoor shower beside the pool. He closes his book, which had taken him far away to places that made him think about things other than his own thoughts, but which lost its power as soon as he'd felt Ex's tongue pushing toward his throat. He throws the book down hard on the coffee table and despises himself for having become even more useless than the book has become; more useless, he realizes, because the book's spine is still gloweringly intact after the impact, the back cover has closed back onto the pages, pressing them down into the crisp clean volume that it has been since it came off the press, and protecting the words inside that can never be anything but those immutable words.

A reckoning is in order, he thinks, but about what

exactly? He can't locate anything specifically that has been done, or not been done, around which to commence some type of full frontal – only a growing weakness and subjugation that has been overtaking him since he first saw Ex, said "Hi," turned away and then turned around to say more. And who is to blame for that? Nevertheless, there is a temptation to cast aside all of the gentility with some harsh gesture, like a magician who suddenly pulls the tablecloth out from a fully set table, except that Andrew wants his gesture (in this case words) to cause the glasses, plates and flatware to come crashing to the ground. The pipes stop their gurgling. He walks to the back door, where he can see Ex toweling off, pokes his head out and, despite the floating rage that is making his body shake, says, "Hope you had a good day. I'm heading off to bed. See you tomorrow." As if to make matters worse, he smiles as he closes the door behind him, gently.

"Let's have a child together. A little girl. We'll name her Clare." Ex has snuck up behind Andrew, who is staring out the window at the morning sunlight as he works through a series of syntactical conundrums drafted by a non-English mother tongue technical writer who has inserted the information that Andrew requested in order to advocate more strongly for funding for women's training in microenterprise development. He feels Ex's hands settle lightly on his shoulders, his long fingers extending to his cliff of collarbone and pushing their way underneath. He closes his eyes and hopes that Ex is able to eke out some pleasure from his exploration and isn't grossed out by the thinness of flesh, the prominence of fragile bone. "What do you think?"

Andrew can't conceive of where such a proposition could have possibly come from. "Tell me more."

"I can imagine it."

"Imagine what?"

"You and me, and Clare."

"Tell me more."

"What more is there to say?"

How simple it could be, were it not for the list of practical questions that presents itself immediately to him and makes him realize how incapable he is of genuinely letting go: Who will change her diaper? Who will wake up how many times in the night to let her suck on the nipple of the bottle of formula that has been prepared (by whom)? Who will have the presence of mind to be completely present with her when the urge is to be anything but, and when her need – and right – is to be the center of the universe? Etc. But Ex cannot know these things or, if he does, chooses not to consider them. His desire or his calculations emanate from elsewhere. But from where?

How he would like to abandon his mundane plane of pragmatic concern and join Ex in the airy place where he is, a place enviably ignited by impulse and fantastical conjurings that truly seem possible and wonderful – if that is where this particular scenario is coming from. "A family unit?"

"Yep. A kind of fourth generation in the house. Zee, you, me and Clare. And maybe even another kid. After a year or two. A boy this time."

"So that would make me her grandfather and you her father?"

"Kind of."

"Which would kind of make me your father."

Ex's eyes harden. "Why do you have to define this?"

"Good question."

Ex eases up the pressure on Andrew's collar bone, slides his hands up to the sides of Andrew's face and gives each cheek a light slap. "Chill, will you?" His palms are clammy and have a faint whiff of that metallic odor. As he heads down the hallway, Andrew listens carefully for the footsteps to tell him which bedroom he is going to.

Chill indeed. He will be permanently chilled soon enough, and at this he thinks of his father sleeping in bed and hopes that when the final day finally comes it will be one morning soon. He will peek into his father's room to see why he hasn't yet gotten up (the coffee will have been ready for some time and will probably need to be microwaved), look for the slow rise and fall of his stomach under the white Hanes t-shirt he wears as a pajama top, see no movement there or anywhere else along the contours of the blanket, and realize that his father has slipped away, mercifully, sometime during the night while he was sleeping and dreaming what Andrew hopes were literally breathtaking overlooks to that final place. But he, Andrew, is not there yet, although its approach makes itself known and felt constantly, like a dust mote in the eye or glochid in the thumb. In the interim, he doesn't want to be not with him, merely for the exuberance and thrall that Ex incites by his blind-peacock presence, and for the need to have something to commit to, something personal at stake, something capable of disorder, mayhem even, so that the time he has left does not dull him into a complacence brought on by habit or by past meaningfulnesses that seemed to work at the time. The now presses on, with its admonitions of finiteness. And he needs to be with him so that there is some emotion, some feeling, that will periodically jolt him and, before he himself dies, makes him feel inside-out alive.

Which bedroom will it be this time, he wonders. Will his bed be colonized by the unwary sprawl of this long-limbed demigod and his fragrances, or will his sleep zone be smooth and spacious and consoling in his plight of (or striving for) solitude? He will not venture down the hallway yet. The idea of Clare (Clare or Claire, he wonders) needs more thought. He can remember (not how many times, although they were many) his mother saying to him, "You would make such a wonderful father. That's what I regret most" and how, despite his desire to oppose her, he couldn't, having said the same thing to himself within months of understanding that only men could satisfy his need for physical communion and appetite and that men do not have a uterus. It was the Eighties. Men who liked men were too busy enjoying the newly opening buffet of taste-testing – the propulsion of cock, the lure of entry into a tight ass, the texture of leather, the transport of poppers – to think about the domestication of their desires to the point of raising a family. The party was in full swing, and he danced and fucked with the rest of them, but his hair was already starting to recede and the noise soon began to grate on him and he dreaded going home – either alone or latched on to a stranger with a promising bulge whose presence, especially if he were to spend the night, would amplify his solitude. AIDS took so many of them away, but somehow, amidst the flesh-fest, he was spared and survived to witness so many of them waste away to a horrifying gauntness, wraiths barely able to speak for the weakness, and die. It was the Eighties, he was Ex's age, brimming with the sense of possibility (except that of having children), and surrounded by so many of his age and of his kind, dying.

He opens the window to let real air mingle with the air-conditioned air. He sits and watches the palm trees swaying outside before going down the hallway to discover which doors are open and which are closed. The sky is clear and the moon is full. Claire de lune. One day

Ex will have his Clare, he thinks. But not with him. It is too late. Besides, something about the way Ex's tongue slipped in his mouth and pulled out so quickly, as if his first taste of male was and will continue to be repugnant, suggests strict limits to where they will travel together in bed, and out of bed. Ex will find a woman, they will live together and have a child, which, if she agrees, they will name Claire (or Clare).

He closes the window and goes down the hallway. Ex's door is open. Clothes, towels and legal tablets litter the floor. The bed is unmade and empty. He continues down to his bedroom. Ex is lying on his stomach, his arms and legs stretched almost to the four corners of the mattress. He is uncovered and naked. If Andrew wants to slip in to join him, he will have no choice but to wake him up in order to make room. First, however, he will leave the hallway light on, stand over him, and pretend that he can spy on his dreams, or slip inside his real desires.

CHAPTER 21

Sheila calls in the morning. She would like to drop by on her way to show a client several beachside condos a few miles south of Andrew, who has come to expect her occasional visits to be the second, and less important, bird that she can kill with one stone. As always, he tests his theory by asking her, "Why don't you come for breakfast?", to which she comes through resoundingly with, "Sure. One less meal to cook." Three birds for sis.

He has already decided how to present Ex to her: a young local with whom he spoke regularly during his daily beach walks and who recently was looking for a room to rent since his family had relocated. Keep it unelaborate. His sister is quick to judge, and although he doesn't fear her judgment, he prefers to avoid it, strident and unyielding (and tinged with hurt) as it can be, especially when it comes to men, who are often the main topic of conversation ("bashing," as she calls it) when she gets together with her divorced girlfriends (and they are many) at local bars with names like Bunky's or The Shack and by the time a few sips of watermelon martini and bites of pot sticker have reached their gullets men have already been reduced to something less evolved than a platypus. She relishes spilling to him all of the silly talk, assuming he will get it, since he is her brother and is gay (and he knows when to laugh), and therefore doesn't "count" as a man, which in itself causes him to bristle. But as much as he bristles when she tells him about these fruit-concentrate martini-fueled evenings with their banal epiphanies ("men have dicks for brains" and so on), he eggs her on with attentive eyes and silence. Sheila, like many, can't tolerate silence. It makes her squirm, as if something has gone wrong, a connection has been broken, a rift revealed, and so she keeps talking and, in doing so, unravelling, which is precisely what Andrew is interested in, that point when the spool has unwound and the end of the thread is tugging in the tiny diagonal slot meant to prevent it from slipping out and creating a mess of unruly coils. That's where he wants her to arrive, at the tug. There she will go all righteous and he will have understood another type of barrier that one constructs to protect oneself against hurt.

He scrutinizes the refrigerator to see what he can prepare that will impress (he likes to be responsible for something memorable) and hold her at the table with these three men for more time than if he were to simply lay out a medley of cereal boxes. He wants her to linger and enjoy the ease of the male threesome so as to not question or suspect it. There is cream cheese and just enough lox to make an omelet, although there are no olives (Ex must have finished them again), which she loves to slice up and arrange on her bagel like oversized dotted Swiss. He checks the freezer. Six "everything" bagels are nuzzled on the door shelf. That should keep things light and breezy. It does, until he finds her damned reading glasses.

"Hello?" He has taken the stainless-steel whisk to the eight eggs floating in the stainless steel bowl that are waiting to have their yolks furiously merged when he hears her voice at the front door, and appreciates that she knows when she should let herself in, when she should ring the doorbell and then let herself in, and when she should ring the doorbell and wait for someone to answer.

"In the kitchen!" He knows that she will see Ex and their father in the living room as she makes her way to greet Charles with a peck on the cheek.

"Who's that?"

"The roommate I was telling you about. Lex. Or Alex. Or Ex. You have a choice." He doesn't look up from his whisking. He can only imagine the expression on her face. She intuits a lot, and easily.

"Let me go say hello. You need any help?"

"I'm fine. I'll call you all when breakfast is ready."

She helps herself to the pot of coffee (she knows where to find the mugs, teaspoons and sugar) and goes to the living room. Andrew whisks more loudly, and when he has finished beating the eggs he starts pulling out pans and lids and plates and flatware with enough clattering to prevent him from hearing anything but snippets of the conversation taking place in the other room. But the snippets are sufficient. By the time he is carefully slipping the perfectly folded semi-circle omelet onto the serving dish and the last batch of bagels has popped up in the toaster, his sister's direct but benevolent interrogation of Ex has produced all of the responses that he had been avoiding knowing about: He is completing the paperwork to re-enroll in university in the fall; he might major in performing arts but is also thinking about psychology; he left his job at Ace Hardware because of the hours and is looking for another part-time job; and he used to have a girlfriend but doesn't now. Incorrigible sis.

"Breakfast is ready!"

They gather at the table. Sheila and Ex approach the same chair, the one facing the picture window; she defers.

"Help yourselves." There is much passing around of platters – the omelet, the bagels, the sliced tomatoes, the cream cheese – until all settles down. Andrew is terrified of the potential language and gesture codes already established between him and Ex that could display themselves during breakfast and reveal to Sheila a dynamic that she is certainly already suspicious of, especially when he was laying down the plate of tomatoes, saw that the crystal was back on the table, exchanged glances with Ex and saw that his sister was watching them watch each other.

"How is everything, Dad?" He thinks to direct his attention to his father, who, unlike his sister, is easy to keep clueless about certain things.

"Excellent, son."

"Zee, can you pass the orange juice?" Ex asks.

At that word, "Zee," Andrew can feel Sheila's hazel eyes focused on him laser-sharp. He can't resist a passing glance at her. "Sis, can I have the salt?" She hands it to him in silence.

As breakfast proceeds, he busies himself serving and clearing and replenishing, leaving it up to the others to carry on with talk, which they do, and it remains light and fluid, at times with moments of laughter, especially when Charles asks Ex if he can burp on command and Ex obliges with a low dry rumble. Andrew would like to join in but instead takes several private long quiet breaths.

Finally, the last bites are taken. "Gotta run, guys. Lex, it was so nice to meet you. You boys keep out of trouble."

She gets up from the table and Andrew walks her to the door.

"Thanks for the breakfast, bro. He's a sweet boy. And so cute. He'll be good for Dad, too."

"Thanks for coming by." He reaches over to hug her.

As she walks toward her car, he notices that her bag, shoes and nail polish are the same color: blood red. He also notices her reading glasses. They are sitting on the catch-all table by the front door. He picks them up and runs out to give them to her.

She unrolls her window. "Android to the rescue again."

"That's *moi.*"

"But really, bro, did you have to fall in love with him?"

At that moment, he hates her. He hates her for being the heiress of their mother's know-it-allness. He hates her for inability to try to be gentle in her pronouncements. He hates her for bashing even him, her brother. He hates her for spewing devastating conclusions that aren't tempered by considerations of delicacy. He tries to not hate her (but fails) by thinking that she is probably jealous. And in the end, he hates her most for being spot-on.

Shapiro

CHAPTER 22

Metal. His father likes working with it, although he prefers wood. Charles considers metal to be part of the skeleton of things seen and admired – the wire-holding rod encased in the mahogany lamps (that he has built), the bolts fastening the sides of a desk or bookcase (that he has built), the components of circuit boards deep inside of televisions (that he has built). Essential but hidden. Andrew has never given much thought to metal, let alone its smell (except for the incidents with Keith, years ago, when he was Ex's age), until the scent and flavor of it entered his mouth by way of Ex's tongue, at which point it too became essential. The taste of metal predominating from a tongue that has taken in so many other inputs in the course of a day – meals, snacks, energy drinks, sea air – speaks to some chemical sovereignty and its power to take over an entire human organism (body and not-body), a horrifying colonization that Andrew slowly begins to consider, dismiss, fail to dismiss, and consider again. He wants more of Ex's tongue for its wet and erotic come-hither dance of tongue against tongue, but also to enable him to taste and test the disturbing chemical ingredient, like a technician conducting an assessment. He wants to one-up Ex by being privy to something that Ex doesn't think that he, a middle-aged man, is capable of being privy to.

That smell. It is not easily dismissed. It is the smell of Keith in particular and the overall smell of the chemically enhanced sexual abandon of those days, whose night segments he had abandoned himself to with the help of products that contained variations on a theme of that smell in order to get through whatever sex presented itself in whatever bodily form and starlit hour of the night. It was a short-lived revel. He quit his job at the restaurant-discotheque-cocaine palace, the point of entry for his nocturnal releases, and took an office job instead. The party, he decided quickly, was over.

Except for Keith. Keith seeped out at night, unable to resist the quick and simple popping of a pill that would egg him out to the streets, suck him into some bar or club, and lead him to the destination of male flesh. But unlike the others, Keith seemed measured, calculated, when it came to his doses of drugs and sex: Andrew strongly sensed something strategic and philosophical – perhaps even metaphysical – about Keith's intense forays into drug/sex abandon, as if this handsome, articulate, buff, thirty-something had figured out – or was devoting his soul and intellect into attempting to figure out – a functioning balance between depravity and rectitude. (He lost touch with Keith and was never able to discover whether he had come through, alive.) Andrew was attracted to him and to this idea that he had decided drove Keith. He was attracted to him ideologically, physically, sexually. They ended up in bed together regularly, and often with a third party. And every time that Keith sweated (which was within five minutes of every time that their bodies were rubbing against each other), it smelled metallic.

Thinking of Ex's tongue as Andrew strains to cheerfully wave good-bye to his sister from the driveway and head back into his house and the two incongruous characters inhabiting it (but for how long?) in this phase of his life that both wrenches him backward in an effort to understand, and yanks him forward in an effort to accept (regardless of what he may have understood), he remembers that smell, in its past and in its present. In its past, it is a chemical emanation and overflow, spilling out in beads of sweat (especially in the concave depths of Keith's armpits where tips of the hairs are sweat-beaded) resulting from saturation – of Quaaludes, cocaine, PCP, windowpane, poppers, and he doesn't remember what other adult candy (although surely there were others). And in its present? He is behind the times and decides, for better or for worse (if he can make the distinction) to seek out Ex's tongue again, somehow. And if not his tongue, his armpit or, if need be, a stealthy rummaging through the hamper to locate the armpit section of a tee-shirt, the crotch section of shorts, the toe section of socks, anywhere where such emanations will secrete a suggestion of their origins before being tumbled clean in a long, hot wash cycle.

As he enters the living space, his father and Ex are talking; Charles is on the sofa, Ex has usurped the green Danish lounge chair. They are facing one another and the volume is higher than usual. As Andrew approaches, he hears the word "Illuminati" pronounced in the form of an accusatory question by his father and fears that a first

213

major rift is in the making. Yes, Ex is off and running to that exopolitical zone where he travels whenever he feels cornered like a rat by what he considers to be considerations proffered by silly, clueless people (usually older, or at least more accomplished, than he is) who are, he feels, making him account for himself, and so he provocatively lands in that place – the Illuminati – to shake up, disorient, give an impression of rising above and beyond, and hopefully save himself from having to save himself.

"Zee, you don't understand," he says. Indeed, Andrew thinks. That is the point. To not be understood. Charles holds his own.

"You're probably right about that," his father replies. "But young man, I don't think you care whether I understand or not. You care about whether I agree or not."

As much as he would like to hear how this will play out, Andrew bolts into their space. "Anyone want to take a walk on the beach with me?"

"Talk to my walker," Charles says.

"I'm good," Ex says.

"Sorry if I interrupted," Andrew says, knowing that he has done just that, that the same rift that he has had with Ex and that has led nowhere but could have led somewhere with his father (who has never been blisteringly disadvantaged by having Ex's tongue in his mouth, or Ex's body usurping his bed) now has nowhere to go. But it's too late. The two of them, in a stand-off, will revert to other topics – classes, Ex's family, whether Ex has a girlfriend – and Andrew regrets not having lingered on the driveway after his sister had pulled out, to think about metal and why his sister is so absent-minded about her eyeglasses. He would like to take that walk on the beach, knowing how well it would serve, but he can't quite tear himself away from the buzzings inside his house, even if he doesn't know where in this rattled sanctuary he should park himself.

"I'm going to lie down," his father says.

"I'm going to take a walk," Ex says.

Andrew looks at the two of them. Their eyes betray the onset of fed-up-ness.

"All-righty." He watches them saunter off in different directions and is at a loss as to where he should go. He chooses to trail his father down the hall.

Charles stations his walker to the side of the bed, sits on the mattress and pries off the heel of his left sneaker with the toe of his right foot, and vice versa. Andrew stoops down and places the sneakers squarely under the walker. He is tempted to flatten the turquoise gel pads that are inside the sneakers and have arched up, leaving pockets of empty space that undermine their purported benefit, but he resists. "That sounded intense."

His father props up the two pillows, pivots his bony frame onto the length of the bed, and lowers his head until it makes a gentle crash-landing onto them.

"Strange boy."

"What do you mean?" he asks. He knows exactly what his father means, but he wants to hear an observation or explanation or description, something that is audible outside of his own head.

"Troubled boy."

"Why do you say that?"

Father looks at son intently. Their blue and thirsty eyes are so similar in what they reveal and in what they demand. Words are not necessary. But Andrew wants words. He needs their hard currency. He waits.

"Such a good-looking boy. Smart. Inquisitive. His eyes

are always red. Maybe he has allergies. Maybe he cries a lot when no one is around. Who knows? But something is off, son. Way off. Dangerously off."

Andrew waits again. Only now does he fully understand and accept what his father, in his accumulated years and wisdom, has to say. The tendency to diminish him, because he is just his father, and so old, dying even, vanishes in an instant. He feels him as a whole human being who has suffered and rejoiced and puzzled through eighty-five years of having to live and observe because he is still in the throes of being alive and, like everyone else, has to come to terms with and make some kind of sense out of his life as much as he does out of his death. Like the small child he once was, he waits for instructions.

"Be careful."

"Of what?" Andrew sits on the bed next to his father. Charles lifts himself from the pillows into an L shape, opens the drawer to his nighttable, removes a sheet of paper, and hands it to his son.

"Read this. Ex left it on my bed last night. Poor kid. Don't know whether he's trying to make a connect or build a wall."

Andrew takes the paper, sees the word "exopolitical" at the top in 14-point bold, and smiles. "Oh, this. Crazy shit. I know. He tries to talk about it with me, and I listen politely for a sentence or two and then change the subject."

"You do wrong." Charles looks hard into his son's eyes. "I agree. It's crazy stuff. We all do crazy stuff. Me too. Did I ever tell you about the time in engineering school during break when my roommate left the campus to visit his family? I took his car, a white Volkswagen bug, and disassembled it where he had parked it in the lot. Then I carried each part, piece by piece, into his bedroom, and reassembled it. Maybe I did tell you that. And that was tame. We all do crazy stuff. Don't get me on the subject of your mother. But mind you, this boy is possessed by a huge schtick of crazy. And don't you make light of it just because you don't get it. You're smarter than that. Read it. He lives in that place, he thinks in that place, he tries to make sense of things in that place. I can tell. Crazy. Dangerous."

"Please, Dad."

"Here. Read it, dammit." Andrew takes the sheet of paper and obeys his father.

Isis Astara, my beloved soulmate, has left the physical plane. She was often brutally attacked with directed energy weapons and the attack on January 25th was one attack too many. We could not protect her, her heart could not make it. The Resistance could not intervene directly otherwise toplet bombs would be triggered.

She has successfully transitioned through plasma plane and is now with her spiritual guides, surrounded by Love, joyful that she is finally free. After the Event, she will return in a cloned body that will look exactly the same as her physical body looked in this lifetime. She will be living in an area of Light, anchoring energies of the Goddess and living a joyful life in the Golden age she always wanted to live.

This was a direct attack on loving feminine Goddess presence with serious exopolitical implications.

Until now, the Light Forces were using a slow cautious approach to planetary liberation not to trigger the dark forces killing too many hostages (surface population). In a hostage situation, this phase is called negotiation phase (or standoff phase). During negotiation phase, there is not much apparent progress and there are many delays, because the longer hostage negotiations last, the more likely it is that hostages will survive unharmed.

With killing of a key person such as Isis Astara, the hostage liberation has shifted in the final, termination phase. During termination phase, there is swift physical action to liberate the host."

He looks up at his father.

"Finished?"

"Yeah. I get it."

"What do you get?"

"That it's silly. It's crazy."

"But do you get that he really believes this?"

"Dad, I was a Jew for Jesus when I was sixteen."

"And two months later, you weren't a Jew for Jesus. But this boy. I don't know. And I don't think you know this boy."

"Dad, don't worry."

Charles slams his hands down against the mattress on both sides of his body, as if to jolt his son out of some trance or hypnosis. "Like hell I won't."

Andrew remains calm, his voice steady, thoughtful, low-toned. "I'm tired, Dad."

Charles's hands recede. "I need to get some sleep too, son. And you. You need to wake up. But before we go beddie-bye, I'd like to ask you one simple, crude question."

"Fire away, Dad."

Charles hesitates. "Please don't take offense. It's probably not my business. In fact, it's definitely not my business. But I just want to…"

"Ask me, for Christ's sake."

His father raises his head from the pillow so that his face and eyes can be closer to his son's, even though Andrew is staring at a painting on the wall (an original he'd unearthed at a retro furniture store in Ft. Lauderdale, where he'd gone for a weekend because it was reputed to have some sort of gay community or "gay ghetto" area, which his area doesn't, and where he'd almost had sex, but didn't) of three hand-holding moustachioed boleros on the beach. He asks, "Have you had sex with him?"

"You're right. That's none of your Goddam business."

"Now that we've established that, have you?"

Andrew relents. "No."

Charles takes his son by the chin, pivots it toward him so that their eyes have no choice but to meet. "As long as it's not my business, I'll continue with one simple piece of advice. To borrow one of your mother's favorite expressions, Fuck him. I mean literally. Or get fucked by him – whatever your preference. But do it. Soon. And when you're finished, fuck him. Figuratively, this time. Have done with it, and then have him pack his bags.

"Fuck you, Dad."

Charles sinks back into the pillows. His breathing is strained. Andrew can hear a troubling wheeze each time his father inhales and exhales. Charles lowers his knees and lets his legs run the length of the bed. The veins pop out on his feet like miniature cobalt sewer pipes. He inhales and with great effort manages to utter, "No. Fuck *him*, son. I'll be fucked soon enough." And with that proclamation, his eyelids relax and descend, like some sage and wizened lizard that can't resist the pull toward repose.

CHAPTER 23

On his way out, Andrew closes the bedroom door, pulling it swiftly toward its frame but then slowing down so that the gold-colored metal tongue at the side of the door eases into the corresponding hole in the frame with a light click. He walks the length of the hallway and passes through the living room to the front porch, where he peruses each shelf of the black pseudo-bamboo shoe rack to the side of the front door: Ex's unmistakable size 12/13 flip-flops are not there; neither are they to be seen, flipped and flopped, on the polished cement floor of the living area when he goes back inside. Yes, he is gone for now. Andrew knows two things that he would like to do while his father sleeps and Ex is out of the house. Thing one: He would like to get out of the house, too, and take the beach walk that he had proposed to take with either or both of them. But walking beachside alone holds little appeal now, unless each step would bring with it the possibility of seeing, in the distance, a pavonine creature gazing into the horizon with a certain weight on his shoulders like some fallen divinity and who would then turn his head to the right, see Andrew in the distance, and emit a smile, as if to say, "You have arrived! Disencumber me. Lift me up. Elevate me!" Thing two: He would like to make an about-face, tiptoe down the corridor, turn left at the threshold of Ex's bedroom, enter into it and begin rummaging – under the bed, inside drawers, inside the still-unopened boxes in the closet – until some object announces itself as the thing that will make everything make sense.

He removes his Birkenstocks and, as he does so, feels the grains of sand freeing themselves from the soles of his feet and littering the floor like constant reminders of the grating imperfections of this world, this life, as he heads back down the hallway. When he reaches the bathroom he rarely uses (across from Ex's bedroom, whose door is held open by a conch shell), his cell phone rings. He looks at the screen and sees the photo of an attractive, air-brushed, middle-aged woman in high-school-graduation-picture pose, complete with shoulder-length Tahitian-glossy hair whose improbable color of mahogany suggests polished furniture rather than hair. What does his sister want now? He lets his voicemail take it. The walnut mini-blinds in Ex's room have been pulled up and compressed into a one-inch block of wood, and the windows are wide open. (He checks on the windows regularly; he knows that Ex would never think to close them before leaving the house, even during a cloudscape that suggests the possibility of rain.) Somewhere through the disarray that Ex stirs up everywhere (except his body, whose pure and perfect contours are inviolable), the room's intention, as set forth by Andrew when he had finished the renovation and had embarked on the furnishings, was supposed to evoke a quality of spareness that was not radical, but could also embrace qualities of comfortable and comforting: queen-size mattress sitting on simple metal frame and covered with hand-made patchwork quilt; dresser (celery green and unevenly painted so that bits of wood reveal themselves along drawer edges and burnished handles); nighttable (bamboo legs with bamboo inlay set into the ebony top); reading chair (Bentwood, with coffee-colored leather seat cushion); desk (teak, built by his father) with lamp (here he allowed himself to fall into the non-descript); and several pictures on the eggshell-colored walls – all of them with different frames and rigorously unmatching, like the rest of the house and, like the rest of the house, stringently eclectic. In this, at least, Andrew can say with confidence, "I do know what I am doing."

He steps into Ex's bedroom. The grayish light filtering in from the open windows seems to resemble to Andrew, at this moment, an open hand with pointed index finger that has pinpointed each and every item of Ex's and proclaimed a resounding verdict of chaos. He scans the space. What a fucking mess. Where to begin looking? When to stop? If he knew what it was he was looking for (the thing that would make everything make sense, he reminds himself), perhaps he could opt instead for Thing One: walk out and take that stroll on the beach after all. But he hasn't a clue as to what he is looking for, a hard fact of his life in this moment that holds him slave to the room, eyes scoping out all of the material proof of Ex's carefree and careless life in this house as he tries to figure out where to begin. A hard fact of life indeed. He sits on the bed, turns the phrase over in his head, and is quickly taken in by its other connection – the birds and the bees. He thinks back to the repugnant parental discourse he suffered about the insertion of penises into vaginas (weren't those silly organs just things that existed, tucked away, to let the pee out?). The dreaded topic came about when, at the age of ten and bored on a rainy day, he was sleuthing in his parents' night table drawers (for what, he doesn't remember). In the bottom drawer of the glossy blond-wood night table next to his mother's side of the bed (which matched the headboard and other night table on his father's side), and nestled in that same drawer against the small blue metal safe-deposit box that was locked, he came upon another box, this one smaller and made of cardboard – the kind of generic box that gifts are placed inside of before they are wrapped, although this box had a layer of rippled cardboard between its smooth inner and outer walls that suggested a manufacturing process specifically designed to ennoble this item. He lifted the lid to find rows of many items, uniform and wrapped in thin square aluminum packages, like the kind that individual After-Eight mints are wrapped in, although After-Eight wrappings were mostly green and these wrappings instead were the shade of serenity blue of the safe deposit box saddling up against it. He extracted one of the packages from the middle of a row, plumped the row back up to conceal the missing piece, and opened the confection by biting on the corner with his teeth and pulling. Inside was a perfectly formed latex disk. As he was beginning to examine it, his mother walked in the room, carrying a white plastic mesh basket filled with folded laundry.

"What are you doing?"

"I was looking for Zee's mezuzah. I wanted to try it on and see if it's still too big for me to wear. What are these balloons?"

"Andrew, never look through other people's things. Drawers and closed boxes are there for a reason. It's not right."

"Sorry, Mom. What are these balloons?"

Edith hesitated. "Right. Balloons. You never know when you might need balloons."

"Can I have some?"

"No. These are boring. All of them are white. I can get you some colored balloons."

"Okay. When?"

"Do you think you should be grounded for going through my drawers?"

Andrew lowered his head.

"Do you think I should tell your father what you did?"

He kept his head lowered and continued to not answer.

"Why don't you leave the balloon you opened on my bed and do your homework or go outside and play tetherball or croquet with Jill. I heard her a minute ago. I think she's outside."

"Okay, Mom."

He deposited the balloon and its wrapping in the middle of the bedspread, whose blue background registered in his budding sense of aesthetic a pleasing sense of conscious coherence on the part of his mom and dad: the color was almost the same as the shag carpeting and the safe deposit box. How cool is that?

Balloons. He didn't believe it himself (how could he?) when he'd told her that that was what they were. Balloons came in small cheap plastic bags and were randomly tossed inside regardless of their color or the shape they assumed once inflated – some round and pink, others elongated and blue, some with tips that were darker and looked like nipples and challenged you to blow just a little more to diminish them, and others that simply burst after a few exhalations. But these. These were something else, perfectly uniform and smacking of a precision and a precise if cryptic purpose. He resented her for thinking that he could fall for such an inane explanation (but what were they?). Wasn't it she who constantly pulled him against her breast and called him her Messiah? If he didn't know everything, wasn't it she who was mandated to guide him, the Messiah, toward the knowing of everything? And if not knowing everything meant that he wasn't the Messiah, then what was he really for her, for himself, for the world?

"Mom. C'mon. I'm not that stupid. What are they?"

She settled herself next to him on the bed and told him how they were not objects to blow up and thumb-tack to walls or to tie to ribbons for parties, but were sheaths to unfold onto a penis so that the penis could be inserted into a "vagina without spilling its seed inside ("Seed?" he asked) and swimming to find the egg ("Egg?" he asked) to fertilize in order to create the baby," and so on. He hadn't the faintest clue as to what she was talking about; he felt only disgust and a wave of nausea.

Sitting on the bed, he remembers another box that had been discovered, or unearthed, two years later, when he was raking leaves under the maple tree while his mother was digging up a cracked flagstone step on a small slope of yard that she had been meaning to replace for some time, even though the flagstone steps were never used by anyone to arrive anywhere since they didn't arrive anywhere in particular or in general. As she struggled to pry the flagstone up from the ground where it had become embedded, she noticed a turquoise square that was level with smooth surface of the ground formed by the flagstone's underbelly. She dug her fingers around the perimeter of the blue square in a clockwise motion, deeper and deeper, until she reached one of the bottom edges of the square, about one inch down. She yanked it up. It was a small plastic box that she had forgotten about, and inside was a ruby ring that she had also forgotten about.

"Andrew. Can you come here for a minute?"

He let the rake drop and ran over, slowing his pace as the turquoise object in her hand became visible to him.

"Oh. That."

"What? Tell me."

"I buried it to make a lost treasure. I forgot about it."

"Where did you get it?"

"I don't know. I mean, I don't remember."

"Have you buried anything else in the yard?"

"I don't remember."

"Well think."

"But, Mom, if I remembered it, then it wouldn't be lost."

"Andrew, why on earth would you want to lose things?"

He trundled back to his rake, picked off the leaves that were impaled on its tines, and continued amassing his pile of autumn colors and crunches. "I don't know. I guess so I can find them. Geez."

He gets up from the bed and peruses the room. The temptation is to select certain bits strewn about on the floor that have rubbed up against Ex's flesh – underpants, socks, t-shirts – slowly lift them up to his face and, yes, inhale deeply. But he knows that this is off-point altogether, has nothing to do with finding a harsher and more meaningful something. So he ignores the lure of recently worn and pungent intimate wear and opens first the file cabinet (legal tablets and envelopes with letters tucked inside), then the drawers of the chest of drawers (clothes only), then the night table drawer (pens, incense, index cards, tabloid clippings, a scattering of minor crystals), then the closet (a few shirts and slacks hanging neatly on white plastic hangers, while dozens of white plastic hangers hang empty to the right). He brushes aside vast mounds of clothes on the floor with his left foot, gets on his knees and looks under the bed: large, flattened (and therefore probably empty) backpack; CDs and DVDs scattered individually like loose tiles or stacked in twos and threes; and a shoe box placed dead center under the bed. He gets himself in stretching-cat position so that his fingers can barely brush against the shoe box, coaxes it closer (after several failed attempts), nudges it out from under the bed and open its lid, which is not completely closed because the contents of the box rise above its upper lip.

It's a Nike shoe box, and the primary object obstructing the full closure of the lid is peeping out from the lid's lip like a flaccid periscope. It seems to be some kind of flexible tube. He opens the lid, and out springs a tan and rubbery snake-like coil, whose length would suffice to tie tightly around an upper arm in order for enough veins to exclaim by the protrusion and pulsation provoked by the coil if it were to be tied around said upper arm, "I'm good for this round. Do me." Underneath the tube are syringes. Each one is sealed in plastic (front side), and a thin foil (back side) shares the same recipe of the condom-balloon casings that he had come upon in his parents' night table: hermetically sealed, protected, protective and suggesting an activity entirely foreign to him. For an instant, Andrew hopes that the box is a memorabilia box, and not a toolbox. But he looks at every other item in the room that is immediately visible to him, or that he has ransacked in order to be made visible to him, and understands that there is not a single haphazardly discarded or stored item in this room that doesn't serve some present purpose that makes sense based on what he understands of Ex. He cups his hands over his eyes as if to obliterate all that he sees, or thinks, that he is coming to understand, or to obstruct the tears that are welling up in their lower front corners. The darkness introduced by the pressure of his hands persists when he removes them to call Sheila and ask her if he can bring their father to her house for the rest of the day, knowing that she won't dare to ask why and will simply say "Sure," because in the end her brother has taken their father in – despite the home that she had bought to accommodate their father and the hasty sale of his house that she had pushed so that she could make her commission – and she must do her part.

"Sure," she says.

"Dad." He shakes his father's shoulders lightly. "I need to take you to Sheila's for the day. Something came up with work. I'll explain later." His father rouses slowly as Andrew pulls the small black duffel back from the shelf in the closet and sets about gathering the usual necessities for a day (or two) visit – the weekly pill box, a package of Depends, a change of clothing, the iPod and earbuds, a sweater and sweatpants (Charles needs layers when the temperature drops below seventy-five), cell phone charger, computer. He doesn't notice his father struggling to get up. He doesn't notice the effort of his lungs to expand and contract. He no longer sees his father as anything but an object, and a temporary impediment, that needs to be transported from one place to another in order to make room for another more compelling trajectory that needs to be pushed forward until it is finally seen through.

"Ready?"

Zee hobbles to his walker. "As ready as I'll ever be."

Andrew makes his way down the hallway, wishing that his father didn't exist so that he could just turn right, into Ex's room, and plunge deeper. He can hear his father's walker and feet behind him as he continues down the hall, without turning his head right, into Ex's room, or behind him toward his father. His only thought, and how he hates it, is to rid himself of this dying annoyance of a man and his walker and his accessories.

When they finally arrive at Sheila's, Charles can barely manage to walk down the driveway and into her house. Andrew rings the doorbell even though he has the key. His sister opens the front door after an interminable minute. After their father passes through and has gone a short distance away from them toward the sofa in the living room, she asks, "Is he okay?"

"He's fine. A bit groggy. I had to wake him from his nap to bring him here. I really hated to do it, but something's come up." He looks over at their father, hobbling and then pausing to look back at his children with great effort to form a vibrant expression on his face as if to hide his humiliation over having been reduced to little more than a heap of bones and burden. Eighty-five years of thoughtful, difficult living. How much he must have known. How much he deserves to be trusted, honored. For that matter, his mother too. Andrew decides to go to the beach to feel the blinding light and heat and to find Ex, and when he does, he will bring him home one last time and, like a contrite child, decide that his dead mother and dying father know more about most things than he does.

CHAPTER 24

He arrives at the beach and is surprised to find himself breathless after jogging from the parking lot to the dunes, a distance of less than a city block. He turns to the right, in order to walk the stretch of beach with the high-rise condos that line the dunes without pause, and that pump out onto the sand the elderly residents or snowbirds who don't confine themselves to their balconettes to experience the breadth and majesty of the scene before them. However, they come armed with their lotions and potions and radios and cellphones and earbuds and coolers filled with phosphorescent energy drinks and bags of snacks 'n things. The turf they claim is larger than their balconettes, and combined with the accessories they haul with them as if in defiance of simplicity itself, the beach has the feel of clusters of human invasion and density much like that of the sand crabs at sunrise. But to turn left would mean to turn toward unpopulated and quiet space, the kind of space where he might find Ex, the last thing he would want to find now (did Ex even go to the beach when he left the house?). Walking at a very slow pace that he is trying to impose on himself as if in an act of spiritual discipline, he focuses to the left, on the ocean and the perfectly straight edge between sea and sky that for millennia had convinced humankind (and how could it not?) that the Earth was flat; on the choreography of the pelicans that glide overhead in a chevron formation that occasionally breaks as one of them darts down bomb-like into the lapping waves to seize some prey; on the scattered clouds that, masterminded by the sun, spread lines of pinks and blues and yellows that merge into each other and swell into an ever-changing psychedelia of shape and color; on anything but the stretch of sand in front of him and all of the people lying on it, sitting on it, fishing from it, among whom, God forbid right now, could emerge some young figure standing tall, seductive, beckoning and destructive. His entire desire to cleanse himself, both body and soul, of the infection of Ex is fed solely by his hope to find him here, on the beach, to approach him, feel the heat and the impossible possibilities that unnerve him in a way that he feels he must be unnerved one more time before he, like his father, is on the cusp of dying.

But the monolith of Ex is not to be seen, and despite his lolling pace and deep breathing, which are studied exercises in the art of feeling presentness, the beach is just a beach, the sun the same old sun, the sound of waves a tedious refrain. He will turn around to go home, to head down the hallway to Ex's bedroom, in order to arrive at an object which, he has known from the moment he stepped out of the house and toward the beach, was the intended destination: a shoebox whose lid doesn't close properly because of a piece of all-purpose tubing whose shape and color resemble a swollen, jaundiced vein. There will be two stopovers: the credenza in the living room, from whose top drawer he will pull out a roll of silver wrapping paper and a spool of wide white ribbon; and his desk, from whose side drawer he will remove the scissors and the Scotch tape dispenser from the black mesh organizer. He will clutch the four items in his two hands, carry them into Ex's room, and open his fingers, releasing them gently but haphazardly onto the desk.

After the shoebox has been wrapped and criss-crossed with the ribbon (he resists scraping the scissor blade along the underside of the ribbon ends to make curly-cues, opting instead to clip them close to the knot), Andrew takes it to his bedroom directly across the hallway and places it on the top of the thrift-store dresser, between the framed photo of him trekking in the Himalayas (shot decades ago, when he was Ex's age) and a tall, narrow, wooden square canister that he had succumbed to buying while the house was being renovated, thinking that it could be useful for storing something that has yet to be stored (perfect for a liquor bottle except that he doesn't drink). He lies down on his bed with his hands behind his head on two propped-up pillows, in order to rest but not fall asleep, waiting to hear the eventual sound of the front door opening. At some point, he must have closed his eyes, because he is startled and feels the effort of opening them when the word "Hey" crosses the threshold of his room to his ears.

"Hey," he responds.

Ex sits on the side of the bed as Andrew rises up to so that his right hand can free itself from behind his head, make its way to Ex's flushed cheek and stroke it. Ex's eyes are flushed too. "Everything okay?"

Ex closes his eyes and pushes his cheek into Andrew's hand with the unabashed neediness of a cat at the strum of human fingers against its chin. "I'm feeling better now."

Andrew tries to extend his other hand to Ex's other cheek but he can't quite reach. "What was not making you feel good before?"

Ex releases a long, audible exhale of breath. Andrew takes his index finger and traces the line underneath the merged upper and lower lashes along Ex's closed eyelids. All is damp. "Have you been crying?"

"I really can't talk about it." He moves his face, takes Andrews hands, places them together and squeezes them gently into a dome so that he can position his mouth and nose inside. His lips graze the concave interior.

Andrew moves his face closer to Ex's hands and to the face that seems to be drinking from them. He can smell that metallic smell. "Would you kiss me?"

Ex opens his eyes and pulls back. "What's with you?"

Andrew retracts his hands and sits upright. "Nothing's with me. *You're* not with me."

"What's going on?"

"Why don't you tell *me* what's going on?"

Ex gets up from the bed and walks toward the door.

Andrew remains seated where he is. The mattress is soft, the four pillows promise comfort. "You like Zee, don't you? You even admire him, don't you?"

Ex stops and turns toward Andrew. "Of course I do. He's amazing, he's so wise. He gets me."

Andrew laughs. "He is wise. And he does get you. He truly does. And you know what my father told me in his infinite wisdom and getting of you? My father told me, the very flesh and blood of his loins, to fuck you, or to be fucked by you, whatever my preference was, and to be done with it. How about that? Right you are, dear sweet Ex. Zee is amazing, and oh-so wise."

Ex slowly backs himself toward the door, hunching over ever so slightly, like someone who has had to suppress himself for years and has finally decided to lunge.

"Stop there. I'm not finished. So, I thought about what he said. But I decided against it. Not that I wouldn't want to, you know, fuck with you. That's beside the point." He points to the wrapped box sitting on the dresser. "I decided on something else. A gift, even though it already belongs to you. It's over there. Take it to your room, open it or not, and put it in your backpack."

"What is it?"

"Just take it to your room, open it or not, and put it in your backpack."

Ex approaches Andrew. "You're crazy."

"I might be. But I'm tired. And old, and angry. Take it. Go. You're in my way."

"I *am* your way." Ex walks to the dresser, leaving flecks of dark sand as each foot moves along the terrazzo floor, picks up the box and turns toward Andrew. His bristled posture has relaxed into sunkenness, sullenness. He stares into space.

"The door is that way. Now go."

Ex pauses at the doorway. Andrew can make out a thin line of tears on Ex's cheek, glistening like a filament freshly made by a snail as it makes its way from any place to any other. The tall confident body is shuddering too. Andrew gets up from the bed, stands in front of Ex and places one hand firmly on Ex's breastbone, in precisely the place where he liked to nestle his hand in order for them to fall asleep when they shared his bed. "Please. Just go." He rests his head against Ex's chest, and then pushes his hand hard against it. "I'll bring some boxes for your things. Now go. Away from this room. Away from this house. Very away."

He finds twelve cardboard boxes in the garage. Three trips of four boxes stacked up, secured underneath by

Andrew's fingers, which are extended at the level of his knees, and at the top by his chin, which pushes like a vise against the upper-most box. Each time he arrives at Ex's room, he stoops down and releases the precarious stack like some precision and mono-purposeful Deere vehicle. And with each trip down the hallway, he pauses at Zee's closed door to listen for any sound that might indicate that his father is awake and therefore possibly privy to the repetitive shuffling to and fro – and each time he is greeted with a competition among silences: the neutral silence of a man he imagines is having a nap; the disquieting silence of a man who is serenely relinquishing his lust for life and accepting that this lust, and the very life being lusted after, are at the tail end of the process of being extinguished; and the cruel silence relishing the fact that a cheap piece of wallboard between a bedroom and a hallway is sufficient to insulate, or even sever, two intimately connected lives in the throes of two wholly unconnected turmoils. A fourth silence he has overlooked completely: the simple and factual silence caused by the simple fact that his father is not in the room or the house, that his son has relocated him elsewhere until the debris has been cleaned and cleared up and out.

"That'll do it," he says to Ex as he stoops down the third time. "I'm going out for about an hour. That should be enough time for you to not be here when I get back." Not be here. Where will he be? His thoughts return to a recurring image of Ex sleeping on a bench under a Bismarck palm by one of many man-made lakes in one of many local parks, and then to another image of Ex flailing about on a prison cot as he tries to fend off the glowering eyes of his cellmate.

He reaches the living room, whose eastern half is infiltrated by direct sunlight, especially on the mosaic coffee table in the center of the living space, where books, magazines, and various remotes and coasters cover much of its surface at clean angles. Among them is an object, unrecognizable because of a single ray that has struck it just so, causing smaller beams to bounce off it and blur it, as if it were some still-forming angel-embryo fallen out of a womb. A cloud passes, the beams vanish, and the object identifies itself: Ex's peripatetic crystal. He snaps it up and fits it into the large bottom pocket of his navy-blue khaki shorts before heading back to the beach to pass the hour that he has promised Ex to give him in order for the creature to collect his things and slink very away. He opens the front door. Overhead, slightly to the west, clouds are forming. There could be a downpour. But if it is brief, and the sun burns it off, a rainbow or two might appear. That's what usually happens.

Going down the driveway, he pauses beside the door to his car. A change of plan: he unlocks the lock with his remote, gets inside, immediately opens the windows to push out the unbearable heat that can be seen in rivulets through the front windows, and drives across the causeway, inland-bound, where all sense of beach vanishes among the sprawl of chain restaurants, shops and megastores that are set back from the highway and are reached, in clusters, by turning right or left at the traffic lights that are almost as numerous as the telephone poles and that keep the highway in a perpetual state of stop and go. He has never been to a Walmart, a Chick Fil-A, a Cracker Barrel, or even a Starbucks. None of them have ever offered him a convincing solution to emptiness of any kind. He looks for his landmark – a small one-story pink stucco building with pink picnic tables out front where pulled pork is served – that signals to him to move into the left-turn-only lane to enter the Barnes and Noble parking lot. Books, and people perusing them, are what he will surround himself with during the hour or so that Ex reluctantly but dutifully eliminates himself from the house like some clogged drain being opened up with the help of a chemical agent. As usual, the parking lot is about three-quarters full, which surprises and reassures him every time. People still read words on paper, turn pages, make marginalia, refer back to understand better in order to move forward better.

First stop, the "New Releases" aisle, where he rarely picks up a book (they must prove their worth by enduring the initial promotion and strategic placement) but enjoys quickly reading all of the titles as if, taken together, they will indicate some kind of pulse or trend that needs to be taken note of, if only to be *au courant*. Several aisles back, the "Fiction" section begins, his second and usually last stop. A dozen or so long aisles hold books (rarely more than one of each title) arranged alphabetically by author, and customers walk down them with their heads cocked at a forty-five-degree angle to read the titles on the spines. More often than not, Andrew doesn't find what he is looking for. But today he isn't looking for anything in particular. He simply wants to read titles, extract a book from time to time, open it randomly, dip into a sentence or two or a paragraph or two, and put it back. He thirsts for the quiet noise and distraction of other people's ideas encased between two covers, which he can close at will, with no apologies or explanations needed for his judgment or his indulgence. Blessed books.

By the time he has reached the "G"s, his mind is almost empty of Ex and Zee. It isn't until he arrives at the beginning of the "H"s (where he has slowly nudged "The Scarlet Letter" off the shelf and has just begun to slowly leaf through its pages hoping that, on his own, he will remember Hester's last name – damn this old age – before it appears on the printed page) that his father and his...his... (his what?) rush back into his head from the vibration of his cell phone in the pocket of his khaki shorts that is above the pocket holding the crystal.

"Hey Bro."

"Hey Sheila."

"I stopped by your house, but you weren't there. So I let myself in. I thought you might be napping."

"That's fine." He realizes that it may not be so fine. What if she had found Ex in the midst of loading boxes into his car? He takes a deep breath. "Everything okay?"

"He's gone."

So she did see him in the throes of leaving. Did she stop him and ask him what was up? Did Ex tell her (and what exactly did he tell her?)? Or did they just greet each other politely as if packing boxes into a car and shipping out (where, he wonders) were as routine as dropping of a small package at the FedEx center? He wants to know each and every detail, but he is in a bookstore perusing spines of books in order to not think about wanting to know these things. "Yes. I know." He pauses for the second that it will take him to invent a story sufficient to prevent his sister from interrogating him, if that's what she has in mind. He begins, "A friend of his was looking for a roommate, so he decided to…"

"What are you talking about?"

"Ex. He's gone. I know." He can hear her crying.

"Andrew. I'm not talking about Ex. I'm glad he's history. I hope he's history. I'm talking about Dad. He's gone."

Andrew looks at his watch and breathes a sigh of relief. "Not to worry, sis. He always makes his afternoon rounds at this hour. The lady's man. He's so cute. This is when he slips out to take a walk with his walker and scope out the territory. He casually makes a bee-line to Debbie's house. She lives two blocks away and does her gardening in the front yard in the afternoon. Poor Dad. He keeps trying to engage her in a conversation that will lead to dinner out or a concert or a movie, but she doesn't bite. He keeps going back, though. Do you think it's a sexual thing or just a female company thing? I mean, he didn't get much of either from Mom."

"No, Andrew. I mean he's gone gone."

"What the hell is that supposed to mean?"

"I mean he's dead. I was checking on him when he was lying in his bed. His breathing was super-shallow. I took his hand and started talking to him and then the breathing stopped, like some unwound wind-up toy. Dad is dead."

"I'll be there in about twenty minutes." How dare she, and how dare his dad. He feels consummately cheated. He was the one who should have been there, the one who should have been by his side and comforted him, as he had been doing all these months. How dare she be the one to be there. How dare he wait for the daughter to be there, and for the son to not be there, when he died.

Sheila breaks down. "Oh my god, bro, it's happened," she sobs. Her voice is bereft of any desire to show the strength, harshness or hardness that over the years has convinced him that she was carrying on in their mother's footsteps. He can almost hear her tears. "We're orphans."

And so they are, he realizes. Orphans. At this age. Does it make him feel younger or older, he wonders as everything compelling about living or dying is suddenly drained from him and replaced by the commotion of no-feeling. He shoves "The Scarlet Letter" back onto the shelf and moves quickly, but not frantically, to his car, thinking of Ex heading off God knows where in his beat-up car away from him. Ex, too, gone. Absences as acute and palpable as their presences. The two of them – his father and his (his…his…what?). A sobering slap-in-the-face conspiracy to restore him to his place. Shifting into Reverse, he can feel the persistent arthritic ache in his ankle as he looks at his eyes in the rear-view mirror and observes a wide-eyedness in the blue and white globes he inherited from his father that still have so much to receive and embrace. He asks himself where that place might be.

PART III - LATER

"...so too the love god, in order to make spiritual things visible, loves to use the shapes and colors of young men, turning them into instruments of bewitchment by adorning them with all the reflected splendor of Beauty, so that the sight of them will truly set us on fire with pain and hope...for man loves and respects his fellow man for as long as he is not yet in a position to evaluate him, and desire is born of defective knowledge...." Thomas Mann

CHAPTER 25

The ashes, which the crematorium director has placed inside a heavy-duty zip-lock plastic bag couched in a heavy-duty cardboard box (no Grecian-style urns for them, God forbid), will not be scattered for some time because of Hurricanes Chantal and Dorian, which, based on the weather forecast, may arrive one upon the other. The dense, gray powder which once had been their father will sit in its low-end box on a shelf in the walnut hutch that houses the special dinnerware Sheila had claimed when Edith died. The setting for eight (dinner plates, soup bowls, saucers and one serving platter and salad bowl) had been a wedding gift for Edith and Charles more than five decades ago, and neither of their children could remember a single occasion that had been special enough for their mother to use any of the pieces, which were square with rounded edges that lifted slightly up at the corners and were almost visionary in their design, even in their pattern of large, abstract brown and green leaves. Andrew thought they were beautiful (he often wondered what friends of his parents' could have given such dinnerware to them, and why that friendship couldn't have been spared his mother's inevitable disdain and dismissal on the basis of the dinnerware alone), even if in principle he was relatively indifferent to the idea of "dinnerware," as long as it wasn't too cheap, like the everyday cutlery his mother used whose fork tines bent if he jabbed them into a piece of meat that was too thick and too tough. He was pleased that his sister wanted the set – finally it would get some use – although he pretended that he was making a bit of a sacrifice in ceding it to her, in order to win what would have been a difficult battle over the mosaic coffee table, which he was able to claim without the slightest voiced objection or evidence of a scowl. It was only fair.

One half of the scattering should have been easy because it is to take place nearby – where the ocean breaks on the sand, as they had done with their mother. The second half – to take place in the yard of the house where they had grown up in the suburb of Philadelphia (and where Andrew had flown to with only one small piece of carry-on luggage into which he had stuffed half of his mother's ashes in order to fertilize his childhood lawn with what remained of her) – would come later. Unlike the first batch, the second scattering would require some planning, especially if, this time, unlike the time with their mother, it was to be a joint effort: Although she had insisted on participating, Sheila was loath to board any transport that was destined to carry her beyond fifty miles of her house. She didn't do planes anymore.

About the first hurricane, Chantal. If the forecast is accurate, Chantal will hit in early summer, shortly after his father's death and be Andrew's first experience in the tropics of something beyond a very rainy day with occasional flash flooding. He will be glued to the television, seduced by the meteorological models – not unlike fashion models, with their voluptuous, undulating curves and pithy and unpredictable movements. Were it not for Ex, he would have evacuated. But Ex, who at times like these prided himself on being a native Floridian (how often had he bragged about the primordial value of breathing salt air and riding waves from birth), would have scoffed at such ratings-induced media scenarios and convinced Andrew that in the end, and at most, it would just amount to a very rainy day. Andrew would have decided to trust him, a sentiment that was in a gradual but steady state of diminishment since Ex had moved in, quickly made himself at home, and then been told to leave. Ex would have offered to go out and stock up on water, candles, canned and jarred foods and other provisions, and Andrew would have opened his wallet and handed him whatever amount Ex deemed necessary to get through Mother Nature's scolding of humankind over such hubris. Ex would surely have returned from the crowded shops with at least ten plastic bags draped on both arms like giant gaudy bracelets. After depositing them on the kitchen counter, he would have handed Andrew the receipts and the change. But Ex will be gone well before the winds and the threats accelerate.

Charles, too, would have decided to hunker down, having himself lived in Florida long enough to understand that the probability of television sound bites corresponding to what ends up taking place on the ground is slim. He also would have agreed because, as he couldn't have helped but knowing by then, his days were numbered and he would rather expire here, in this house, crushed by a gust-loosened joist or collapsed section of roof, rather than holed up in some seedy motel or, if time were to be generous, a hospital bed with guardrails and a panoply of disgruntled nurses who wake him up at all hours of the night, charts in hand, and tiny paper pill cups wheeled in on squeaky carts.

The media hype will be hype. Chantal will strike. It will rain all day, at times lightly, at times heavily, but never enough for Andrew to feel the need to step out back and begin to drain the level of the pool water. There will also be the drama of wind, but at an intensity that the mature palm trees scoff at, as if they were being bullied by the usual band of wannabe perturbations. When what is in the end barely a Category 1 hurricane passes after several hours, Andrew will be relieved, but also disappointed, thinking that it could have been one more memorable episode to remember. He will honor the self-satisfied expression that Ex, the veteran of storms (young as he may be), can't help but flaunt. He will imagine kissing him above the space between his eyebrows, wishing for the nth time as his lips touch Ex's smooth forehead that the intentionality behind his affectionate gesture will arouse in Ex the latent desire for a kiss that is more aggressive and turgid, wetter and sloppier, a foretaste of a series of wetter and sloppier acts that will follow and become a regular part of their domain as they set up house together and have Clare after all. But once again, Ex will accept the kiss tentatively, pull back gracefully, and say, "I love you." And once again, Andrew will be at a loss as to whether this most sacrosanct of all possible declarations – "I love you" – is a strategy or an outpouring, and at the same time will be perfectly aware that he may not want to know or be able to know. Ever. But Ex will not be there when Chantal touches land.

Sheila will also be of the hunker-down school, although more as a matter of either convenience or denial than of hard deliberation. Sharing a motel room with her brother, even if it should have two queen-size beds and a "living" space with bistro table, desk and love sofa, is not to be done under any circumstances. She loves her brother. But her love has more to do with continuity of contact than of connection during contact. Connection has too much potential for disappointment, hurt, and outright rejection. Simple contact is smooth and easily accomplished with lots of smiles (Sheila exploits them by applying whitening strips twice a year) and the ability to keep the eyes wide open and sparkling with interest (Sheila has applied a subtle line of permanent eyeliner to the top of her lower lid in order to accentuate whiteness and sparkle), accompanied by light chit-chat of any sort...*et voila,* the secret recipe. "I give you permission to kill me if you see I'm turning into Mom," she has said to her brother on so many occasions, referring, among other things but especially, to Edith's habit of striving for intolerance and imperious dismissal of others. Andrew will never be able to indict his sister on these grounds. She doesn't go in for hate. That is far too abrasive and indelicate. Sheila creates distance through animated eyes and gleaming smiles – and she wouldn't dream of accepting her brother's invitation to hunker down with him in his house, let alone evacuate together to a motel.

When the wind picks up and the sky darkens, he will close the accordion storm shutters on all windows and doors, turn on a light in each room (hoping they won't succumb to a power outage) and sit it out. Once again, the absence of his dead father and of the banished Ex will be more acute than their presence. And the ashes of his father will remain on Sheila's shelf.

In the end, when the wind and outdoor clatter subside like bored provocateurs and Andrew dares to open the hurricane shutters, he will observe only modest vestiges of Chantal's aftermath – branches and twigs from the jacaranda, leaves and pods from assorted bushes and plants – that have littered the back yard or sunk to the bottom of the pool or floated on its surface, transforming its liquid-heaven blue into a kind of army-green broth. Had Ex been holed up with Andrew, he would have offered with enthusiasm to dive in and clear out the muck, and Andrew would have agreed without a moment's thought, knowing that in this way he would be able to savor the double satisfaction of re-contemplating this creature contort his naked splendor into every conceivable shape as he moved about to grab a leaf or twig, and of having his pool restored to liquid heavenliness.

"Why don't you wait until Zee is napping?" he would ask (had his father also still been present), if only to be able to watch Ex in his exquisite protean condition without the possibility of being interrupted by his father asking for something, or calling him to wherever he may have been sitting or lying down in order to offer some narrative about something or other that would begin with "S'what happened was…"

"Sure," Ex would reply, and then vanish into his room, door shut, to do who knows what.

Andrew would make his way down the hallway, unable to keep himself in those parts of the house that could be a source of productivity (the study, where he could get some work done; the kitchen, where he could prep the next meal), and cup his ear against Ex's door. He would hear silence, as he has the so many other times he has cupped his ear against Ex's door, a silence that gives rise to questions: Masturbation (thinking about whom?). Light guitar-strumming (a ballad pining over whom?). Phone calls (to whom? Scribbling on one of his piss-yellow legal pads (about what or to whom?). Or simply daydreaming (about whom?). Whatever he is doing behind that closed door will be off limits. He can only hope that he figures into whatever it is that Ex is doing behind that closed door. So ridiculous, but so irresistible. At his age, however, he has nothing to lose by opening his arms to such juvenile foolishness.

Eventually, Ex would emerge, clad in his perforated nylon shorts, which he would remove to dive into the pool and set about removing the debris. Andrew would watch him from the safety of the kitchen window as Ex happily bolts through the water eel-like and in his element, grabbing leaves and twigs, and all of the encumbrances heaped upon his love for this boy/man will have floated away and he will feel again, if only in those excruciatingly intense and fleeting moments, joy.

But Ex will be gone when Chantal arrives. The box of ashes will remain on the shelf.

CHAPTER 26

Should the weather forecast continue to be accurate, the second hurricane, Dorian, will arrive just a few weeks after Chantal and, unlike his predecessor, will ravage the area with a fury. In those few weeks between female and male incursions, there will be no discussion between brother and sister of scattering the ashes. In fact, there will be little contact between brother and sister at all as they try to arc back into that simpler and roomier pocket of time when Sheila had her life entirely to herself and Andrew did too; to that time when their father still maintained his house, cooked his meals, did his laundry, and the family get-togethers consisted of a weekly group Skype or phone call to catch each other up on the minutia of their separate lives – for Sheila, for example, the temporary dance instructor or the latest saga of a real estate client; for Charles, the most recent HOA meeting, a computer glitch that he couldn't resolve or, if he was in need of company, an offer to deal out leftover supermarket coupons to whichever of his children would meet him somewhere, anywhere. Andrew didn't contribute his own anecdotes unless he was explicitly asked, "What's new with you?", and he was rarely asked. The weekly sessions annoyed him. They served no purpose beyond necessity, he thought, except to allow a moment or two of uncensored me-ness, and to maintain, in this perverse way, the minimum required to give the aging family nucleus a sense of solidarity. No one really listened anyway, no one really cared about the other's insistence that the other had a life. He could feel that the listener didn't at all need to be a member of the family; it could be anyone who would lend an ear. Yes, it did annoy him, but he accepted it, understanding that that is how it was, and probably was, for many families. When at some point one of them remembered to inquire, "How are you?", he responded with a simple "All is good," waiting for, but not expecting (although hoping) to receive another question that hinted of "Tell me more, I'm interested." It never came. "All is good" must have been enough for his sister and his father, if only to allocate them more time to soliloquize in the twenty or so minutes that each conversation lasted.

So in the short interval between Chantal's demise and Dorian's real and present threat (and with Charles dead and Ex gone), Andrew and Sheila will gratefully rebound into their separate lives, although Andrew will spend much of his time pacing his house (something new to him) in an effort to retrieve the hard-earned but shaky satisfaction of solitary solitude (as opposed to the buffered solitude that the temporarily shared household had thrust upon him) that he had worked years to arrive at and that had weakened as soon as he had loaded up his car to bring his father's belongings and his father into his home, and that had quickly crumbled altogether when Ex managed to insinuate himself into his sanctuary as well. As he paces, he will clutch the cell phone in the pocket of his shorts, hoping if not to feel then to will the vibration of an incoming call that will be Ex; or he might pull the cell phone out of his shorts pocket and click the device sequentially up until that last click that will cause Ex's phone to ring and possibly be answered. His father is dead; Ex is as good as dead. He will miss them immensely. Their absence will be more unsettling than their presence, and he will spend most of his time, during this time between Chantal and Dorian, passing time; pacing, lingering at the threshold of Ex's bedroom (which he will have straightened up and made squeaky clean in an effort to cancel him), before he slaps his face hard and returns to his desk to get a bit more work done or another chunk of his father's estate settled. Where did that crystal end up, he will wonder, but he won't search for it, deciding that it will appear at the right place at the right time, carrying with it all of his vague affinities with Ex that had caused everything else in his world to recede as the creature added to his life, erased his life, poured into his life, transformed his life by his every gesture, word and scent, giving him no rest, and continuing to do so even in his absence.

In those few weeks between tropical storm and bona fide hurricane, he will call his sister just a few times to update her on the progress of settling their father's estate. It will not be complicated as a whole, but still it will have its complexities (funds, bonds, veterans' benefits, etc.) that he will want to walk through with her, if only to assure her that he is not making decisions single-handedly, even if in the end, as he knows, she will defer to him without exception because she trusts him in such matters and doesn't want to be bothered with such matters. When he hangs up the phone, he will regret that she didn't find her way to segue into some saga of a client tale, if only to add extra minutes to the time that she can distract him with before he begins pacing again with his fingers clutched around the cell phone in his pants pocket like an addiction, and unable to suppress what he thinks of as a corresponding image of a heroine-filled syringe waiting to be extracted from its hiding place (perhaps a pants pocket as well) and jabbed into a hungry vein that has announced itself as the victor, thanks to the band of rubber tubing wrapped and knotted tightly around the arm above it. Sometimes she will come through, and he will feel the relief that he craves, even if it bores him terribly to hear about the next installment of a story that he could care less about.

More often than not, however, this will not happen, and it will fall on him to fill those endless minutes with something else, anything else, before he goes to bed – when once upon a time, not long ago, he knew that his father had been attended to during the day and was sleeping contentedly in the bedroom down the hallway, and he could afford to feed off of the possibility that Ex, prone on the sofa in the living room composing music or watching a film or looking at who knows what on the computer nestled in his lap, would find his way into his bed and spoon up against him wanting something that neither dared to get to the bottom of but were willing to do anyway. Occasionally, his perambulations will take him beyond the confines of his house and out into the neighborhood, where he will feel disconcertingly like his father, thirty years his senior, as he turns left, then right, then left (or right again) in order to come upon something that will remind him that he must, above all, keep his feet planted on solid ground, that the place and time for running off-leash and getting irretrievably lost must be contained.

He will wend his way through the streets of his neighborhood and feel old and defeated as he passes other elderlies taking their self- or physician-prescribed constitutional to air out and uncreak. He will set as his mission the life-and-death imperative to exempt himself from what must be bleak motivations to make rounds of the neighborhood. A series of questions will serve his purpose: Have they shared a bed with a twenty-something? Have they felt and smelled and tasted such young flesh lying by their side calling out for some kind of need? Or is this walk of theirs just another physician-advised instruction to accompany the medications that have been prescribed in order not to feel their ailments, their conditions, perhaps not to feel anything, but rather to amble along the sidewalks and pedestrian walkways (some with walkers, some managing on their own two feet) like zombies too lit to care about whether life or death is preferable, or even distinguishable? He will feel saddened by them, and sad for them. He will also feel superior to them, he the deserved recipient of some great tall vibrant sweet blessing – until he remembers that Ex is gone. Then he will feel as old as they are, and more pathetic.

"What are you going to do?" he will ask his sister when the various media begin to back off the entertainment dimension of their weather programming, realizing that Dorian is going to be the real thing and it's time to get serious.

"My friend Carol invited me to stay at her house. I think you met her once. She lives in North Carolina. A bit of a schlep, but what a house. Her husband has his own business. I don't remember what it is, but they're loaded. It's worth the eight-hour drive."

He will wait for her to return the question, which he doesn't expect to happen, and which doesn't happen.

"Oh. That's good. I'm not sure what I'll do. It's probably too late to find a hotel or motel. Anyway, I'll get on it."

"You'd better, bro. I'd ask you to come with, but, I don't know Carol well enough to ask her. She's more of an acquaintance than a friend."

"So I can just stay back and maybe die because you don't know Carol well enough to ask her if you can bring your brother. That's cool. No problem," he will think to himself. What he will say to Sheila will be an abridged version: "That's cool." He will figure out something. He always has. He has been in more difficult predicaments, he reminds himself.

He also remembers that there is the predicament of Ex. Where did he go when he loaded up his car? Where is he now? And where will he go? Andrew has resisted his cell phone but not the obits and arrest records on line. That can be done easily from his desk. He needn't get in his car and scour the multitude of park benches that serve as makeshift habitats for the homeless, or the sand dunes with their protective coves of sea oats and sea grapes that shelter all living things. In any event, it needn't be so dire. Ex could be couch-surfing with a friend (does he have friends?). But Dorian is approaching. The meteorologists are sober in their announcements. Surely in such a moment Ex will have no choice but to call him or show up at his house. Dorian will bring such hope, and Andrew will decide, for this reason, to stay put.

"Would you take Dad's ashes with you if you evacuate? I don't believe in these things, but in case I'm wrong, Mom'll be waiting for him. And he's probably waiting for her too. A kind of private hurricane. Would you do that?"

"Dad's probably thrilled to have the break."
"Maybe. But maybe not. What do we really know about them? If you evacuate, could you do that? And drive

carefully."

What did they know about them really? They could have made an endless list of reasons why their parents, together for fifty years, shouldn't have been together beyond the initial passion of the first year or two; but they couldn't have even filled a three-by-five card with reasons why they should have remained together for even a year, let alone fifty. But for fifty years they woke up each morning in the same bed (lovingly, indifferently, glaringly), went about their business (together and apart) in and out of the house, faithfully reuniting by dinner time at the kitchen table (first a rectangular oak table and four chairs given to them by Edith's mother, then the oval walnut formica table and six black leatherette swivel chairs that they'd bought once they'd saved enough money without having to pull from college funds), every day for fifty years, and going about their business in those 2,400 square feet (together and apart) until they climbed into twin beds bolted together inside a single wrought-iron frame (she on the left, in a sheer but unsexy nightgown; he on the right, in a fresh t-shirt and the boxer shorts he'd worn during the day), having to come to terms with each other in some way in order to share the 4.5 by 6.5 Sealy Posturepedic and sleep soundly in preparation for the next day.

How could my fallen messiah know how to love, with a mother and father like us? But there was something about your father. It was underneath him. Inside him. You felt it. Don't deny it. So sweet and innocent, like a pixie. I thought I could get through to him. God knows I tried. Your poor father. Damaged goods. His lovemaking was so careful and sweet, never aggressive. That's not a good thing, you know. I don't think he was attracted to me. In bed at night he arched over me as if he were getting ready to have his way with me. But that arch had more to do with engineering than sex. He just wanted to position himself to be able to extend his arm until he reached my night light. Only after he pushed in the tab would he even kiss me. That was his way of letting me know that he wanted to play around. I kept my nighttable light on on purpose. As soon as he made that arching position to turn it off, I knew. But when he started feeling around in the dark I felt like he was thinking about something else when he touched me and explored me, like I wasn't really what he wanted, but that I was just an instrument of some desire of his that would do. Do you have any idea what that feels like? Maybe I shouldn't have let myself go to seed so soon. But even when I was in my prime — you know, you've seen the pictures, I was quite the catch — he didn't compliment me or look at me like he couldn't wait to eat me up alive. He just didn't have it in him. Or maybe even then he wasn't attracted to me. A wall. An impossible wall. Fifty years I put up with it. For a lot of those years I tried to knock it down. It wore me out. I stopped wearing make-up. I let my hair go gray and chopped it off by myself. Remember how you used count the chop marks and ask if you could smooth them out with the scissors? That's when I decided you were gay. Not that there weren't signs before. You used to comb your sister's Barbie doll's hair when you were little. Even then I was concerned. But then you cut it all off, tied a noose around her neck and hung her from the skyscraper you'd built with the Kenner's Girder and Panel kit we got you for Hanukkah. When I saw that display on the rec room carpeting, I was confused but reassured. Your best friends were girls. God knows what you did with them locked in your bedroom for hours, but I heard lots of giggling, that typical high-pitched giggling that comes from nervous girls. I could make out your giggling too. It had that same pitch and femininity. I was concerned. But then, lo and behold, you'd go out and enthusiastically play baseball with a bunch of smelly boys and I'd be confused and reassured again. It took a while, until I saw how you eyed my chopped-up hair. Then I knew. I also let myself *get fat. I wore the same clothes for four or five days in a row, except my panties. It's something, what not being desired can make you stop caring about. There was a poison in the household. He may have triggered it because he was so stern and unfeeling, but it was me who spread it because I thought it was my duty as wife and mother and woman to heal him. Believe me, I didn't mean to spread it. But I did. I only wanted to spare you and protect you and your sister. Now I look down on you and your sister, both of in your fifties and both of you alone. It breaks my heart. I failed, and I hate myself for it. Yes, I could try to "understand." Your sister, for example. She made some bad choices. She did get a son out of it, and a wonderful son she sees once a year if she's lucky. She's ended up alone in that huge empty house of hers. All those rooms! Why did she have to buy such a big house anyway? Does she really think that at her age, and with what she has gone through with men, she will be able to set up house with another one and use all of that space? She should have gotten a one-bedroom condo on the beach when she decided to move for the umpteenth time. Mind you, I have nothing against hope. But foolishness is another thing. There. I understand. And you, you're something else altogether. So good-looking, so smart, so sensitive, so as close to perfect as anyone can get. Why do you think I called you my messiah? And look at you. Not only alone in your fifties, but you've never not been really alone. You with your relationships that were always aborted before they could even gain some momentum. What the hell is that all about? And now this Ex character holding you like no other. What fucked-upness is that all about? I've said it before, and don't think I can't see your eyes rolling, but this time I am not saying it because you are my son: You are as close to perfect as they come. Scheinkeit, let me tell you something else: You are so stupid. I'm on a roll. You want to know something else? I am your mother. Remember when you were a hottie and spending your nights drugging and dancing your sweet tuchas off in some discotheque hoping to find a trick for the night? That's exactly how old I was when I was pushing you out of me and wondering why your father* wasn't pushing himself inside of me like he used to. That's how young I was when I had to figure out how to take care of you, your sister, your father and, in last place – by choice, I admit it – myself. Wear that like a Hazmat suit and see if you get it. I was that young. You've seen the black and white snapshots of us in the albums. What you don't see is the color, what you don't understand is the "snapness" of those shots. They only captured a moment, but the moment wasn't just a moment. It lived on, carried on, minute by minute, hour by hour, day by day, year after year. Do you understand that? In all those minutes and hours and days and years, I was your mother. Don't you think that gives me the right to grieve over your being alone at your ripe age? There's nothing worse than being alone except dying alone, of coming to understand that your life has not been shared, for better or for worse. Yes, I was your mother, which also gives me the right to lash out at you and your stupidity. But it also gives me the right to blame myself, if not entirely, then almost entirely, for your stupidity despite your gifts. How did you manage to shun a life partner? Why? Where did I go wrong? At least your house is the right size for a bachelor. My fallen messiah, do me a favor. Scatter your father's ashes on mine. And do me one more favor. Find it in you to forgive me.

CHAPTER 27

He will go online to find a checklist of the preparations, precautions and provisions recommended for a hurricane. From nine sites that he navigates, he will assemble a list of what he thinks will see him through whatever Dorian will hurl his way. He will make quick trips to local stores, lists in hand, to acquire as much as he can and will be dismayed to see that the stock of many items he has written down has already been depleted by the many who are more seasoned than he is in these matters. Nevertheless, he will have nabbed enough supplies to feel able to get through. After all, he reminds himself, he is alone. How many cans of beans, bottles of water, packages of batteries and candles, and assorted flashlights does one person need to ride out a day or two or, if worse comes to worst, a week? He will have plenty to keep him nourished, illuminated, alive. As he unbags his provisions and puts them away, he will begin to feel bold and excited until he considers the Armageddon-like havoc that might unfurl outside while he is holed up in the semi-darkness (should the power go out) behind his shuttered windows and doors and from which all of his senses will be deprived of receiving input except that of sound: of wind and of objects (coconuts, trees, patio furniture left outdoors) flailing about, crashing against his roof and cleaving tidy slits and irregular gashes into the shingles so that numerous founts of water cascade inside from above, while below, other water sources seep through his expensive flooring and rise steadily throughout the house, like an aquarium being filled. Then he will begin to panic, wondering whether being only in the company of cans of beans, batteries, candles, bottles of water and flashlights will in the end be enough to get him through. If they are, then what? He doesn't want to live through this alone. As a matter of fact, he doesn't want to *live* alone. Or to die alone. Once again, his hand will reach into his pocket and with more resolve extract his cell phone. This time he will muster up enough weakness to call Ex, wherever he may be. There is no answer. There is no answering machine.

Before he shuts himself in, he will take a quick drive to Sheila's house, not to make sure that she has secured it properly (she has been through several hurricanes and knows the deal) but to monitor her sensitivity to things outside herself and her immediate needs by checking to see if the box of ashes is still on the shelf in the hutch. As he drives up the almost empty coastal highway, he will debate the one merit of finding the box on the shelf – he will have been "right" about her and her insensitivity to things outside of herself and her immediate needs and can thus pat himself on the back for his perceptiveness – versus the value of finding the shelf empty – she isn't as self-concerned as he'd surmised, and he will have the self-righteous task of re-tweaking what he has assumed she is in order to be fair to her as a sister, a daughter, a person.

The five-minute drive along the coastal highway at this hour will not forebode anything out of the ordinary. Traffic will be light. An occasional bicyclist outfitted in a spandex one-piecer and helmet will be pedaling furiously or casually north or south on the wide sidewalks flanking both sides of the highway; parking lots to the public-access beaches will have their usual share of cars (perhaps just a bit less), each stationed equidistant between the two white lines painted on the asphalt for each (and each space so much wider than in most other parts of the country in order to accommodate the many pick-up vehicles that long-time Floridians in this area possess – mostly via credit card purchases that will sink them deeper in debt – in order to haul kayaks, surfboards, fully grown palm trees purchased at a nursery for instant landscaping, and other accretions that signal their belonging); individuals or family constellations will be walking in shorts or in bathing suits carrying towels, coolers, pails and shovels, umbrellas and Styrofoam noodles. Life as usual – except for the shops and gas stations, which are closed and boarded up. Along the brief stretch of ocean highway that he travels to his sister's house, Andrew will study the people he sees – on foot and bicycle, in cars and pick-ups – and divide them into the deniers and the defiers of Dorian, and eventually decide among which group to seek admission.

He will pull into the narrow driveway of his sister's house and notice off the bat that her rippled translucent plexiglass panels have been screwed onto all of her window sills (what has she done in return for a neighbor, surely male, who has taken care of this for her?). This will come as no surprise to him, as do certain pre-hurricane details in the house itself that he himself hasn't considered: all plugs removed from outlets, except for the refrigerator; file cabinets in the ground-floor office elevated with bricks; three ice cubes nestled on the racks of the freezer (if they are no longer there when she returns, it will mean that the freezer went off and she will have to resign herself to throwing out the chicken tenderloins, bag of jumbo shrimp and boxes of weight-watcher three-course dinners to avoid the possibility of food poisoning). It will also come as no surprise to him that the box of ashes is still on the shelf.

Looking out from his sister's lanai, he will see that the sky has begun to darken and the wind to be taunting the higher palm fronds as if to say, "I'm not fucking around." He will take the box of ashes off the shelf, put them in the passenger seat of his car and drive home. When he arrives, he will pull all of the accordion storm shutters across their tracks under and over the windows and doors. (Before he left to inspect his sister's house, he will have already placed candles, lighters and flashlights throughout the rooms of his house, and have turned on every light to give a semblance of afternoon.) He will deposit the box on the knee-high bamboo and parchment-paper table next to the front door, what he calls the "To Do Table," where he keeps his keys and anything he needs to remind himself to take with him the next time he gets in his car to do something that requires him to back out of his wide driveway and remove himself from the sanctuary. Once the box is set on the table, there will be nothing more to be done, and he will not know what to do. He will call his sister.

"Did you make it okay?" he will ask her as he throws some chicken breasts and lamb chops from the freezer into the broiler to have around in order to complement his canned provisions for a day or two.

"Made it. Once I got out of Florida, the traffic wasn't bad at all. Android, you wouldn't believe this place. I feel like I'm on vacation. I have my own bedroom and bathroom, Carol's husband is out of town on business, I never liked him anyway, and she has a cook."

"Maybe you won't come back."

"Nah. I'll be back. I need the tropics. But she has quite the set-up."

"Except for the husband that you don't like."

"At least he's not mine. And he's not here. Thanks, bro. Be safe."

As much as he will want to say to her, "Screw you for not even thinking about me," he will resort to one of his variations on a theme of spinelessness and say, "Not to worry. Enjoy" before he hangs up. He knows his sister well enough to know that she holds men on a lower evolutionary rung, and he is probably no exception (God only knows what she has to say to others about him, if the subject ever comes up.)

The wind will gather force outside, vanquishing the short spurts of silence with its progressive whirrings, whistlings, hummings, knockings and bangings coming from all directions and with different intensities, but with a coherence and musicality that aren't unlike some atonal segment being orchestrated by the gyrating baton of a maestro who knows exactly where he wants to go. Andrew will gird himself – no joke, no game, it's really happening this time. He will hear no sound of rain yet, but a light knocking sound will persist in the vicinity of his front door with a steady, monotonous rhythm that is in defiance of the coherence of the maestro's baton. He will press his ear against the storm shutter to try to identify whatever substance might be beating against the front door, but to no avail. His auditory faculties, without the aid of his sight, will be useless and it will finally come to him (something he had considered many times) that if he had to choose between being blind and being deaf, he would choose the latter. The beating will relent for longer intervals, but as soon as he removes his ear from the storm shutter and turns away it will begin again with its three-pause-three beat. He will slide open the shutter just a sliver to see if he can make out the cause. The gap will reveal nothing but the length of his driveway and the house across the street, bathed in a dark gray bluster that is Dorian on his way. He will slide the shutter open several more inches to see if there is more to see. As the white laminated metal shutter skirs open along its track, he will hear a voice – "Hey. It's me." – and this time will not need his sight to identify the source.

"I'm sorry. I didn't know where else to go."

Ex will be soaked from head to toe, surely with drizzle, probably with sweat, and possibly with tears. He will be wearing his sand-coated flip-flops, and will have swathed his black perforated Nike shorts and loose t-shirt with some kind of army-green tarpaulin that could be a poncho, a tent cover, or a tent-subflooring, which balloons out with each blast of wind. The smooth and bloated mass of tarpaulin, coated with beads of water that drip off its edges, will also be wrapped around his head and cover one eye. Strands of wet bang clusters will stick to his forehead, sending more droplets of water down his cheeks, which seem sallower than usual. This gaunt, frightened creature will seem reduced to a smaller version of himself.

"And here you are, complete with gravy. Let me understand something. Are you here for advice about where you can go? Or are you here because this is where you were assuming you could go in a pinch?" he will say as he opens the door for him, making sure that he is not smiling.

"Really, I wouldn't have come but…"

"But you did. Chill and be still." He will take Ex's hand and lead him down the hallway to the bathroom. "Strip down." He will bend over the tub and start the water, adjusting the two spigots until he can see steam rising on on the sides of the faucet and his hand is barely able to withstand the heat of the water. He will then think to light one of the candles that he has placed on the sink and turn out the too-bright light over the mirror. "I'll get some tea going. Do you remember the word for herb tea in Italian?"

"*Tisana.*"

He will not react to the correct response, which he has expected from Ex, whose thirst for knowledge of the acquisitive kind – names, dates, places, facts – has been evident since that first encounter by the tiki bar jutting out on the strip of beach where Andrew had never arrived at before. He will gather Ex's wet clothes, turn away, continuing to not reveal his delight and relief with a smile, and leave him standing naked in the tub. Before stuffing Ex's wet clothes into the washing machine, he will make a stop at the kitchen to turn on the burner under the tea kettle, watching the circle of red coils grow brighter and brighter under the black glass-top stove, and remember how he had once concluded that Ex was passionate about the idea of being knowledgeable, but that there was too much of "Florida" and "drift" in his veins to bring him up to speed or to enable him to fully commit to that passionate idea, so that occasionally he could strike a hit (as with *tisana*) but more often than not was embarrassingly off-mark (like when he thought that Rome was a country, or when he confused Dylan Thomas with Bob Dylan when they had experimented with the subject of Poetry).

After depositing the laundry into the machine, he will return to the kitchen to wait for the kettle's whistle. As he watches the vapor escape through the hole of the spout he will come to understand that he may be about to become entirely undone despite Dorian. There he is, Ex, back in this very house and naked (a diabolical miracle), defeated, and shrunken by circumstance. What's more, he mustn't forget, in this very house there is also a small box, the size of a three-layer cake box, which holds Zee. Just as the kettle begins to hiss and spit, a blast of wind will shake the house. The power will go off.

In one hand, he will hold a candle that was on the ready on the kitchen countertop; in the other, the cup of tea, whose water had boiled in the nick of time. When he arrives at the bathroom, Ex will be still there, lying motionless, eyes closed, knees and thighs bent and protruding from the filmy surface of the water like steep hillocks, hands crossed over his crotch to push his floating penis under the surface of the water.

"Here." He will place the cup of tea on the corner of the tub nearest to Ex's arm and deposit the candle that he has carried with him on the sink counter. The dim light will remove the dimension of depth.

Ex will sit up and reach for the tea. "Where is Zee?"

Andrew will close the lid of the toilet and sit down. "He's in my study. In a small box. He died. Take a sip of tea. He died. Let me shampoo you."

"I'm sorry."

Andrew will squeeze the cream-colored bottle of tea-tree-oil shampoo into his upturned hand until an extra-large dollop of transparent colorless syrup has oozed into it. He will squeeze the bottle slowly in order for Ex to have enough time to elaborate on what it is, of all the possibilities, that he is saying he is sorry for. Ex will take a sip of tea, remain in his upright position, bend his head forward, and say nothing, waiting to have his head lathered up.

Andrew will place his hands lightly on Ex's head as if he were about to give a benediction, except that his fingers will then quickly stretch over the skull and begin to dig in and work the shampoo. "What can I say? He was dying. And then it happened. He died." He will push further into Ex's scalp in attempt to understand from its grit and grease in what condition he has been living. He will regret that he had hadn't smelled it before applying the shampoo.

"Wow. That's intense."

"What is? Death or my massage?"

"Both, I guess."

"Stand up. Let me do the rest."

"Okay."

Ex will rise slowly. It will seem interminable, and Andrew will want it this way, a never-ending vertical eruption of perfect form, notwithstanding the hard hits it may have taken. The bathwater is brown and turbid as he continues to rise like some golem whose benevolence or evil has yet to be determined. But Andrew won't care. His father is a box of ashes, Dorian is en route, and Ex is naked in his bathtub.

"How did he die?"

Andrew will laugh. "He was old. We have a shelf life. Like parmesan cheese or yogurt or a bag of romaine. You know."

"Right. I'm really sorry."

Andrew will remove his hands from Ex's head, dip them beneath the filmy surface of the bathtub water to rinse off the shampoo, and rub the bar of olive oil soap into his palms until a fresh bout of lather seeps through his fingers. He will place his hands on Ex's neck, eager to begin an unhurried journey downward. "Tell me what you're sorry about. You've said it twice. Are they the same sorry, or different sorries?" he will ask as his hands are arriving at the latitude of Ex's armpits and nipples.

"I don't know."

Andrew will pinch Ex's left nipple. Ex will push his hand away. "Yes you do. I know you do. Tell me. Otherwise I'll wrap my hand around your cock and I won't let go."

"What are you talking about?"

Andrew will move his hand down and begin circling Ex's stomach. "What are you apologizing for?"

Ex will take Andrew's predatory hand and bring it to his face, kissing the tip of each finger lightly before he guides the index finger to one eye, where he has it trace his wet lashes. "I don't know."

With his free hand, Andrew will reach over to the towel bar and yank off the neatly folded white towel. "Here. Rinse off and dry yourself. You're shivering. I'll get the bed ready."

"Okay."

"My bed."

Ex will begin with his hair. He will rub the towel rigorously along his head and face, slackening the pace as he moves down his chest and arrives at the upside-down triangle of hair surrounding his cock. As he proceeds downward to the taut, narrow space between his thigh and his balls, causing his cock to dance like the trees outside must be dancing to Dorian's wind, he'll look at Andrew (who hasn't yet been able to pull himself away) and the right side of his lips will veer upward into the first semblance of a smile since Andrew eyed him through the gap in the shutter and let him in. "Okay."

As he steps out of the tub, the power will be restored.

"Hallelujah," Andrew will say.

"I guess it's good. The candle was nice though."

"I like candles too. They take edges off things, make things softer."

As he steps out of the tub, beadlets of water will slowly wend their way along his leg hairs like dew on a spiderweb. Some will find their way onto the blue furry bathmat that Andrew will have placed on the floor next to the tub (and which he knows that Ex would have never thought to do, even though the mat is draped over the side of the tub). As Ex steps out onto the mat, folding the towel in half before wrapping it around his waist so that the bottom of the towel barely covers his left testicle (which is slightly lower than the right), he will say: "I do love you."

Andrew will scuffle with the smile of intoxication that seeks expression as he leaves the bathroom to turn down the top sheet and light-weight blanket on his bed. Intoxication need not preen. The wind will pick up, and as he walks down the hallway the bombardment of rain against the roof and the storm shutters will begin. Turning into his bedroom, he will say out loud to himself: "It's about to happen. All of it."

CHAPTER 28

The bedroom will be illuminated by one tall white candle rising from its ceramic holder on the night table next to the side of the bed where Andrew doesn't sleep when alone – a candle that Andrew has always kept on the ready, in the event of power outages or sexual encounters. Before he lights the candle, he will realize how long it has been since he has needed to light it: the exposed half-inch of wick is white and fresh, bent over like a dormant blossom. With his thumb and index finger, he will stroke it upward into a vertical position before taking the lighter out of the night table's upper drawer and lighting it. When Ex arrives, he will collapse on the bed immediately, in his position of languid sprawl that bespeaks a crucifixion – simultaneously ingenuous and erotic – that each time that they have ended up together in the same bed has left Andrew powerless and hungry for nothing but this creature, even this time, with Dorian making its own equal or greater vigor felt through the first few hours of the night.

Ex will eventually retract into a crescent, slowly easing backward until he feels Andrew's body and wills it to spoon up against him as he rummages for Andrew's left hand in order to guide it around him until he can press it into his sternum and feel the length of Andrew's arm trail behind like the streak of a shooting star until it settles around his back, forearm and chest. Andrew will position his face against the nape of Ex's neck and begin maneuvering ever so slightly here and there until he finds that spot where the fine baby hairs on Ex's neck cease to tickle. He will find that spot (how well he knows it) and relax his body, his nose nuzzled behind Ex's left earlobe, which he will be tempted to bite but, knowing better, won't.

Dorian's ardent symphony will soon be relegated to a secondary aspect of white noise, brutal but with a regularity that will serve as a kind of cushion to the deeper and more unbridled disturbances that these two men will feel, notwithstanding their being melded together in form and temperature like two ingots of metal risen to molten temperature and oozed into a single unit that will enable them to drift easily into a sleep-hibernation.

Sometime in the middle of the night, Dorian will have run its course. By early morning, Andrew will have begun to stir, first aroused by the click of the air-conditioning kicking in and jarring the steady sound of silence: Dorian has passed through. The power is on. A good sign. Much ado about…

He will extricate himself from the cleaving, remembering that he never did close the storm shutter to the front door after he'd decided to allow Ex to cross the threshold. As he makes his way down the hallway, there will be traces of natural light and heat (and with them the reminder of the natural world) that lack the exquisite heat, light and form of Ex; as he makes his way toward the front door on flooring that has no traces of water infiltration from above or below, he will be hopeful that, notwithstanding Dorian and Ex, he will have come through unscathed and whole.

The natural light will grow, and by the time he arrives at the front door a thick shaft of sunlight, combined with the hum of the air conditioning, will have announced that all is well. Small branches of jacaranda, sea grape and Texas sage will have been loosened from their moorings and strewn about the front lawn, and a large vase holding a Christmas cactus will be on its side at the entrance to the house; as for the rest, it will be as it was before Dorian threatened.

He will slowly and quietly slide open the other storm shutters, peering out from each to see at most only an occasional branch rent from its host trunk, and many leaves and blossoms (especially from the bougainvillea in full bloom) funneled by the wind into heaps throughout the front and back yards, or floating singly in the swimming pool like offerings at a Buddhist temple. One by one he will slide the shutters open along their tracks, praying that each one will reveal nothing more than much ado about… since all he wants to do is to work his way back to the bedroom, find Ex in his crescent position, undisturbed, and reposition himself into that disquieting harmony for as long as it (and he) will last. But the phone will ring.

"Hey bro, you alive and dry?"

"Yep." He will wait for the instruction. And it will come.

"Thank God. Would you do me a favor?"

"Yes, I'll go to your house and check things out and call you with a damage control report."

"Thanks. I'm glad you're okay. I'm having such a great time here. Not sure when I'm coming back. I guess it depends on if there is any damage that I need to take care of it right away."

"I'll let you know."

"You're the best."

"Warning. I might not get to it right away. But I'll head up there sometime today or tomorrow."

"Okay. But let me know as soon as you can. I need to know if I can stay or if I have to come back."

"Sometime today, probably."

He will laugh at how predictable she is and remember how often she has said to him, "If you ever see me becoming too much like Mom, either tell me or kill me." He will do neither, letting it slip through yet one more time and feel one more time the incremental growth of rancor accruing over his lack of balls and spine and his not knowing who to incriminate more: himself or his sister.

"I'll give you a heads-up later on."

"My messiah. I have committed grave injustices. You turned out sensitive, which I prayed for, but you are spineless. Ardent in empathy and hopeless in taking a stand. And your sister. Your sister. A go-getter but getting only things that can satisfy her for the moment. A child with a giant, colorful lollipop that dissolves too quickly. It could be worse, but it could be better. I tried to protect you from the many evils of this world. I tried to make you perfect. What mother wouldn't do that for her children? You I admire. Sheila too, but less so. For you, I had great expectations, and still do, even at your age, fool that I am. For your sister, less so. I admit it: I do have a favorite child. Is that treasonous? Cause for a call to some hotline and incarceration? Maybe. You can do it. Call. Have them throw me behind bars and have done with me. But I warn you. You'll still

want to come and visit me. *You won't be able to resist, and you'll bring me cakes with small serrated saws tucked inside one of the iced layers so that I can break out and away and continue to love you because you could be almost perfect but hate you because you insist on giving into weaknesses that make you fall short. Infuriating. That's the way it has been and will be. So what else is new?*

I know that you love to hate me. It's easier that way. You can avoid the intricacies inside of me that would force you to consider me as all the things I am outside of being your mother. I get that. But I can't believe that you've chosen that route. Maybe you aren't all that sensitive. Maybe you're even stupid, and I've failed. It shocks me, disheartens me. You can find forgiveness for the creepiest characters. Case in point – Ex. But for me, your mother, you reduce things to reduce me. How dare you. Go figure.

Am I being too rough on you? Are you thinking "What about Sheila?" Probably you are. But you are you, and Sheila is Sheila. I'm not saying stand up to her. I kvell when I think that my two children get along, that they don't fight, they have such putting-up-with strength for the sake of not severing, not breaking. But still. A bit more chutzpah, son. Could it hurt? A bit less of the I-embrace-whatever-comes-my-way shtick that makes me bristle. Would it hurt you to have more spine or balls or whatever anatomy you want to attribute it to? Speaking of which, why don't they ever tell women to have more clit? Think about it.

You have quiet relationships with those around you. You're measured in your dealings with those around you. You keep things so steady that intimacy eludes you. And that, maybe more than anything else, worries me. Something's gotta be brewing under there. An unwatched pot always boils over. Like you do with me. Never in my life have I felt such wrath unleashed. Do you hate me that much? Do you love me that much?

I know. I was like that with your father, too. One minute I'd be pinching his cheek to stem a flow of love that I felt I couldn't handle; another minute I'd be fantasizing about bashing his head in with my cast iron griddle to take care of a frustration I couldn't handle. Most of the time, I did neither. What did I do instead? I resigned myself. I sulked. I hated the world for decade upon decade. Then I died.

You will too. Die, that is. The first time I told you to fuck off was when you were eight or nine, I think, give or take a couple of years. You should be used to my crudeness by now. Your father was never crude. He was steady, he was measured. Like you. Now he's just like me. He's dead. You were so good to him. You were good to me too in the final stretch. But with you with him, your goodness reminded me of the long bouts of pleasure I took in braiding your sister's hair when it went down to her waist and was freshly cream-rinsed and smooth. With you with me it was more of a final reckoning, a kind of cancelling out of years of friction through a few stoic months of putting up with me. With patience and affection. With that careful measurement of those around you that I felt honored to be exempt from, even though it hurt so much. In those last months, I felt betrayed by your patience and affection, but I was too weak and morphined to blast you with my variations on the tired theme of "man up or fuck off."

G'neeg. The hurricane is over. You have things to do. You need to check Sheila's house. And you need to get back to him, see what shape he has taken on in your bed and how it fuels your malaise – is that the right word? You need to try to figure out what you're going to do with him and what you're going to do about him. And maybe even figure out what it is that he wants from you in exchange. I have my ideas, and they make me shudder, but you won't want to hear them so I'll bite my tongue for a change. You know them anyway. You are so much more like me than you think, which is probably why you fight me as a knee-jerk reaction. That's too bad, my son. In certain things, mothers are right and they always win. It's encoded in the umbilical cord.

One favor, though. Your father's ashes. Scatter them already. Don't wait for Sheila. Your father and I don't need any fancy-schmancy ritual to bring us back together. We know each other too well. It comes with time. I miss him and the routine of us. We all need company.

Get on with it. Go to your room, do what you need to do with that young man. Get on with it. Or better, yet, get off it. The hurricane has passed.

Her voice will arrive at him with an unfamiliar tone, as if an emery board had been taken to each word and filed away the abrasive edges. He will hear the other-than-your-mother in her, feel the weight of all the years she had lived before she died, and he too will lose his abrasive edges and feel unsettled but consoled by (and attentive to) what she has said. As he walks back down the hallway, his left knee will make clicking sounds, he will feel a mild pressure on his lower back that he has been meaning to go to the doctor about for some time, and he will not fight to the death the things she has said simply because it was she who had said them.

Passing the bathroom, he will relish the prospect of soon discovering the shape that Ex will be in, regardless of the actual shape itself, and the smell of him, if he should dare get close enough. At the same time, he will feel his desire being tempered by the need to be able to study, without having to manipulate Ex's body and risk waking him up, the unhaired under-side of his arms so that he can look for tell-tale punctures or track marks along the geography of those gloriously robust veins.

There is also the matter of his father, compressed into a plastic bag of ashes stuffed into a cardboard box that he has placed on the To Do table among the keys, outgoing mail, and pale yellow post-ems stuck here and there with hastily written tiny scrawls about tiny matters to accomplish that day or, at most, the following day. No, he will not forget about the box of ashes, or the conspiracy of fallen branches and leaves that have sullied his devoutly ordered space in the back and front yards. So much to attend to with the return of sun and the torpor of its heat – Sheila's house, his father's ashes, Ex's body (and his hungry veins). The sun will continue to intensify, but Andrew will wonder whether the hurricane has passed.

CHAPTER 29

Arrived at the bedroom, at that flesh, those arms and, first things first, those veins. Andrew will be in luck: At some point between when he tiptoed out of the bedroom and when he has arrived back at the doorway, Ex will have shifted onto his back, monopolizing the queen-size bed in his crucifix position that consistently suggests respite more than martyrdom. The unhaired under-side of his arms will be in full view, ready for scrutiny.

Before he enters the room, Andrew will think about the evening not too long ago when, relaxing on the sofa with Ex's head nestled on his lap under the dimmed recessed lighting of the cathedraled ceiling of his living space (the mood music was no longer necessary and Charles was safely in his own bedroom sleeping), both of them had felt the contentment of their budding domestic rhythm and had concocted the idea of having not one but two children, a boy and a girl. Not right away. It would take time. A few years. At most three. And during that time, something strange (to others) but natural (to him) would have happened: Each day during that gestation period of the first child (the girl, Clare), as Ex would grow older, Andrew would grow younger. The creases inscribed on the sallow cheeks of Andrew would fill out and the gray around his temples revert to its dirty blond, while the malleable quality of Ex would begin its slow stiffening until he and Andrew met almost halfway – Ex at thirty-five and Andrew at forty-one – and Andrew would have regained as much handsomeness and vibrancy as the aging of Ex would have obscured and relinquished. They will not be dull, but they will not be brilliant, perhaps not even outstanding. They will simply be a handsome couple, content, settled in their ways, resigned to their customary habits, especially the habit of inseparability as they raise their family.

Clare will come first. An angelic child. Easy, and easing the way for Leo, who will follow two years later and be alpha and demanding. The energy of the couple will naturally be funneled into the welfare of the children, but not enough to prevent them from occasionally looking at each other hard and understanding the preposterous situation they have put themselves in, what with Andrew of heart-attack age and Ex still a child himself. But they will simply sigh and slog on.

Andrew enters the room, he will rewind and play this out again, but no further than he and Ex have played it out before, wanting to contain it in the realm of bliss that could very well come crashing down when he walks toward the bed to inspect those effulgent veins. He is not sure what exactly to look for. He has heard of the term "track marks" but has no idea what it means and doesn't want to backtrack down the hallway and through the living space until he reaches his computer, where he can Google "track marks." Ex could reposition himself in the meantime, and he has come this far. How does a substance-abuser's intravenous habit, coupled with impending doom, reveal itself on an arm?

He will quietly position himself on the corner of the bed, lean over so that his eyes are almost against Ex's outstretched arm (he has left his reading glasses somewhere), and look. Perhaps that will be enough to know, to understand, despite the pain he feels in his lower back as he stretches himself toward Ex's body, which is completely exposed except for his left foot, which has found its way under a ripple of top sheet bunched up at the bottom of the bed.

The right arm under his scrutiny will be pale, although the skin where the serious hair begins will have a darker, sun-burnished tone that deepens as it curves around the side of the arm toward the hairier front part that is against the mattress and hidden from view. This paler, balder stretch will reveal a matrix of bluish veins, the larger ones delicately pulsating near the crease at the inner elbow. Several flat beauty marks will dot the otherwise unblemished landscape of this segment of Ex's flesh, where three particularly voluminous veins will each host one small dot ringed in red that looks like a mosquito bite aggravated by a finger that has been unable to resist scratching. And well they might be, he will think. Or maybe not, he will also think, realizing that he will never really know, that he will simply have to decide based on what he already knows or what he has already decided he knows about Ex, which, he knows, is very little. And if they are not insect bites? If, instead, they are what he doesn't want them to be? What then? If he were to connect the dots, another scalene triangle would be formed, even if things geometrical are not his concern at the moment.

He will shift his glance down to Ex's right hand, its palm facing outward and fingers lightly curled, and recall that his young hands are almost educated, except for the rough and stubby nails, which he can't see since they are facing the sheet. His eyes will travel back up to the three dots and he will conclude that, at best, Ex will grow to be mediocre and will spread mediocrity, with or without Clare and Leo. The hypothetical son or daughter that he will push in a stroller will also not make a difference, help change the world, which is sorely in need of a reprieve from all human enterprise. Ex too may grow up (and will grow old), and as he does, the few historic buildings of the area will have fallen down or been demolished, asphalt split, pavements cracked, and through the gaps and crevices and other wounds of demise will emerge splotches of color – a tuft of grass, a clump of weed, a wild flower – and the earth will once again breathe in tiny spots and simply be, and this thing called Life will again show a shimmer of promise, of hope. Will that be enough for him to stay by Ex's side on the mattress, and after he has woken up, taken a shower and expects breakfast?

Ex's hand will begin to close into a fist, his face will tighten, perhaps some not pleasant dream or dream fragment making an inroad. The movement will startle Andrew. He will swiftly but carefully get up from the mattress, back away from the bed and, when he reaches the doorway, turn and pad down the hallway. He will notice a reflection of light on the hallway wall coming from the window of the spare bedroom and wonder where the crystal has ended up. He will look for it and think about when to scatter his father's ashes and check on his sister's house, all the while wishing that his lower back would stop throbbing, his knees stop clicking, and that the erections that used to come so readily to him (they stopped altogether several years ago unless his furious hand coupled with some shameful fantasy did their magic) would return, as if by miracle. He'll look for the Burmese Citrine Cluster and its supposed manifestations under sofas and cushions, behind tables and credenzas; he will pan rooms for any shapes of light being refracted on walls, but nothing will announce itself except numerous puncture marks left from picture hooks that he has relocated and has neglected to smooth over and seal with spackle. He will have decided what he must decide the scalene triangle must represent, and will feel himself to be a kind of cauldron, whose vast liquid inside has heated, hissed and bubbled, slowly evaporating all the while until the last drop has sizzled away, leaving on the cauldron's inner walls only a membrane of white film, the thinnest coating that holds the essence of all that liquid, all that furious motion whose heat could in the end only produce the evaporation of itself, down to that chalky essence, which, were it really chalk, and were a finger to use it as such – dipping into it and applying it to some surface like a clown applying pancake to his face, or some disaffected youth scrawling graffiti on a public sidewalk or wall – its import would be so stupefyingly simple: Ex was just a kid who needed to be heard, to be understood, to be loved, a kid who did not himself feel the need to hear, to understand, or to love, because his own needs were as yet unmet.

As he arrives at the living area, he will glance out the window and notice all of the trees and shrubbery intact. The picture window will frame an abundance of vegetation, flowering and not, that will bring to mind a home he had rented in the mountains one summer not long ago, with its density of green forms that was almost suffocating. Individual blades of grass arriving at the metal criss-cross cyclone fence that demarcated the property line and dripped with ivy leaves creeping up a wooden lattice-work leaning against trees of varying thicknesses holding branches of various thicknesses and up and up and up until just a small patch of unobstructed sky – blue finally! – could be seen, like a rip in some fantastically plush fabric. How beautiful it was, but a busy beauty, distracting in its exaggeration of abundance and crowdedness. So unlike the beach with its two simple and endless striations – sand and sea – whose power lay in its stark simplicity. Had Ex appeared for the first time along a forested mountain pathway and its variegated profusion of distraction (he will wonder, as he looks out the window), would their approach, their intersection and their "Hey, how's it going?" have been an anomalous blip with no consequence?

He will stop trying to find the crystal. Its import will no longer hold the promise of abundance and manifestation. In fact, it will seem like so much silliness. At his age, the coarse and thuggish texture of Ex's fingers together with the scalene triangle depicted by puncture marks along the veins, can point to only one decision, one that Andrew would be a fool not to heed, especially given his years (damn them). The search for the crystal will stop, as will the desire to Google any contingencies about what is already crystal clear. Oh dear God, he thinks. It must end.

CHAPTER 30

Back to the bedroom then, to make noise, to settle the score. As he reenters, he will shuffle his feet, clear his throat, skim his elbow against the door – anything to rouse Ex, memorize and memorialize him as he de-crucifies himself (for the last time in this space), and then lure him out and away from here, to wherever the consequences of who he is so far will lead him.

"Good morning. Afternoon, actually."

Ex will stretch with a quality of bliss and ease that for an instant will make Andrew regret the action he has decided to pursue.

"Hey." He will continue to stretch, as if the ability to reach and reach had no end.

"Welcome to the post-hurricane universe."

"Wow. And?"

"Minimal damage. Give me your arm."

Ex will yield his arm, awaiting some kind of sensual compensation for existing, and particularly in this house, this room, this bed.

"You slept through Mother Nature's wrath," Andrew will inform him as he moves his index finger along the most bulging of the bulging veins, blueish and with gentle curves that make their way to the crease at the elbow, where this vein and all the others submerge back under the pale flesh on their journey to the heart. "How do you do that?"

"Was it that bad?"

"I wouldn't know," he will say as he reaches in his back pocket with his free hand. "It's all relative. This is my first hurricane. You've probably had dozens. You're hardened." He will notice a budding woody.

"That feels good."

"Good. That's the idea. Good is good." As Andrew's finger arrives at the first puncture, he will extract a marker (black, with a phosphorescent pink cap) from his back pocket, snap the lid (it will fall onto the floor and bounce three times before settling under the brown-painted metal bedframe) and place its edge on the lower-most red-ringed aureole. From there, he will draw a line to the second dot, and then to the third. "Well look at that. Three points. X, Y and Z. Connect the dots and *voila* – your very own pink triangle."

Ex will lift his head to see the tattoo, and bring his arm to his nose to smell it.

"Getting another buzz?"

"Sweet. Does it come off?"

"In time. Get dressed. We're going to the beach. Let's see what Dorian has done there."

"Is there any coffee?"

"It's finished. Get dressed." He will watch Andrew struggle to get out of bed and with his right hand pluck each piece of clothing that is scattered on the floor while he tries to shield his woody with his left hand. "Meet me at the front door with your backpack. And don't be your usual pokey self." He will be pleased at his resoluteness, even though his eyes will linger on this naked youth as if to create a tableau before he sets off down the hallway toward the front door, stopping only to stuff the box of ashes next to the crystal in his small army green backpack hanging on one of the three hooks (one holds an umbrella, the other a royal blue waterproof windbreaker) on the wall adjacent to the front porch door. He will stand by the door, fiddling with the loose handle as he waits for Ex, dressed and packed up, to arrive.

"Ready."

"Let's go."

"What's in your backpack?"

"Zee's ashes. I'm going to scatter them."

"Wow. That's intense."

"It is."

"I'm not sure I can handle this."

"You don't have to. Don't worry." How he would like to yank the backpacks off their backs, lead Ex to the bathroom where he will scrub off the triangle, and steer him back to the oasis of the bedroom, where he can witness another time that sprawl and spoon up against its magnificent edge, waiting for his hand to be taken and pulled across the chest as if to shield it from harm. "Let's go."

"Are you angry with me? I'm sorry that I appeared like that. But I needed you."

"I know you need me. I need you too."

"I love you. You know that, don't you?"

Andrew will smile and walk slightly ahead of Ex so as not to listen, not to hear, not to speak. They will have to pause together at the highway until the coast is clear. Ex will sprint across the four lanes and arrive first, turning his head toward Andrew, who continues at a slower pace. "Did you see that the roof over the gas tanks at the gas station blew off?"

"No." Andrew will quicken his pace in order to resume his position of being ahead of Ex as they make their way along the narrow passageway to the beach. The ocean will be surprisingly placid.

"Which way do you want to go?" Andrew will ask.

Ex will turn his head toward the north. "The usual way. Our way." Andrew will watch him adjust his backpack, and Ex will proceed north, head turned slightly toward the horizon as his feet leave deep imprints in the still-wet sand. Andrew will also turn his head – toward the south – and begin walking, hoping that Ex will not eventually call out to him or run up behind him, place his hand on Andrew's shoulder and say, breathless, "What are you doing?" Ten, twenty, thirty paces. No sound, no touch. Twenty more paces and he will turn around. In the distance he will see a tall figure, ankle-deep in the ocean, peering out over the horizon, backpack several yards behind him lying face up on the sand. Andrew will come to understand, with a shock but not a surprise, that he may have already been dispensed with, forgotten about.

As he stoops down to remove his backpack and extract the box, he will feel his back pain work itself up his vertebrae. He will untie the twist-em, open the plastic bag, and bring the box back to his arms, cradling it as he, like Ex, goes ankle-deep in the water, where (unlike Ex) he will take long strides as he scoops up handfuls of ash, swings his arms wide, and unclenches his fist to release the fine gray powder into the tiny waves. But not before he takes the crystal from out of his pocket and flings it as far and as high as he can, hoping to see a last refraction of light before it sinks into the ocean.

When the box is empty, he too will turn toward the horizon and remain still, listening carefully for some evocation with which his father might bless him for the act. He will listen for something. Anything.

Thanks, son. I'm glad you decided not to wait for your sister. I was getting impatient. I miss your mother, as hard as that may be for you to believe. I know. We were at each other's throats. We made each other miserable. Or so it seemed to you. And you were right, if personal fulfilment is your barometer. But you were also wrong on other scores. Most, actually. Eight-five. Not bad. Maybe I could have held out for another few years. Would it have mattered? Does more life make death more acceptable? Silly talk. In any event, I missed your mother, hard as that may be for you to understand. You probably think that our love was poisoned by hate, if there ever was love to begin with. But it was the opposite. Our hate fueled our love. It was like a drug. Speaking of which.

But nothing will come during, or between, the delicate curling of the waves, which suck in his father's ashes and make them vanish.

He will want to turn his head to see whether Ex is still within view or whether he too will have vanished from sight. But he will not turn his head to the left to find out. He will hold steady for several minutes before lowering his head and settling his gaze on the waves smacking against his calves. He will think about Ex and resolve that although he, too, was only ankle-deep in water, he will not have proceeded deeper but will instead have simply floated away. He will think about Zee, too, and repent having performed the ritual of scattering the ashes with so little sanctity (who will scatter his one day, he wonders). As he lifts his head once more toward the horizon, a slender white streak will be piercing through the otherwise unblemished sky, its tail end dispersing as its front end is converging. He will think about Adeline Virginia Woolf (his beloved VW) and how she was able to grant Lily Briscoe a vision (but only at the very end), and how VW probably had to have Lily have her vision so that she, VW, could allow her own muddled madness or piercing clarity to goad her take those long, deep, troubled, but assured strides into the ocean, never turning her head while her body sank lower and lower in the water and her head was finally under.

He will also decide that when he leaves the beach, after the streak has dissipated completely, he will check on his sister's house and, before returning home, will stop at the store to pick up some fresh fish for dinner. Hopefully there will be a nice pompano, his favorite. Back pains and sore knees notwithstanding, he will stoop down to rinse the ashes off his hands and bring them to his face to cool himself with the wet salted daub of ocean that coats them like custom-make gloves. He will feel tiny rivulets of water working their way down the creases in his cheeks. He will feel refreshed but, like Lily, will be overcome by a sense of extreme fatigue. His knees will make their old-man clicking sounds as he takes those first few steps out of the water and starts home, reminding himself to stop at the store and hoping that the man behind the fish counter will be the good-looking one who always treats him special and makes him wonder whether it is possible that he is still desired, desirable. No matter. Whoever is manning the counter, he will ask for the pompano, his favorite.

The end

Made in the USA
Middletown, DE
26 September 2022

11249261R00179